'I had a dream…a memory.'

Cade stopped combing her hair as she continued.
'Your brother told me if I needed anything,
anything at all, I could count on you.'

Cade's gaze delved into hers, as if to unearth
every secret thought that she herself had no
conscious knowledge of. With a shudder she
glanced away. Careful to keep her thoughts close.
Careful to keep her heart close.

Especially when he took up his task again, tugging
the comb through her hair with a long, full stroke,
tugging her back, for one moment, against him.

If ever a man *had* brushed her hair in that murky,
unclear past of hers, Sara knew such an
experience could not compare to the vivid here
and now of Cade McGivern.

It was heaven. It was hell. It was oh-so-right. How
could it be wrong?

Dear Reader,

Welcome to April's six super Silhouette Special Editions®! This is a rather special line-up, with some of our most popular authors *and* our most popular themes.

First up comes our THAT'S MY BABY! title *When Baby Was Born* by Jodi O'Donnell, where a heavily pregnant amnesiac turns up on just the right man's doorstep!

Next comes Lindsay McKenna, one of our very favourite writers, with a new MORGAN'S MERCENARIES story, *Man of Passion*, her impressive fiftieth book for Silhouette®. *The Millionaire She Married* is Christine Rimmer's latest CONVENIENTLY YOURS—Jenna Bravo has 'forgotten' to divorce her husband before getting engaged to someone else! There's another Bravo's story next month—*The MD She Had To Marry*.

Sherryl Woods continues her AND BABY MAKES THREE books with *Dylan and the Baby Doctor*; Dylan is a heroic private detective who's searching for a kidnapped child. In *Married by High Noon* another child is at the centre of a custody battle and Leigh Greenwood shows us that a hasty marriage *can* still be a good one. And Peggy Webb's *Summer Hawk* is heart-wrenching and very unusual...

Enjoy!

The Editors

When Baby Was Born

JODI O'DONNELL

SILHOUETTE

SPECIAL EDITION

*Silhouette, Silhouette Special Edition and Colophon are
registered trademarks of Harlequin Books S.A., used under licence.*

*First published in Great Britain 2001
Silhouette Books, Eton House, 18-24 Paradise Road,
Richmond, Surrey TW9 1SR*

© Jodi O'Donnell 2000

ISBN 0 373 24339 1

23-0401

*Printed and bound in Spain
by Litografia Rosés S.A., Barcelona*

To Pam Johnson, for being there.

My warmest thanks to Rick Haddock, ranch manager, Texas Longhorn Cattle Co., for patiently answering my numerous questions on Panhandle ranching.

JODI O'DONNELL

grew up one of fourteen children in small-town Iowa. As a result, she loves to explore in her writing how family relationships influence who and why we love as we do.

A *USA Today* best-selling author, Jodi has also been a finalist for the Romance Writers of America's RITA Award, and is a past winner of RWA's Golden Heart Award. She lives in Iowa with her two dogs, Rio and Leia.

Dear Reader,

When baby was born… What memories those words evoke! In a family of fourteen children, as mine was, such a phrase is apt to produce a spate of 'remember when's,' like 'Remember when Tom was born? Dad was on the road working, so Mum had cousin Ellen drive her to the hospital, and they barely made it!' Or 'Remember when Evy was born? Dad was on the road again, and the Lutheran minister's wife drove Mum to the hospital in the Cadillac. She said that car spoiled her for any other after that!'

Yes, each and every one of us has a story that begins with 'When you were born…' because the birth of each and every one of us is unique. I firmly believe there are no routine births; each is its own miracle, capable of transforming the lives around it.

That's exactly what happens to Sara and Cade in *When Baby Was Born*. Fate has conspired to bring them together for this most memorable of births. And indeed, this baby changes their lives, and continues to change them even as fate seems to conspire to keep them apart.

It's impossible, however, for Sara and Cade to deny the bond they forged when her baby was born. Such is the power of this kind of an event. Such is the power of love.

So for the child in all of us who loves to hear about that moment when we came into the world, forever changing it, here's *When Baby Was Born*. Enjoy!

Jodi O'Donnell

Chapter One

With only a towel about his waist and one slung around his neck, Cade McGivern gingerly sat down on the side of the bed in his darkened bedroom. Twenty minutes under a hot-as-he-could-stand-it shower, and it had only taken the edge off his aches, the merest bite out of the chill that seemed to go bone deep. He could still feel on his face the raw sting of snow driven by straight-line winds.

Yup, from the looks of it, it was shaping up to be one hell of a new year.

Hunching forward, he finished toweling his hair dry, stifling a groan at the twinge of pain through his right shoulder, the result of trying to coax a particularly ornery steer out of a drifting-over washout.

Not that there was another soul in the house to hear him if he did let go with a holler or two. As it stood, he was completely alone, with nothing for company but the wind outside. It was howling a blue streak of its own.

No doubt about it, that was one wicked storm out there. He was glad to be out of it after nearly twelve hours of working against time to ensure the safety of his herd. At a certain point, though, it all came under the category of damage control, meaning he'd learned as a matter of course not to hold out hope for a whole lot of success.

Yet both such circumstances, he realized, might be about to change, with any amount of luck. Luck, that was, and Destiny.

Cade didn't know what he'd have done today without the chestnut gelding he'd been training up. Destiny had been a trooper, never faltering throughout the hours of gathering cattle and driving them to closer pastures.

Then there was the letter that had come just yesterday. He reached out in the dark toward the bedside table to touch the still unopened envelope. What message it contained, he didn't know. Forgiveness would be nice, although he'd done nothing wrong. Cade was ages past looking for justice, however. Simply having fate give him another chance would do.

As for no longer being alone—well, that'd be nice, too.

Yup, despite this blizzard and the prospect of losing cattle to it, Cade was aware of a certain…expectancy in the air that augured better times in the new year.

In any case, he sure as hell was ready for a change.

If he had the gumption, he'd see midnight in, just for the curiosity of finding out whether this hopeful impression would bear out. But he was just too dog-tired to stay up another minute, much less three hours.

Casting the towel in his hand toward the doorway and giving the one around his waist a fling in the same general direction, he eased under the thick covers.

That's when he did smell something for real: the faintest waft of wood. Sandalwood, to be specific. He knew only because his brother had favored it, even if Loren had taken any amount of grief from Cade for being so city-slickered as to choose a "scent."

Lying on his back, Cade again put out a hand, finding the letter on the bed stand and bringing it to his nose. It smelled only faintly of ink and paper, nothing more.

He shook his head at such foolishness, much unlike him. What was he waiting for, anyway? He may as well open it and get it over with.

But he *was* waiting for something, he realized, even as he pushed himself up onto one elbow to turn on the lamp on the opposite bed stand. He was waiting for, wanting, expecting, something more—

Cade's heart stopped cold. He stared, blinked, then stared some more.

For lying on her side in the bed, her back to him, was a woman, sound asleep.

He was too stunned at first to move. Had he got so chilled out in the storm he was imagining things? Except he felt in perfect command of his senses.

From his vantage leaning over her, he could see that she was fairly young, with skin as smooth and white and flawless as the snow-covered plain outside. Long lashes lay against her cheek like tiny feathers. A dark braid of hair curled over her shoulder. She'd evidently been pretty chilled herself, for she'd drawn the down comforter up to her chin, making her look like nothing so much as an ebony-haired Sleeping Beauty in the midst of the hundred-year sleep whose end would come only with the kiss of her princely hero.

But he was no hero, princely or otherwise.

Truth be told, though, the whole scene she presented, sleeping peacefully in his bed as if truly secure in the trust that a certain someone would soon ride in whose return would make everything right in her world, had a feeling of…of rightness about it—like the answer to a question he hadn't even known he'd asked.

She must have heard him, for the woman stirred, brow furrowing in momentary distress, making him wonder what dream he'd disturbed her from. He couldn't tell whether it had been good or bad from the little sound she made in the back of her throat, half sigh, half moan. Half pleasure, half pain.

It occurred to Cade that it was one of the most intimate things you could do, watching someone wake up. He was helpless to look away, though, even if it made him feel like a voyeur in his own bed.

Her lashes fluttered, then opened. She glanced around drowsily before settling her gaze on his hand, propped on the mattress in front of her. Her eyes followed a path up from wrist to forearm to biceps to shoulder to neck before finally meeting his own gaze.

And Cade found himself looking into a pair of the biggest, deepest, darkest blue eyes under the sun. He'd never seen anything like them, nor the expression in them, completely, utterly trusting.

"You're home," she said simply. As if she *had* been waiting for him. Or someone else.

Which seemed highly unlikely, given the way she closed her eyes again, as if to fully savor his chest pressed against her spine, her backside nestled against his—

He realized only then that he was naked as the day he was born. And just as vulnerable. At the mercy of the elements, so to speak.

At the mercy of this woman.

It had been a long time since he'd been surprised into such a disadvantage. Seven years, in fact.

If his face hadn't already been red from windburn, it surely was now as Cade cast around for something to make him decent. Luckily—if you could call it luck, which he was beginning to think he was on the *wrong* end of—there was the pair of jeans he'd thrown over the footboard earlier before heading into the shower.

With a mumbled "Pardon me," he swiftly reached for the jeans and pulled them on under the covers before swinging out of the bed, back to her, to zip them up, barely preserving his modesty in the process, and only a fraction of his composure.

For when he turned around, it was to those singularly captivating eyes staring at him as if he were the answer to a wish.

But hadn't he been the one doing the wishing?

Without a doubt, the cold *had* done a number on his reason, Cade decided. He noticed the letter on the coverlet, where it must have slipped out of his hand. It had gotten crumpled, probably during his exertions getting his jeans on. He snatched it up and tossed it back onto the night table, making a mental note to be sure and read it as soon as he had a private moment. Best to get back to reality with no more delay.

"If you don't mind my bein' nosy, just what're you doin' in my bed?" Cade asked, embarrassment making him short.

She pushed herself halfway up on the headboard, the thick comforter mounding around her. "There wasn't another one made up in the house," she said, as if that explained everything.

Once more, sarcasm got the better of him. "Not much reason for a man livin' out in the middle of the Texas Panhandle to keep a guest room ready on the off chance some strange woman'll want to make herself at home."

He immediately regretted his abruptness. Even with her face half in shadow, he marked the shock in her expression, as well as another emotion he couldn't make out.

"You *are* Cade McGivern, aren't you?" she asked.

"I am," he said, wondering how she knew his name. Of course, one had only to look on the mailbox at the end of the lane, or on any number of papers and such lying around the house.

Yet she murmured on a breath of relief, "At least I'm in the right place."

Her words sent up a flag of warning. Who *was* this woman? How did she get here? More important, why was she here?

Well, he was more than ready to end the mystery.

"You mind tellin' me what's going on here?" he asked, gesturing toward her and the bed.

She pushed herself the rest of the way upright with some difficulty, swinging her legs over the far side of the bed and rising. "Actually, I was hoping you could tell me."

"Tell you what?"

He took a hit of confusion when she turned and he saw what her position in the bed and the comforter had hidden from him: She was pregnant. Heavily so.

He must have stared, for her arms went protectively around the burden under her navy corduroy jumper.

"T-tell me how you know me," she said, that unnamed emotion coloring her words and sending up another flag of warning.

"Ma'am, I've never seen you before in my life," Cade said in dead earnestness.

"I...see." She closed her eyes briefly, as if absorbing another shock. Her mouth trembled in fear.

That was the other emotion he'd spied a minute ago: fear. Again, the warning went off in his head, like an alarm, but at least now he understood what it was about.

For in the next moment an unmistakable shiver of pain crossed her delicate features.

"Oh no," she moaned. Her hand shot out to grab the bedpost as she bent forward, clutching her belly.

Cade didn't need a medical degree to know what was happening. In an instant he was around the foot of the bed to take her elbow. "It's the baby, isn't it?" he said. "That's why you stopped here."

"No!" She shook him off. "It's not time yet! It's too early!" She gasped for breath, then seemed to ask of some-one besides him, "Why? I did everything I could! Every-thing I could think of –"

She doubled over. In one motion, he lifted her and laid her back on the bed.

To his dismay, she locked her arms around his neck to keep him from rising.

"P-please," she panted, obviously still in pain. "Please…tell me the truth. Are you sure you don't know me?"

Bending over her, Cade could only shake his head. "Why do you think I should?"

"Because," she answered, her gaze searching his face desperately, "I've been sent to you, Cade McGivern."

"Sent to me? But…why?"

She shifted slightly, and her belly brushed against his naked stomach. The scent of sandalwood rose up to meet his nose.

"It must be…for you to deliver my baby…and not why I'd thought."

The warning in his ears suddenly sounded louder than ever, like the *bong-bong-bong*ing of a thousand clocks striking midnight.

Because she was looking up at him, hitting him again with that blue gaze as deep as the ocean. And what he now saw in her eyes was aloneness—crushing and soul deep.

It reached out to him, grabbed hold of him and drew him in as nothing else on earth could.

"What did you think you'd been sent to me for?" Cade asked through a throat gone sandpaper-dry.

"To tell me who I am," she whispered. "Because I don't know."

Cade climbed the stairs with a heavy tread, dreading what he had to tell the woman in his bedroom. He couldn't imagine what it would be like for her, finding out she'd only a ham-fisted cowboy—and perfect stranger to her, to boot—to depend on as doctor, midwife and partner in the delivery of her baby.

But then, she was pretty much a perfect stranger to herself, apparently.

He sure as hell wished Virgil would get home. The old ranch hand would be useless so far as helping him with the actual delivery, but it'd be handy to have someone to sterilize whatever needed sterilizing and to keep the fresh linen coming.

But Virgil must have stopped for the night at the Oldfield Ranch next over, rather than trying to ride the six miles back on horseback in a blinding blizzard. No one in the county knew West Texas terrain and weather better than Virg, but not even the most experienced cowboy looked to have any truck with Mother Nature when she got her back up.

Hopefully the hand was safe and warm at the Oldfields', but Cade had learned that, more often than not, hope bought you more trouble than it was worth.

The proof of that was upstairs in his bedroom.

Mentally bracing himself, he entered the room to find the woman walking its length, back and forth, chin against her chest and one hand on her back, the other flattened on her belly.

She glanced up when he came in the room, relief chasing the fear out of her eyes. But not the desolate aloneness that had a way of pulling him in, despite himself.

That feeling of trouble on the hoof struck him once again.

"I got through to Doc Barclay back in Sagebrush," he said a little more curtly than he meant to. He'd had a moment to put on a shirt. It made him feel a little less vulnerable, at least physically.

"Doc Barclay?"

"He's the G.P. in these parts." Cade decided he may as well give it to her straight. "He said there's no way with this storm blowin' full force that he can get here to deliver your baby. We're lucky we've still got phone service."

"And d-driving—" she pressed her fingers to her mouth for a moment, then tried again "—Driving to the doctor?"

"To be frank, you'd have to be related to yourself to be so simpleminded as to go out in this weather. It's a total whiteout out there. Even in my dually four-by-four, we'd like as not end up goin' off the road and get stuck in a ditch."

"I see." She bit her lip in a way that very nearly distracted him from the emergency at hand. "I guess I'm lucky to have found you."

It was a narrow opening, to be sure, but he jumped on it. "Yeah, let's talk about that a minute, if you don't mind."

He jammed his fingers into his front jeans pockets, knowing he was being contentious bringing the subject up when the woman was about to give birth, but he had the right to at least a couple of questions before then. "I didn't see a car outside when I rode in, but that's probably because it's half-buried under a drift of snow. You said you don't know who you are," he said leadingly, "but what *do* you know, like how or when or why you came here?"

Her stance turned wary, her arm around her swollen belly protective, which did nothing to improve his confidence in her truthfulness. "I must've gotten here...oh, I guess two or three hours ago—by car."

"Did you stop here at the ranch 'cause it was the first place you came to when you realized the weather was getting ugly?" he tried again.

"But I told you," she answered. "I thought I was coming to *you.*"

Cade steeled himself against the appeal in those blue eyes. "Look, you said that before, but I'm obviously not making the connection. How on earth could you know you were comin' to me?"

"I had a...a note in my coat pocket with your name and address on it," she said, glancing around. "I must have left it downstairs."

"A note?" Was it just him or was this whole situation becoming less believable by the second?

"Yes. It said 'Sara—'"

"Wait a minute," Cade interrupted. "So now you *do* know your name? You said before you didn't remember."

"I *don't* remember." She looked at him pleadingly. "All I know is that I have a note to *a* Sara, sending her into your care."

Nope, it wasn't just him, Cade thought. This was definitely the strangest situation he'd ever been in, bar none. "Well, if you don't mind my askin', *who* sent you?"

"The note didn't say."

He had to ask. "Y'think it could've been your husband?"

At the question, they both glanced at her left hand. She wore no ring, and Cade didn't like the ensuing relief he felt. Didn't like that he was being drawn yet further into a situation that had all the earmarks of trouble.

In fact, her next words only notched up his suspicions.

"Cade, please, I know it's difficult to understand," she said rather urgently, taking a step toward him. "Heaven knows I don't. But all the way here I thought, if I could just make it to you, everything *would* make sense. I thought you might be…oh, I don't know—that *you* might be my husband, or at least someone who knew me. Cared for me…"

Her shoulders slumped in discouragement. "But you don't. You don't know me at all."

Her voice cracked, and she half turned from him, one palm still pressed to her belly, the other over her mouth, as if she sought to hold back her tears along with the birth of her child.

She was apparently successful, for she went on fiercely, her fingers closed in a fist, "I have to believe I had the right instinct in coming here."

"The right instinct," Cade doggedly pointed out, "would have been to stop fifteen miles back in Sagebrush where there's a doctor with some skill at handling these sorts of situations."

She pivoted back toward him. "I know for sure I didn't pass through any place named Sagebrush," she contradicted. "Besides, you're a cattle rancher, right?"

"What the hell does my being a cattleman have to do with your giving birth?"

"You've probably delivered hundreds of calves, that's what," she said, her voice rising with panic. "You know how labor progresses and how—"

"They're calves!" Cade broke in, his own voice sounding close to panicked, even to his own ears. "Deliverin' a baby would be completely different!"

The room echoed with his doomsday words.

"In any case, no matter how I got here or why I was sent to you," Sara said with just the whisper of a quaver in her voice that sent self-disgust slicing through him like a knife, "you're all I've got right now, Cade."

Abruptly, her face contorted with pain, and she sagged

forward, hands spread on her stomach. Cade was by her side in a single stride, supporting her under her elbow as the contraction intensified, her fingers gripping his forearm, before it finally ebbed.

"How far apart are they?" he asked, still steadying her while she caught her breath.

She rubbed her forehead distractedly, as if that caused her pain, too. Had she hit her head and that was the reason for her memory loss? Cade wondered. Or had someone hit her?

The thought roused a fury of protectiveness in him.

"Maybe ten minutes or so," she answered. "I haven't been keeping track."

"Well, let's make sure we do that next time." Her face sheened with perspiration. "Should you be up walking right now?"

"I don't know! I've never had a baby before...at least I d-don't think I have," she said, that quaver creeping back into her voice, making him even more ashamed.

She was right, of course. The doctor had been extremely clear about a lot of things, but mainly that if Cade was this woman's only source of support to get through this, then it was up to him to convey to her complete reassurance and trust in him. "The more fearful she is," Doc had said, "the more she'll like to have trouble. You know that, Cade. One of your mama cows goes into labor, 'specially for the first time, it's a loving hand and calming voice that's going to see her safely through."

But this is no cow! Cade had thought, as just now he'd said.

Which he shouldn't have. He hadn't mentioned the amnesia to Doc, his own instinct deeming such information best kept to himself for now. Who knew the trouble this Sara might be in, or who in actuality had "sent" her here.

He decided he'd also keep the observation to himself

that whoever or whatever force *had* sent her was about as reliable as the Texas weather outside, and she'd be wise to hitch her hopes to a different star from now on. Because while he'd delivered hundreds of calves, it wasn't a process that came to him instinctively. That had always been Loren's particular gift.

Whatever the case, as she'd said, *he* was all she had to depend on right now, as much as Cade might wish differently.

He noticed her watching him, as if actually looking for that sign, just as she had when she'd gazed at him from his bed.

Cade realized he still held her arm, and he released it.

"All right, let's forget the third degree for now about why you're here," he said, pushing the hair off his forehead and back across his scalp. "The next contraction that comes, let's keep tabs on how long it goes on and how long till the next one. Do you feel more comfortable walking around?"

"For now, yes."

"Do y'know if you had a suitcase or some clothes other than what you've got on?"

"Th-there was nothing in the car. Not even a purse."

The question seemed to upset her again, so he moved on. "When was the last time you ate?"

"I seem to remember stopping for…something on the way here," she said with that certain vagueness he'd seen in her before. He chose to ignore it, since it tended to make him second-guess anything she told him.

"So that was some time ago. Doc said we need to keep your energy up but didn't think you'd be wantin' anything solid."

She confirmed that assumption with a nod.

"I'm afraid I don't have much in the way of broth or

the like. I think there's some orange juice, though. Would you like some of that?'' he asked gruffly.

"Oh, yes," she said with a grateful smile, the first he'd seen from her. And damn if it didn't take him by surprise, stealing his breath away.

It was just a shade crooked, with one corner denting in, creating a dimple, while the other side of her mouth curved up. Combined with those blue eyes, it was about as fascinating as finding the first wildflower in spring.

Which made it doubly hard to do what he needed to next. He may as well get it over with.

"I…uh, I also need to get an idea of how the baby's going to be presenting, so I can tell Doc." Cade extended one hand, indicating her bulging waistline, and asked, "Do you mind?"

She shook her head.

Uncomfortable as hell, he hovered tentatively over that roundness before he gritted his teeth and touched her. Even through the corduroy of her jumper, he could feel how taut and smooth her skin was. He moved his hand downward, feeling for the baby's backbone, hoping—there was that word again—to detect it pressing up against the wall of her womb. If the baby wasn't in the normal position and they'd be dealing with a complicated birth, Cade didn't know what he'd do.

"You're right, I've done this hundreds of times with a pregnant heifer," he murmured, more for himself than for her. *But never a woman.*

His touch, he was glad to note, seemed to calm her, for she put her hand over his and moved it over a spot on her belly. "Is that a foot there?"

The firmness of her swollen pregnancy captivated him, so much so he didn't answer her. Every bit of her was baby, and despite the fear she'd expressed that she wasn't ready to go into labor, he didn't see how she couldn't be.

She was so fine-boned and slim, he wondered how she had been able to carry such weight. Wondered how she would look without it.

Who *was* she and why couldn't she remember that? He'd have to find that note of hers and take a good look at it, see if he could tell who'd sent her into the great wide lonesome of West Texas to hook up with a perfect stranger.

And by God, where was the man who'd given her this child? If it'd been him, Cade knew nothing between heaven and hell could have made him leave her side.

He lifted his eyes to find Sara's upon him, questioning— but hardly indignant at his familiarity. And oh, so very blue. She may doubt it, but some real instinct of his own told him: Sara was her name.

And he would have to get a handle on himself if he was going to make it through this.

Cade stepped away. "Far as I can tell, the baby is presenting properly. I'll call the doctor back and get instructions on what to do next if you'll time any contractions while I'm gone."

He grabbed up his watch from the nightstand and handed it to her without even asking if she had one. But he needed to get out of there, away from her, just for a while, like a man needing to fill his lungs before diving back into the deep blue sea.

Cade gathered an armful of clean blankets and sheets from the linen closet and swung by the downstairs bathroom for a box of sterile gauze, a bottle of antibacterial soap and some rubbing alcohol before heading upstairs to his bedroom again. Doc Barclay had given him a bunch of instructions and told him to round up the supplies he'd need, most of which he didn't have on hand and would have to improvise. He was going to have to use a couple of large plastic trash bags in lieu of a plastic sheet to protect the mattress. Luckily, he'd found a new pair of shoestrings in a drawer. Doc said that would be best for tying off the umbilical cord. The kitchen shears would have to do for cutting the cord after the baby was born. As for a syringe to suction the baby's nose and mouth, all he had was an eyedropper. That'd do the trick.

At least he assumed it would. He and Doc had been cut off in midconversation when the phone went dead. Obviously, the storm was doing its share of damage. Cade took a measure of comfort in knowing that the generator would keep the furnace running, even if the electricity went out.

He'd hate, though, to deliver a baby by the meager glow of a flashlight. He was already enough in the dark as it was.

At the thought, his hands shook so hard he dropped the rubbing alcohol. The bottle bounced off the step and all the way down to the foot of the stairs, from where he retrieved it.

He *had* to get a grip on himself. Maybe he'd do better to separate himself a little from the situation, as he did when delivering calves. He'd have liked a tad more experience with women in general, however. But since Marlene, he hadn't done much associating with the fairer sex.

With a start, he remembered the letter, still unread, on his bed stand. He'd forgotten it in all the commotion. Well, he'd no time to read it now. Yet he knew that particular moment of reckoning would have to come sooner or later.

Entering the room and setting the supplies on the dresser, Cade turned to Sara. "Doc said as long as you felt up to walking you should do it. It increases the effectiveness of the contractions," he rattled off, avoiding her eyes. He refrained from calling her Sara outright. It kept the distance between them. "What are we talkin' about so far as those?"

"The last one was about forty-five seconds long, seven minutes ago."

"Do they feel like they're getting stronger and closer together than they were before?"

She cradled her belly. "Y-yes," she said softly.

"Then it looks like we should get prepared to deliver a baby," he said, matter-of-fact. He brushed past her, going to the bed and stripping it. He wadded the used bedclothes in a ball and tossed them toward the doorway to remind him to put them in a load of wash. He didn't have that many changes of sheets, and they were going to need at least two or three.

With silent efficiency, he made up the bed again, making sure he padded the middle with several layers of towels and arranging the pillows in a stack so when the time came for her to give birth, her back would be supported and she'd have leverage to push through the contractions.

Cade paused, not facing her. "I don't really have anything like a nightgown for you to change into, but maybe that clean shirt of Virgil's on the dresser will at least cover the vital areas. There's some antibacterial soap there, and washcloths in the bathroom down the hall. You'll want to wash up best you can. I'll—I'll give you a chance to change while I check on the water I've got boiling on the stove."

He plain couldn't look at her as he left the room again. She would know as well as he did that modesty would soon take a back seat to urgency.

Talk about really being exposed—and vulnerable.

Downstairs, Cade stalled for ten minutes, busying himself with sundry tasks, before venturing into the bedroom again to be greeted by the fetching sight of Sara in his ranch hand's chambray shirt.

She swam in it, the tails hanging to her knees and the sleeves engulfing her hands as she clutched the neckline together. The color of the shirt brought out the blue in her eyes, making them shimmer as she looked askance at him.

She seemed so much an innocent girl in her daddy's nightshirt and not a mother about to give birth that he had to remark, "Dang if Virgil's shirt doesn't fit you to a tee."

Her frown was just as engaging as her smile had been.

Cade noticed that the toes of one bare foot curled over the other. "Here, let me get you some socks to keep your feet warm."

He fetched a pair of his own from a drawer, and it seemed the considerate thing for him to put them on her himself, rather than make her struggle with bending over.

Going down on one knee, he patted his thigh for her to put her foot up, which she did while clinging to the bedpost for balance. Cade realized right away that while it was polite, it was also the wrong move so far as his composure was concerned.

Because she wasn't a girl. She was all woman, no mistake. Holding her slender ankle, sliding one of his rough woolen stockings over her soft foot and tugging it over her delicate heel, being close to her and having the womanly scent of her overtake his senses...all of it nearly overwhelmed him, it had simply been so long since he'd been close to a woman this way. It was like that tidal tug he'd experienced earlier, making him want to slide his hand up her calf, over that fascinating indentation behind the knee, and further up—

"Oh!" she cried, and a gush of fluid poured down her legs and pooled on the floor in front of him.

In one motion, Cade came to his feet and grasped her upper arms in support as the contraction rocked through her. Eyes squeezed shut, she clutched her belly, gasping. "Oh...God."

"Deep breaths now," he counseled, even as he tried to count the seconds in his head. Where in hell was his watch? "Exhale. Get that air out for me. Now a deep breath in. That's it."

Sara was flushed and perspiring and shaking on her feet by the time the contraction passed. He eased her down on the bed then sidestepped to the dresser, grabbed a couple of towels, and dropped one to the floor to mop up the puddle. The other she used to dry herself. When she'd done with that, he got her a fresh one to hold between her legs in case of another onslaught.

Yup, so much for modesty.

Glancing up at him in apprehension, she asked, "H-how long was the contraction? I couldn't tell."

"So far as I could make it, it lasted about a minute." He spied his watch lying on the sheet next to her and noted the time. "Looks like we're moving right along," he said as confidently as possible. He was doing a little sweating himself.

She nodded, obviously trying to take her cue from him. He could see she was scared, though. Scared as hell. "I— I think I'd like to lie down now."

He didn't question her, had been told by Doc Barclay to let her decide how much activity and what position felt best for her. Cade helped her up onto the bed, where she curled onto her left side, one of his pillows between her knees. He pulled the worn coverlet up over her shoulders, as he'd done a thousand times over his own.

It struck him then, fully, that this woman was having a baby here, in his own bedroom. In his own bed.

And it was just the two of them. Alone.

"Sorry about the mess on your nice wood floor," she said, her voice tight with embarrassment.

"Don't worry about it." He sat on the edge of the mattress, keeping a close eye on both her and the watch. Thankfully, she seemed more comfortable in this position. She would need her strength for later on, he knew.

And that time seemed to be fast approaching.

With the only illumination coming from the bedside lamp behind her, her face was cast in shadow. Cade wondered if he should turn on the overhead light, but it seemed too glaring for this intimate a setting.

"So what would you like me to call you?" he asked abruptly.

She opened her eyes. "Call me?"

"I mean, if we're goin' through this together, I'm gonna need to call you something. Like, y'know—Sara."

"If that's my name." She didn't quite seem to have bought in to it yet, as he had. "What do you say when you're helping a cow to birth her baby?" she asked.

Cade shrugged. "Well, I'll say 'C'mon, girl.' Or else 'You're almost there, darlin'.'"

"You call your cows *darling?*"

He felt his jaw jut mulishly. His gaze stayed glued to the hands of his watch. "If that's what seems to help her, then yes."

She said nothing for a few moments. Finally, she spoke up, "Well. I guess, then, that you—" A gasp broke off her next words. Her hand shot out to clasp his.

He held on to it as tightly as the contraction ran its course. "Breathe as slow as you can," Cade coached her.

He noticed her biting down on her lip hindered her respiration.

"If you wanna holler, holler," he said, exaggerating his twang. "Cuss and swear as the urge takes you, too. There's no one to hear but me, and nothin' you say's going to shock this old cowboy, believe me."

Her brow furrowed with effort, and putting about as much wind behind it as she would to blow soap bubbles, she said "Damn," making Cade laugh out loud.

It seemed to ease the tension in them both. After what

seemed an eternity, she gave one final, cleansing exhalation, her face now gone pale and wan.

"You made it through that one just fine," he said quietly, now finding it hard *not* to call her Sara. He smoothed a washcloth across her forehead, brushing curling wisps of hair away from her face. Her time was definitely drawing near. He was loath to leave her again but he needed to prepare for the birth. He'd see her through the next one, then go get things in order.

"Maybe..." Cade reflected aloud "...maybe that's how we should go at this whole delivery thing—get through one contraction at a time and try not to worry too much about what'll come after till it comes. Let go of what's past, let what's to be, be. And put all our efforts in the here and now."

"Th-that sounds good to me," she whispered, eyes closed. It was probably pretty apparent to her, however, that such a strategy was more to ease his mind than hers.

Although she was the one giving birth...she was the one who had come out of the storm, *without* the anchor of a past or the prospect of a future—except for the pure, blind faith that a man named Cade McGivern would be able to make things right with her world.

And truth be told, *that* was what scared the life out of him.

"Darlin'," she said.

Cade started. "Beg pardon?"

"You can call me...darlin'." She said it how he had, drawled and dropping the *G*. "If that comes more naturally to you. You know, because of your mama cows."

She swallowed, eyes still closed, and put her hand over his as it rested on her shoulder.

Outside, the storm raged on, fierce and ferocious as a bull tearing full bore through a pasture. Inside, the air in the room hung heavy with both possibilities and portent.

Yet a slow warmth stole through Cade. For sure, they were both all the other had right now.

Amazing, how quickly a life could change and get caught up in another's.

''Sounds good to me,'' he said.

Chapter Two

"Talk to me," Sara pleaded.

She saw Cade's Adam's apple bob. He didn't answer.

The labor wasn't going well. Even knowing nothing of her past, she knew this. She'd hit a period of strong, close contractions, but now they'd been in a pushing phase for the past hour. She'd sweated through the shirt and the sheets as she shifted from one uncomfortable position to another, seeking relief and never seeming to find it.

But keeping, just barely, the fear at bay.

Finally, she'd settled for sitting propped up by a load of pillows, knees drawn up. Cade, trying to be helpful, had suggested she come forward on her knees, or maybe squat and let gravity do more of the work, and she'd nearly bit his head off.

For which she was immediately and profoundly sorry. Even now, half an hour later, remembering the moment made her throat constrict with unshed tears. For some reason, she found it vital she keep them in check. Keep her temper in check. Keep the fear in check.

The problem was, she didn't know how much longer she'd be able to do all three and give birth to this baby— this baby she had no memory of conceiving or carrying, whose father she had no memory of. No memory of her own identity as its mother.

The realization struck her anew. It seemed a failure, an abandonment of her child and where it had come from.

A failure if she was to be unable to see it safely born.

She couldn't think about that. If she did, she'd lose more than her memory. She'd lose her mind.

At least she had Cade. Through a fog of pain and confusion, he was the only sure thing in her world, even more than this unborn child was. Even more than the thin gold band on the chain around her neck.

She'd noticed it when she changed clothes. Still on its slender chain, she'd slipped it onto her left ring finger. It had fit perfectly.

The fact that it had infused her with caution, and she'd decided to keep it hidden for now. She had sensed that Cade wanted nothing less than to be trapped here in this situation she'd literally thrust upon him. The thought that he wouldn't want to be, or that the instinct that had brought her to him might have been wrong, gave rise to that clawing fear in her again. But she couldn't do this alone! She couldn't lose this baby. She'd do anything, anything not to.

"Cade," Sara said, bringing his gaze back from brooding out the darkened window. He had brown eyes, the color of whiskey, liquid and golden. Just looking into them, she found herself calmed. Reassured, as if she feared she'd forget him, too, should she lose for too long the connection between them. It was still so tenuous. "Please. Talk to me."

His features gentled and, for the hundredth time, he brushed her hair from her temple, sticky with perspiration. He'd taken the liberty of divesting himself of his flannel shirt, and still the sweat beaded on his chest, dampened his thick auburn hair. He was worried for her.

"About what?" he asked.

"I don't care." She shifted, vainly trying to relieve the pressure on her back. "The sound of your voice...helps me keep my mind off of...things. Tell me about yourself."

Obviously uncomfortable with the subject, he nevertheless cleared his throat. "Well, uh, I'm a rancher, as you've already confirmed. Been doin' it so long I don't guess I could do much else. Not that there's much else I fancy doin'," he added hastily.

Even from the edge of total fatigue, Sara caught his uneasiness. "Who's this...Virgil you mentioned?" she asked.

Relief eased across his brow at the change of subject. "Virg is my ranch hand. Been around here forever, since when my granddaddy ran the operation."

Again, he offered no further comment. The connection between them waned.

Mustering her energy, Sara persisted "Your grandfather—and your parents. Are they still around, too?"

"'Fraid not. Granddaddy passed on some years ago. Daddy and Mother, we lost them when I wasn't more'n ten."

Strangely, she found herself buoyed by his admission— as if it somehow confirmed that instinct she'd had to find him. He was alone, too.

Still, she apologized, "I didn't mean to bring up sad memories."

Cade only shrugged. "It was a long time ago."

"So you must have been in charge of the ranch when you were quite young." She had noted the rugged yet youthful lines of his face. "You don't look much past thirty."

He blinked in surprise. "I hit thirty-one my next birthday."

"And you've no other family?" Her mouth worked around the next question, trying to suppress it and failing. "Or a special…friend?"

"Nope," Cade replied, returning to his characteristic terseness. "Just a brother. In New Mexico."

The words sparked recognition in the back of her mind. "New Mexico?"

"That would be the state just west of Texas."

She couldn't keep from treating him to a cross look. "I know what New Mexico is. I haven't lost all sense of the world."

"Beggin' your pardon, but how'm I supposed to know that?" Cade said mildly.

"I remembered I hadn't passed through a town named Sagebrush," she reminded him.

Her comment apparently struck a chord with him, too. "That means you weren't coming from west. What was the last big city you went through?"

It was the last subject Sara wanted to pursue right now. To do so brought all the emotions she needed to keep control of from taking over. Yet she'd hazarded into this territory of her own accord in her attempt to engage him.

She closed her eyes, trying to concentrate. Where *had* she come from? The awareness grew, hovering on the edges of her perception and making her anxious, but this time she tried to go toward it. "I think it was…somewhere in Oklahoma."

"Oklahoma?" Cade frowned. "That's in the opposite direction. Was there something about New Mexico that seemed familiar?"

What *was* it that had caused a ripple in the vast, undisturbed surface of her memory? Massaging her forehead, she tried to think back, push the edges of what memory she had, but the effort seemed more than she could stand right now. "I don't know."

"Were you heading to New Mexico?"

She shook her head, which only made it throb even more. "I don't know! I don't know."

Why couldn't she remember?

Pain bit into her, shaking her in its jaws.

"Oh!" Sara's chin snapped forward and she pressed her palms to her belly.

The contraction was a doozy, rolling through her in shock wave after shock wave. All sense seemed to leave her when they hit, chased by that stark, utter terror that was gaining ground on her by the second.

She shamelessly clung to Cade's hand, and he hung with her until the contraction passed, leaving her gasping and exhausted.

With infinite gentleness, he stroked the washcloth across her forehead. "I'm sorry," he said. "I shouldn't've pushed you for information, especially when I told you I wouldn't."

But it had drawn him out of his remote, brusque manner, bringing the tenderness back to his warm brown eyes. Sara didn't want to see it leave again, didn't think she could stand it if it did. But she realized it came with a price to herself.

Because when the next contraction came, just as strong, a few minutes after that, then the next and the next after that, she knew it meant she was going into hard labor. Her baby was on its way. Yet still something held it back, something in her held back, for there was little progress.

She was reaching the edge of her endurance. The edge of her reason.

"Oh, Cade." Sara clutched his hands with both of hers

as yet another contraction came and went, and still no baby. "I don't know...if I can do this."

"Sure you can, darlin'," he countered with quiet firmness as he sat beside her on the bed. "Sure you can."

No, I can't. She could barely hold her head up, much less hold at bay the doubts and fears boiling up in her. Why didn't the baby come? What was wrong with it? What was wrong with her? This was her own flesh and blood, for God's sake! If she hadn't the strength within her to bring her own child into the world, then what *did* she have the strength to withstand?

"No," Sara said, shaking her head. "No, you don't understand."

"You're right, I can't understand," Cade agreed placatingly. "No one can who hasn't birthed a child."

"That's just it! Who knows if I have before?"

Even she could hear the hysteria that rose in her voice. She couldn't breathe. The pain, the confusion, the lack of any mooring in this storm in her head—each was taking its toll.

"C'mon, darlin'." Cade's voice was steady, his gaze unwavering, keeping the connection. But even that was barely getting through to her. Panic prowled nearby, stalking her in her weakened state. "Remember our pact? Just focus on what's directly in front of you. Focus on that baby of yours, ready to come into the world."

"I know...I am...but oh, Cade, I don't even know where he came from, where *I* came from!" she cried, giving in to her fears at last. It was simply too much to contain.

Yet it only cleared the way for her next fear, which clambered up from the depths of her being, fighting her for expression. "I don't even know who we belong to...and why he's not here!"

Another contraction socked her, pitching her forward,

her spine rounding and body shaking with effort. The pain seemed unbearable, the contraction intense, as if every muscle in her body was converging to push out this child.

But it wouldn't come! It wouldn't come, and she didn't know why.

Sara fell back, drained. It seemed impossible she'd find the strength and energy to endure the following wave.

"Sara." The name came to her as if across a canyon, wide and deep. "Stay with me now. Stay with me."

She found Cade's words unexpectedly humorous. He was the one she was trying to keep engaged in the moment, wasn't he? she thought as laughter bubbled up from her chest. What emerged was a sob, then another. Sara turned her head away as she worked to contain them.

"I'm sorry, Cade," she whispered.

"Sorry for what?"

"For...drawing you into this." She squeezed her eyes shut, but still the tears streamed from their corners. She couldn't hold them back, another failure. "You don't know me...and whoever sent me to you...why they sent me to you...it wasn't right. I don't belong...here."

He said nothing for a few minutes. Then his weight next to her on the bed stirred as he released her hand.

Arctic cold, as icy as the wind outside whistling under the eaves, swept through Sara.

Then she felt his palm on her cheek, urging her to turn her head. Weakly, she resisted.

"Hey. Look at me."

Reluctantly, Sara opened her eyes, afraid of what she'd find. Cade's face swam before her, and she blinked away tears to see him gazing at her—no, connecting with her, as she so needed.

"You're right," he said, "I can't begin to know what it's like havin' a baby— or what it must feel like to be without the anchor of a name I knew was mine, or a place to belong. But I do have some experience with goin' without the tie of loved ones. Without someone to belong to.''

His gaze faltered briefly, but then came back home to hers. ''And I won't have you feel so alone as that.''

Like dawn breaking over the horizon, she saw in Cade's brown eyes so many things she'd hoped for, without even realizing it: reassurance, encouragement, confidence—and maybe a little bit of love.

Or was it her exhaustion, the pain, the utter despair she had been fighting that made her think she saw all those things?

Then Cade said, ''I'm here to tell you, though, that wherever both of you came from, you and your baby, you're here now—in my house, in my bed, right where you need to be.''

He wove the fingers of one of his large, capable hands in hers. ''For now, you belong here, with me. And I won't let you down.''

It seemed unreal, but at his words Sara felt the pain, the fatigue, her every doubt and fear for her child, dwindle and wane like an echo across both space and time. They were all still there, most certainly, but manageable now.

Some part of her, though, still doubted. She had to be sure. ''Just…don't leave me, Cade.''

''I won't,'' he vowed, low. ''Not for anything.''

Her eyes spilled over with new tears, for she knew then in her heart that she *had* had the right instinct in finding this man. Or perhaps it hadn't been her doing at all, and she'd been guided to him, not by some mysterious note writer, but by a force much larger than them all.

It was a gift, she realized, this trust in a force—call it heavenly or fateful or whatever—that she somehow had lost faith in, in that slumbering memory of hers.

Tremulously, Sara smiled at the man who had given her such a gift. Cade's gaze dropped to her mouth, then came around again to hers. What she saw there overwhelmed her anew.

It was that connection, to be sure, but stronger than ever, made so by the naked longing in his eyes. The power of it reached out to her, and she couldn't help but respond with an answering yearning that rose up from deep inside her, almost from another life, another time completely—

The next contraction hit.

Cade helped her pull herself forward, her shoulders hunched and her chin lowered as she bore down hard, a guttural moan of effort rising from her chest. His fingers laced with hers, and her nails dug into his palm. He didn't bat an eyelash.

"I can see the head crowning," he told her, not without some excitement. She slumped back as the contraction subsided. "Next one, give a big ol' push, and I bet we'll have him."

"Really?" she panted, not daring to believe it.

"You bet." He massaged her calves, seeming to know without a word from her that they were seconds from cramping. "When the baby does start to come out, though, I'm gonna have to concentrate on it, you know. So I won't be able to hold your hand. You okay with that?"

She nodded. "Yes. Yes, of course."

"Good. I already told you, I'm not goin' anywhere."

And he didn't, even as her agony increased twofold with the next contraction. Yet they *were* making progress.

"C'mon, darlin', you're doin' great," Cade urged, both hands now flush up against her intimately, ready and waiting to receive precious cargo. "Big push now. You can do it, darlin'. You can."

Sara pushed with all her might, putting everything into it, holding back nothing, for now she knew someone would be there to see her through to completion.

"There you go," Cade exhorted her. "I've got his head, just give me the rest of him—"

"Him?" she puffed, straining to see. "Is it a boy?"

"I don't know yet," Cade said, full upon his knees by now, every muscle in him seeming to strain with her in empathy. "Just one more push, baby. One more, just for me…"

She couldn't let him down. Where she found the strength, she didn't know, but it came to her, and one last time, Sara bore down. The last of her apprehension disappeared as she watched the miracle unfold as he received her child into his large hands.

First off, he checked its parts. "Hoo-haw! It *is* a boy! You got yourself a son."

"We do?" she breathed. "Oh, let me see him!"

"In a sec, darlin'." With barely a pause, he snatched up an eyedropper and suctioned the infant's mouth and nose.

From her position, the babe looked a good weight, easing some of her apprehension that he was early. But why was he so still?

"Is he…is he all right?" she asked, fear creeping into her voice despite herself. "What did the doctor say to do if the baby's not responding?"

He didn't answer. "Cade, what did he say!"

"He didn't…we didn't get that far in the conversation," he said curtly, still suctioning feebly.

"But why…?" Then it dawned on her. "The phone— it *did* go out, didn't it?"

Again, Cade refused to answer, his wide shoulders hunched over the tiny form, his face a study in fierce determination. His silence, however, was all the confirmation she needed.

Oh, what kind of woman was she not to protect her child better, to put him at such risk?

It was her worst fear revealed.

"Cade, please, I can't lose this baby!"

"You won't. He's just gettin' his bearings."

Frantically, Sara pushed herself upright, trying to see, trying to reach for her baby. "But he's not moving—"

"He will!" Cade hit her with his bloodshot gaze, and she saw his own fear in it. Yet she saw something else, too, enduring as the day was long. "He's going to be fine. *I promise you.*"

Then, as if in answer to that promise, the baby sputtered briefly, filled his lungs and, with a grimace, gave a mighty cry.

Grabbing a towel, he dried the baby off, and Sara could see for herself that the infant was quickly gaining color. His tiny fists waved about as he gave another gloriously vigorous wail.

Cade placed him on her stomach. "There you go, darlin'—a healthy baby boy."

"Oh, you sweetheart!" She caressed the babe, wet and warm and still connected to her through the umbilical cord. But he was his own person now, even if they would forever be connected.

Hands on his thighs, Cade smiled across the bed at Sara. Even with his dark hair matted with perspiration and his eyes ringed with exhaustion, Sara thought she'd never seen anything so noble and true as this man. She'd hold the image in her heart forever.

Downstairs, a clock chimed, and she could tell he counted the strokes, as she did, twelve in all.

"Happy New Year, darlin'," he whispered.

She couldn't not do it. Whoever she was, wherever she'd come from, she had to reach out to him one more time with her gaze—reach out, grab hold, and connect. Because she knew. Knew there had been a moment of grave danger for her child. And Cade McGivern had seen him—seen them both—safely through the storm. She would never, ever forget that.

No, she'd not lose memory of Cade McGivern. Not for anything.

"Yes, it is, Cade," Sara murmured. "It's a very happy one—because of *you*."

And when she saw the look in those whiskey-brown eyes, it almost made her forget the slender band of gold she wore around her neck.

Almost.

Cade helped Sara to get cleaned up, best she could, changed the padding beneath her and kept the clean towels coming for the bleeding after she'd delivered the afterbirth, anything he could do to make her more comfortable and rest easier until she felt like getting up for a real shower.

He himself did the honors, giving the baby a sponge bath in the bathroom sink, as fascinated as she with the tyke.

What a perfect package he made! Cade couldn't help thinking as he finished up. Newborn calves were precious in their own way, but gangly. Swaddled in a blanket, this babe fit in his hands like he was made to, dinky butt situated in one palm, tiny head cradling just right in the other. The shock of dark hair that stood up on his head like a bristle brush had been impossible to slick down, and in fact Cade's efforts to do so had only made matters worse. He hoped Sara wouldn't mind having a newborn who looked like a startled rooster.

"I don't have a proper diaper for him," he said, coming back into the bedroom. "I imagine I can rig him up somethin' that'll keep him dry—or actually, keep you dry."

Sara let go of Virg's shirt, which she'd been clasping shut at the neckline, as he handed her child back to her. She'd declined a change into another of the hand's shirts.

"I'm more concerned about him soaking your bed," she said.

"Don't worry, I did a load of wash." Still lacking his own shirt, Cade leaned a shoulder against the bedpost, openly enthralled with the picture the two made. "And soon's I have a minute to get up to the attic, I'll bring down the cradle that's been in my family for years. I should get you somethin' to eat first, though. You gotta be hungry after all that work you did."

"You must be exhausted yourself, Cade," she protested, but he wouldn't hear a word of it.

"It won't take me more'n a minute to fix you an egg or somethin'."

"Th that sounds wonderful." Sara ducked her chin, avoiding his eyes. "I want to thank you, Cade, for all the work *you've* done. And for, well, for everything. I've completely commandeered your bedroom, and now I'm going to inconvenience you further by your having to wait on me and my baby till I can get up and around."

"I don't mind," he told her truthfully. "Honest."

But he guessed what was going on—and what he was trying mightily to ignore. They'd just shared an intimate act in delivering her son, almost as intimate as the one that had made him. It hadn't escaped Cade how at the moment of birth she'd called him *their* baby. It *wasn't* theirs, though.

It was hers—and some other man's, wherever he was.

Cade didn't like that he felt disappointed at this reality, but what, really, did he expect?

He expected...something more, for in that moment when he'd set that child into his mother's arms, and she'd looked at him as if he'd performed a miracle, he'd felt anything was possible, anything on earth. And maybe even anything in heaven above, although he couldn't have said what he'd have wanted that to be.

The baby, who'd been fussing, finally cut loose with a full-fledged howl that echoed in the room and brought his attention back to front and center.

"That's some set of lungs," he remarked.

Sara jostled the infant slightly, worry etched between her eyes. "I wish I knew more about babies."

"Hell, what's there to know? He's probably just hungry," Cade suggested. "At least, that's what a newborn calf bawls about."

"That's a thought." Her hands were at the buttons of her shirt before she seemed to remember herself. In flushed confusion, she murmured, "If you wouldn't mind, Cade…"

He got her meaning. "Of course," he said, cutting for the door, feeling a little flushed and confused himself. And unjustifiably rankled.

In the hallway, he leaned back against the wall. So he'd just taken her baby from her body! And sure, it made him feel like he'd performed a miracle. Never in his life had he felt such power of emotion before. And like a miracle, it had been transforming. But she *wasn't* his wife with whom he'd have shared the real miracle in creating this baby.

Was there a chance, though, that she might not be anyone else's?

With that thought, Cade realized he'd do almost anything to recover the feeling he'd shared with Sara—and *that* he definitely didn't like, not at all.

Because heaven and earth couldn't have stopped him in the next instant from turning back into the bedroom with the words of his own hopes for the two of them on his lips.

He stopped dead in his tracks. She'd already opened her shirt, revealing a creamy breast, and was in the process of guiding the newborn's mouth to one rose-colored nipple.

Sara looked up in startlement, trying to pull the edges of her shirt together, but the baby's mouth had already found its target and latched on.

Cade couldn't have looked away even if his immortal soul depended upon it.

For in that instant before Sara's gaze dropped, he caught the flutter of her lashes as she took in his own exposed chest. And instead of hope, raging desire surged through him in a torrent that stunned him, for it seemed an even greater force to be reckoned with—and even more one not to be denied.

Until he caught the glisten of a chain around her neck. On it, nestled in the hollow between her breasts and just above her child's downy head, was a simple gold wedding band.

It glittered in the light, and in just such a flash, Cade saw himself in his own desperate, vulnerable aloneness as he never had in his life.

From the direction of the stairs there came a clatter like a herd of elephants stampeded up them. In the next instant a man appeared in the doorway, steam rising from his clothing, hoarfrost covering his bushy mustache and eyebrows, his face white as the driving snow outside.

His eyeball-popping gaze went from Cade to the woman in his bed to the baby cradled in her arms, then back to Cade. His shaggy head wagged back and forth slowly.

"Lordy, Cade!" Virgil exclaimed. "I knew I was late and prob'ly worryin' ya to death, but I didn't know you'd take to such extremes to distract yourself!"

She could not take her eyes off him.

Alone for the moment, Sara took the opportunity to explore every inch of her sleeping child.

Utterly exhausted but still too wound up to sleep, she made a thorough inventory, counting each finely formed finger, each tiny toe, each delicate dimple. She caressed each satiny surface, reveling in a softness that felt like none she could have ever imagined.

Whatever pain she'd endured, whatever heartache she'd lived through or would live through, it was worth it for this child.

It didn't seem possible that just a few hours ago he had been inside her, a part of her, and now was a separate person—but oh! still so much a part of her, as he always would be.

To her surprise, features that had earlier been unrecognizable to her in the bathroom mirror she now glimpsed in her son: her own nose in the button on his face, a certain familiar look about his cupid's bow of a mouth.

Tears misted her sight as she clung to that recognition like a lifeline. Who knew why she'd forgotten who she was, but perhaps her baby would help her to remember.

Who else was he a part of, though? The question haunted her. What man had she so loved—and had so loved her—they had created a child together?

And where was he now?

Turning, she stared blindly out the window where the blizzard continued to blow, as all the questions she'd managed to keep at bay since her delivery rose up inside her again. Questions she'd seen reflected in Cade's eyes as they focused on the ring she wore around her neck.

The resulting desolation of spirit she'd glimpsed in him had been heartbreaking, for it was her own.

The tears standing in her eyes spilled over. What kind of woman was she? Had she only used that fine man, taken advantage of his good heart and tender feelings to keep him invested in her and her baby through the delivery?

But she'd had to! She herself had had to reach out to him with everything in her. He was real; he was there. The knowns in her life had had to take precedence over the unknowns.

And what had she known? That she was going into labor. That she was alone. That she'd been sent to Cade.

But now...now she had to ask about...him. The father of her child. What kind of man was he not to have been here with her now? Had she been trying to find him, and somehow gotten it in her mind she would discover him here?

Was that in fact her real transgression, not taking from Cade what she needed, but seeking from him what she'd been missing from the man who'd placed this ring on her finger?

"Hey, there," came a soft call from the doorway. She turned.

Cade stood at the threshold to his bedroom as if needing an invitation inside.

"Hello." A warmth having nothing to do with her erratic hormonal state swept over her. Suddenly, it *didn't* seem real—that only a few hours ago he'd been with her on this very bed, the two of them partners in a battle for her baby's life. It simply didn't seem possible that such broad shoulders, such sturdy arms and large hands, could have yielded over their might to the kind of gentleness it took to hold a newborn babe. Seemed impossible that, with his reserved, remote bearing, she could have felt completely cared for and safe. Because right now, the sheer height and breadth and strength of presence of him took her breath away.

She could not take her eyes off him.

And what kind of woman did that make her?

"How's the little mite doin'?" he asked in that provocative, gravelly drawl of his, coming into the room to drop a dark piece of clothing over the arm of a chair.

"He's eaten his fill and is sleeping like a lamb," she

reported, covertly sweeping away the traces of moisture on her cheeks.

"Now that I most definitely can't tolerate."

The wind left her lungs with completeness. "But... why?"

"Sleepin' like a lamb?" He shook his head gravely. "This territory's strictly cattle ranching, and I'm afraid if word got out that Cade McGivern was tendin' sheep on his place, I'd get tarred and feathered within an inch of my life."

Sara was struck dumb—until she caught the amusement in his eyes. Relieved laughter shook loose any lingering anxiety. "Oh...you!" was the best she could come up with, flustered as she'd become.

For a second there, she'd experienced a riot of sheer panic that he meant to turn them back out into the storm.

Which was ludicrous. Yes, she'd done what she'd needed to, to secure the safe delivery of her baby. And yes, he'd seen the ring. Yet neither what happened before or afterward could diminish the moment when he had made her and her child his own.

But it had only been for that moment, he said. And now?

Sara only realized her mind had drifted when she heard Cade clear his throat, obviously not for the first time.

"So," he said tersely, "how's that makeshift diaper Virg made holding up?"

"Just fine. Want to see?"

She obligingly drew back the blanket as he bent close, leaning on one hand on the bed next to her hip. He'd showered, she noticed; his chestnut-brown hair shone slickly, the forelock hanging in spikes over his forehead. It reminded her of how his hair had been when she'd awakened and looked up into his eyes for the first time.

She pushed her own hair, limp and lank, back from her

face. She must look a mess. As soon as she could, she was taking a shower.

The diaper was basically a clean washcloth with some extra gauze padding the front and pinned at the sides. The key component was the waterproof pants Virgil had fabricated out of a plastic freezer bag by cutting a couple of leg holes and rimming them with duct tape to prevent tearing and leakage. Two more pieces of tape secured the pants at the sides.

Cade eyed the whole contraption speculatively. "It sure enough makes him look like some home plumbing work, but I guess it does the job."

"Baby Cade doesn't mind," she said before thinking

His head shot up. "You named him after *me?*"

"Why, yes," Sara said, commanding her gaze not to falter. It was difficult to do, with his face so close to hers. "I can think of no one finer."

Shock rimmed his eyes. "That's because you don't *know* anyone else at this point!"

"I know you," she averred stubbornly. "I know what you did for me and my baby."

"But you've got to see, darl—"

Rather than she, it was he who dropped his gaze. He'd yet to call her Sara—except once, when he'd summoned her back from the depths of her despair.

"I'm just askin'," he said, his voice muted, "what about the baby's father?"

"What about him?" Sara said boldly. She realized what he was staring at, and her fingers went to the chain lying on her chambray shirtfront. "Yes—this ring. Obviously, it's mine. But no, I don't remember who gave it to me or what happened t-to him."

To her dismay, her voice shook and her mouth trembled with more tears. Sara sniffed them back. "But whoever he is, Cade, he owes you a debt of gratitude, and I can't imagine he would begrudge this expression of my—of our appreciation. I—I'll never forget what you've done for me,'' she vowed in an echo of her thoughts at that moment when he'd given her this child.

"You won't?" Cade asked skeptically.

Sara didn't even realize the contradiction in her phrasing until the words were out—for obviously she *had* forgotten, so very much.

Her head had begun to ache again, and she rubbed the knot of tension at her temple. She couldn't let what she didn't know keep her from believing in what she did!

She noticed Cade had gone very still, his expression watchful.

"Does your head hurt because you were injured?" he asked. "Did you hit it somehow…or did someone hit you?"

She wondered what he'd do if she said yes, because from the looks of it, Cade McGivern had it in him to focus a ferocious amount of energy toward protecting someone he cared for.

The thought calmed her, gave her courage. Lifting her chin high, she answered, "I don't know, Cade. I don't know what happened. But there is no way on earth I will ever forget the experience with you of bringing this child into the world. I may not know who I am, but I know that with every bit of my heart."

For a moment Cade didn't speak, his whiskey-brown gaze keen upon her face as if himself searching for recognition in her features, as she had in her son's. Or was he looking for something else, something beyond acknowledgement? For lurking in the back of his eyes, she detected the same yearning she'd seen before, a desperate wanting to believe.

And she wanted to give him the assurance he could, as he'd given her, because what had happened between them *was* worth believing in, *was* worth remembering. But before she could speak, Cade pushed off from the bed, pivoting away, and her chance was gone.

"Speakin' of identities," he said, "I found your coat downstairs where you left it."

He fetched it from where he'd laid it on the chair and thrust the coat out to her with a brief nod. "I didn't want to go through the pockets myself, but I'm thinkin' you might find that note in them."

She again caught the skepticism in his voice. Cradling her baby in the crook of her arm, Sara took the coat from him and drew it across her lap. She didn't know why, but her hand shook as she dipped it into one pocket. Out came a pack of chewing gum and a set of car keys.

"No note?" Cade asked.

"Not here." Turning the coat over, she felt inside the other pocket. Her fingers closed over something. She pulled out a folded scrap of paper.

Opening it, she read aloud, "'Sara—if there's anything you should need—anything at all—contact Cade. He'll take care of you.'"

Relief came in a wave, washing over her. She didn't realize until now how much she *had* doubted of what she knew.

Handing the note to him, she said triumphantly, "Your name, address and phone number are listed, along with some directions from the interstate, but as I said, there's no signature—"

He made a strangled sound.

"Cade?" Sara asked.

All of her apprehension came back as she watched him study the note as if he were memorizing every pen stroke. It was the same way he'd looked at her—except she could see in that note he *was* finding recognition.

"What is it, Cade?" Still he didn't answer her, his

whole stance seeming carved in stone, and Sara instinctively clutched her baby to her breast.

When he finally moved, he did so with a speed that seemed fantastic, and at once had rounded the bed to the opposite bed stand. He picked up an envelope lying there. He tore into it, read its contents like one possessed.

Before her eyes, he turned pale as a ghost, and rather than shocked, as earlier, he looked utterly horrified.

"Cade, tell me, please!" Sara cried.

In two strides he was at her side. He practically shoved the envelope into her hand. His own closed around the sheets of writing it had contained, crushing them.

The envelope looked as if it had been handled tens of times, even though the postmark was only half a week old.

Then she saw what Cade obviously had: the envelope was addressed to him in the exact same handwriting as her note. The return address said "McGivern, Albuquerque, New Mexico."

Meeting his gaze, Sara shook her head. "This is from…your brother?"

"Yes. My brother—Loren." He watched her closely, obviously looking for some sign from her, but the name meant nothing to her.

"So I must know your brother, well enough that he'd give me your name in case of an emergency. He never mentioned that to you?"

"Funny, but it never seemed to've come up. Of course, this letter is the first contact I've had from him in seven years," Cade answered.

He seemed to have distanced himself from her, was more like the cynical man she'd first encountered. Except now she knew what lay behind that hard exterior of his, and she couldn't go back.

"Is that what's wrong, Cade? You and your brother are

estranged?'' she pressed. ''Was there some sort of falling out?''

He gave a mirthless laugh that she didn't care for, not at all. ''Oh, definitely. But now Loren writes to tell me he remarried some months ago, that his new wife is pregnant with his first child. And once that child is born, he doesn't want him not to know his only uncle.''

Foreboding crept over Sara. Strange she should have any kind of presentiment when she remembered nothing of the past. Wouldn't it have to be rooted in some event she remembered as already happening in her life?

But something *had* happened. As short as it was, she did have a past she remembered: she and Cade had shared the experience of her son's birth. And she couldn't go back to before.

She wanted to remind him of their pact to focus on this moment and not let either the past or the future stop them from living this moment to the fullest. She wanted to remind him of how he himself had allayed her fears with his own vow that still rang in her ears: *Wherever both of you came from, you and your baby, you're here now—in my house, in my bed, right where you need to be. For now, you belong here, with me. And I won't let you down.*

It had meant so much to her, kept her hanging on through the worst of the pain and fear. Oh, was she about to lose that, too?

She couldn't!

Sara put a hand to her head, it was spinning so. She felt as if she were trapped and struggling in a quagmire of all the unknowns in her life, both past and to come. Maybe that was why she clung so desperately to the certainty of the here and now. Clung so desperately to Cade.

She didn't want to ask her next question, but she knew she had to. Knew—because Cade knew the answer, and it would kill him not to say so. She owed him more than that.

"Your brother, Loren." The name felt heavy on her tongue. But definitely not unfamiliar. "His wife...?"

Sara made herself lift her eyes to meet his, and wished she hadn't. Memory or no, she had never seen a man look so bleak.

"My brother's wife's name," he said, "is Sara."

Chapter Three

Cade plunged out into the storm, head and hands bare and exposed to the freezing cold. At least he'd stopped to pull his wool-lined jacket from its peg and thrust it on, or he'd be completely at the mercy of the elements.

The icy bitterness felt good, though. It was like a great big hit of reality smack in the face, right where he obviously needed it.

Because the woman in his bed—the one in a moment of insanity he'd vowed was his and no other man's—was his brother's wife.

The very brother Cade had spent the past seven years wondering whether he would ever be forgiven by and, since receiving Loren's letter, had begun to hope he had.

And it got worse from there. Stumbling through a snowdrift, Cade brutally forced himself to admit that yes, even after seeing Sara's wedding band, he'd *hoped* her wearing it on a chain around her neck and not her finger had meant she might be free.

Free—to do what? He barely knew her!

So why didn't it feel that way?

Yet there had to be a reason for her keeping the ring on a chain. Was it something Loren had done? When? From the way his brother wrote in his letter, it seemed as though the pregnancy was recent. Obviously, that wasn't the case.

So what had happened? What *could* have happened, in just a few days? Of course, there was Sara's amnesia, her claim she had no purse. Had they been held up on the highway, and his brother had tried to hold off their attackers so Sara could speed to safety?

Cade endured a moment of mortal fear for his brother's safety, until he recalled the note in Loren's handwriting. His brother had obviously anticipated sending his new wife to Cade, for whatever reason.

So what had happened with Marlene? Or maybe the question was, what happened *to* her, since Loren had loved her to such distraction Cade couldn't imagine they'd split up voluntarily.

It was damned hard to get his head around all the changed perceptions that up until ten minutes ago had been well settled in his mind.

Then another possibility occurred to him? Was this a...a test of some sort? Cade couldn't get behind that, not by a long shot! Loren would never do that to him, no matter how hurt and angry he'd been.

Cade had gone seven years, though, without one single, solitary word from the older brother he'd worshiped since he was old enough to walk.

Which brought him around to the real questions he wanted to ask Loren, the ones buffeting him like the pounding wind: *Why aren't you with Sara? How could you bear not to be with her so close to her hour of need?*

Damn it, Loren had even been careless about her name! He'd written it as "Sarah," over and over again, throughout the letter. But on the note to Cade, it was "Sara." How could a man not know how to spell his wife's name?

Somehow, Cade felt glad. *Sarah*—she was the one Loren had gone on about for pages, his words steeped in love and devotion.

But *Sara*—she'd been sent to him out of the storm, knowing nothing but the one certainty: once she found him, all would be well.

And she'd said it herself: he'd delivered her baby, and she would never forget it. The act forever linked together their lives.

Cade swore soundly. He had to get rid of that thinking pronto. Sara, with or without the *H*, was Loren's.

Only she didn't remember Loren. She only knew him, Cade.

Loren's scent surrounded her.

The questions flew at him like the millions of snow-flakes, confounding him. Then one in particular loomed in his mind: what had Loren told her about him, the kid brother he'd given up on seven years ago—and why?

He practically smashed his forehead into the side of the stable, Cade was so wrapped up in his thoughts. He definitely needed to get a handle on himself. Men had gotten lost and frozen to death mere yards from shelter in such weather.

Feeling his way, he located the stable door, pulled it open with difficulty, and slipped inside.

All three horses stirred, but only Destiny lifted his massive head and gave a snort of greeting into the dimness. Lord, he was one smart horse! Cade had only had him a few months and already the chestnut welcomed his particular presence.

"Damn if you're not about the only one around here who does," Cade said without rancor, making his way to the stall.

The gelding had been an indulgence, no doubt about it, costing upward of twice as much as Cade had planned to spend on a new cow pony. There'd been many a fine piece of horseflesh he'd looked at that could have done the job he needed just fine. Yet as soon as he'd seen the quarter horse in that pasture, head held high and the sun glinting off his chestnut coat the color and shine of a new penny, Cade had had to have him.

Up to then, he'd pretty much abandoned the dream of training horses for a living. But with one look, Destiny had sparked the hope to life again. He didn't know how or when he might build such a business, given he was running a three-man spread with just him and Virgil, but for Destiny, he'd find a way.

Of course, if he wanted to free up some of his time, all Cade had to do was hire a second hand; it wasn't as if the ranch's income couldn't bear another wage earner. The truth, however, was that he'd never hired anyone else because he'd always held a picture in his mind of how his older brother would look when he came back and discovered Cade had never given up on the ranch—or him.

And when he'd gotten Loren's letter, it had taken somewhere in the vicinity of sixty seconds for him to play out the rest of that scene to where Loren asked if he could come back to the ranch to live—for good this time.

Now, though, the prospect of living here with Sara seemed more of a nightmare than a dream come true.

His ears were thawing out, and they itched like blue blazes. Rubbing one, Cade rested his forearm on the stall railing, hand dangling. The gelding snuffled his palm hopefully.

"Sorry, pardner," he murmured. "No treats tonight."

He gave the chestnut a scratch on the bridge of his nose instead, and the caress seemed to satisfy. Cade couldn't help regretting all his shortcomings weren't so easily compensated for.

Seven years. Seven years of living here with no family but Virgil, trying to run the ranch using his spotty know-how where in the past he'd always had Loren to know what to do. Loren had been the one who'd been born to ranch, the one who because of age and skill Granddad had groomed for the job from the first. And Cade had always been the younger brother meant to take the reins in a different arena.

Except their fate hadn't played out that way. And both he and Loren knew the reason why.

Cade swung around, his gaze making a circle of the stable's interior. It had happened here, actually. He could still hear his brother's words ringing in the dusty air.

"You bastard! I can't believe my own brother would do such a thing! You bastard."

"But I didn't do anything! Loren, you've got to believe me," Cade pleaded. *"What you saw, it's not what you think!"*

"The hell it's not! Then why'm I standin' here looking at you with guilt written all over your face?"

"I don't know!" He shook his head, wondering himself at the guilt that pecked and gnawed at his insides like buzzards on roadkill.

Cade held out a hand in appeal. *"Honest, Loren, I was just bein' friendly. I mean, Marlene is your fiancée! When she followed me out here to the stable, I thought she was just wantin' us to get to know each other better, you know?"*

Loren's head had just about come clean off his shoulders at that. *"And your idea of gettin' to know her better was kissin' her with your hands all over her like stink on a skunk?"*

"It didn't happen like that! I was tryin' to push her

*away. Good Lord, Loren, you're my brother! I wouldn't
do you that way. Marlene's the one that—''*

That's when Cade had seen the look in his brother's
eyes, begging him not to go there. Loren had been stone
gone in love with Marlene Lane, in over his head and not
even sane about it.

So Cade had shut up, because there was nothing on earth
that could have made him do his brother *that* way.

Yet it meant Loren had gone away believing his only
brother had betrayed him. He'd been wrong, though. Cade
hadn't betrayed Loren with the woman he loved. He hadn't
had the least interest in Marlene, had never felt for her
anything more than brotherly affection.

That had been Marlene, however. Not Sara.

This time, his brother would have a justifiable bone to
pick with him. And Cade couldn't help feeling that this
time, unlike the last, he'd of his own will brought such
wrath upon himself.

He'd heard the warning about not tempting fate, but
what *were* the consequences when fate tempted him?

Cade dropped his forehead to rest on the wood rail. A
day ago, all he would have asked those fates for was one
minute. One minute on either side of Loren's appearance
that day seven years ago—before Marlene had stepped forward and wrapped herself around Cade, or after he'd freed
himself from her clutches.

And now? he wondered. What would he ask for now—
with Sara?

Straightening, Cade made himself take a fortifying
breath. He had to remember, nothing had happened—yet.
And nothing would, he silently vowed. He knew better
now, knew that he'd been a fool to hope he could have—
even for one minute—the kind of love with a woman he'd
pretty much resigned himself to not being in the cards for
him this go-round on earth.

So. He would care for Sara, as Loren would want, until he came for her himself. Cade had to trust that the reasons his brother couldn't be here were sound, and that Loren had known Cade would look after Sara and the baby's every need.

The thought brought him up short. He was doing anything but looking after them out here.

Cade ran from the stable, lunging through the knee deep snow, arms flailing in front of him. He was blind as a bat out here, couldn't even see the lights from the ranch house. He might wander right past it and never find it.

He had to! He had to get back—back to Sara. He had promised to stay with her as long as she needed him, and he always kept his word.

When Cade came up against a car, he wasn't exactly happy. It was just one more obstacle between himself and Sara. Muttering a curse, he started to feel his way around it when it occurred to him he might find more clues as to his brother's whereabouts.

Or maybe he'd find more clues as to Sara's identity, Cade thought. Maybe…maybe the woman who just gave birth in his bedroom *wasn't* his sister-in-law. Because really, what was he going on so far but a four-inch-square piece of paper in his brother's handwriting? She could have found it on the side of the road or left behind at the grocery checkout—neither of which she remembered, of course. And why didn't she? What sort of blow had she suffered to make her lose her memory? Or was her amnesia all an act?

Barely considering that he was near to hoping he'd been duped by the woman in his house than the alternative, Cade brushed away snow until he found a door handle. He tried it. The car was unlocked.

Its interior was like a tomb, buried as the car was in snow. He couldn't tell the make or model right off, but could see it was a sedan of some kind. Loren was strictly a pickup man.

The dome light was about as illuminating as striking a match. Cade peered about for clues. On the passenger seat lay a road atlas with a route from Albuquerque to Oklahoma City highlighted in yellow. Except no—Sara said she'd come from the east.

What was in Oklahoma City that she'd have been returning from—alone?

He opened the compartment between the bucket seats. Some change, a paper clip, that was about it. There wasn't much else in the car—no clothes, an old receipt, not even a CD or cassette tape which might have given him an idea what kind of person owned the vehicle.

Then he opened the glove box. There, he found an operator's manual—and the registration.

With fingers deadened by the cold, Cade tried to remove it from its plastic sleeve and failed. He held it up to the light and caught only glare off the plastic. Damn it! He turned it, and the names became readable.

Loren and Sarah McGivern.

Cade sat for some time slumped in the driver's seat of the car. His feet were frozen, his hands were frozen. He was numb clear through to his bones, and still he continued to sit staring at the paper in his hands.

He couldn't stay there forever, though. He needed to get back and take care of his brother's wife and son.

The dream was all flashes of impressions and vague images.

She was back in labor, although there was no pain. Just the fear. Instead of wanting the baby to come, she resisted. It was too early, much too early. She couldn't lose him!

It made her cry, great keening wails that seemed to come up from the depths of her being. The sound of her cries stopped dead in the air, though; no echo came back to her, answered her.

Alone. That's how alone I am. The realization was like an arrow through her heart, making her cry harder. She didn't think she could endure it. She had to, though. She had to—for this child she wanted and yet didn't want.

What kind of woman did that make her?

Then she felt Cade's presence there beside her, enveloping her, connecting with her and pulling her back from the depths of hopelessness with his touch and solemn vow: *Wherever both of you came from, darlin', you're here now—in my house, in my bed, right where you need to be. For now, you're mine. You belong to me. And I won't let you down.*

Peace settled in her like a dove alighting on a branch. Yes, Cade was there. He wouldn't leave her, no matter what.

She glanced up, needing to see that confirmation in his face, and found instead some other man, not Cade, stood beside her. He looked like Cade, though, even if his nearness produced hardly a fraction of the same powerful reaction Cade's did. He had Cade's dark brown hair and whiskey eyes—eyes that were clouded with concern as he looked down at her.

"Are you sure you'll be all right?" he asked.

"Yes," she answered, the sense that she'd had this conversation before immediately striking her. *"I'll be fine."*

"I'm afraid it'll be difficult to get in touch should you need something on the road," he said doubtfully. *"Maybe we shouldn't go—"*

"Go! Go and don't worry a minute about me. You won't get this chance again for a long time once the baby comes," she said with affection, touched by his concern.

The man smiled at her with the same fondness—but no more than that. *"Well, at least you've got Cade's contact info if somethin' happens,''* he said. *"Just explain what you need, and I know he'll see to it."*

Regret filled his eyes, even as he said with quiet humbleness, *"He's one of the best, my brother. It isn't in him to quit a person he loves—even when that person quits him. No, I never saw him give up on anything or anyone, no matter if sure defeat stared him in the eye."*

The tears dried on her cheeks as she stared at him in hushed silence, each word striking like the chime of a clock, deep and resonant, until all that remained was their memory in her heart.

The crying, though, went on...and on...and on—

"Sara. Sara, wake up."

Sara came out of her dream like one drugged. With effort, she lifted her head and tried to orient herself in the darkened room. She still heard crying, and with a start, she realized it was her baby, lying next to her in the bed.

"Oh! Oh, sweetheart, I'm sorry!" She'd pushed herself up on one elbow, blindly reaching for the babe, when a large hand on her shoulder urged her back down.

"Relax," Cade murmured. "I'll try to quiet the little mite while you get your bearings."

She heard him pick up the infant, who continued to wail at an ear-piercing volume. Now fully awake, Sara tried to sit up, stifling a groan. Where right after the labor she'd been tired, now she ached all over, as if she'd climbed Mount Everest.

A lock of her hair got caught between her back and the headboard, and she tugged it free, gathering the whole damp mass of it in her hands and twisting it over one shoulder.

"All right, I can take him now," she said, holding her arms out toward Cade's shadowed form, dimly backlit by the pale light filtering in from the hallway. "And you may as well turn on a light. It doesn't sound like he's going to settle back down right away.''

"You sure?" Cade asked, holding the still-fussing infant, insignificant as a peanut against his broad shoulder, and patting his back.

"Well, n-no," she said rather tremulously as her dream spontaneously revived itself, bringing back the failure she'd experienced with a vengeance. "I mean, it's obvious I've got a ways to go to being a good mother if the sound of my own baby's crying doesn't w-wake me up."

To her dismay, tears stung her eyes, and she wondered if the whole dream would come pouring out of her unbidden.

She didn't want it to, she realized. Not yet.

"Sara," Cade said gently. "I didn't mean were you sure about what the baby needed. I meant were you sure about turning on the light?"

"Oh." Already she missed him calling her *darlin'*. She blinked away the moisture in her eyes and peered at him. "Why wouldn't I be?"

He cleared his throat, eyes averted. "Well, it's just that you might want to adjust your clothing first."

She glanced down and realized what he could see in the faint light shining into the room from behind him. The edges of her unbuttoned shirt lay open in a deep V between her breasts.

Cheeks burning, Sara drew the edges of the shirt together, fumbling with the buttons. "I forgot...I was nursing Baby Cade when I fell asleep."

It occurred to her then why he might be crying. "He may need to be burped," she suggested just as the baby let out a tiny hiccup of air. He immediately ceased fretting and quieted down.

"That's all it was," Cade soothed, holding the baby

one-handedly as he stooped to switch on the bedside lamp. "Just a little burp that had to get out. Ready for him?"

Now decently covered, she answered, "Yes."

Cade eased the child into her arms. From the looks of things, he'd apparently been asleep himself. The jeans he wore were unbuttoned at the waist, and the flannel shirt he'd slid on was itself unbuttoned and revealing the defined muscles in his chest and flat stomach—directly at eye level.

She realized she was staring, and that he'd apparently noticed, for he stepped back with an abruptness that wrung her heart.

Suddenly, Sara felt bared in a different way, as if the echoes of her dream still ringing in her head reverberated throughout the room as well.

Yes, she realized, here in this room there was an answering echo. She wasn't alone.

Yet something had changed—in Cade. What or why or how she knew it was so, she couldn't have said. Maybe it was the way he marked distance between them. Or the wariness in his stance.

Or perhaps it was the way all hope and promise had left his golden-brown eyes.

He was here, though. He hadn't left. He wouldn't leave.

Sara noticed Cade looking at her, puzzled. "Your hair's wet," he said.

She fingered back a lock of it. "Y-yes, I couldn't stand it, so when the baby was sleeping, I took a chance he'd be all right for ten minutes and got in a quick shower."

"But...how did you manage?"

"It wasn't easy," she admitted. "I'm still pretty shaky on my pins, but I figured I'd just sit down if I started to feel I couldn't support myself."

Cade thrust his hands into the front pockets of his jeans, which inevitably drew her eye straight to that undone button at his waist. "You should have called for me to help, Sara."

"I did," she answered rather breathlessly. "You must have been asleep—o-or outside. I heard the door slam."

Giving undue attention to her perfectly content child, Sara waited. Perhaps Cade would broach the subject and end this awkwardness between them. And she so wanted it to end! She didn't like the distance between them, missed the closeness they'd shared intensely. In fact, it made her rather desperate, because even more than it had a few minutes ago, fear rolled over her, engulfing her like a cloud of smoke.

She shivered suddenly. No, she didn't want to go there.

"Are you cold?" Cade asked, taking back the step he'd retreated.

"No." Sara shook her head, trying to rid it of that feeling at the same time. "No, it's just that my hair's still a little damp. If you've got a brush, I'll get the tangles out and put it back in a braid again and off my shoulders. It'll be dry by morning."

"Let me see what I can find."

She used the time while he went in search of a brush to pull herself together. Thankfully, Baby Cade was sleeping soundly, nestled between her blanket-covered thighs, and seemed none the worse for having his mother fall asleep on him in the midst of a feeding. Now that she could think about it rationally, she'd bet she wasn't the first new mother to do such a thing—as well as to feel completely inadequate at motherhood.

Unable to resist, she wiggled his chin with her pinkie finger. Immediately, his rosebud mouth screwed into a pucker, making smacking noises. When no nipple presented itself to be suckled, he whimpered briefly before settling back into his dreams.

And that's all mine was, Sara thought. A dream. There

was no way on earth she couldn't have wanted this child to be born even for a second.

"Will a comb do?" Cade asked as he came back into the room. "The last person to live in this house who might've used a hairbrush was my grandmother, and that was twenty years ago."

He handed the comb to her. "I'm surprised going so long without a female influence hasn't made you McGivern men wild as savages," she ventured to tease.

Cade did another one of his turned-to-stone numbers. "You tell me," he said, and she realized he meant not himself, but Loren—her husband.

Yes, they'd both tiptoed around mentioning him, had both avoided the subject of what she remembered of him, or of what Cade might tell her to help her do that.

And they both knew why.

Sara lifted her arms to attack her tangled hair with a fervor and immediately regretted the sudden effort. Her stomach muscles protested, and she gave a huff of frustration. "I guess I must have overdone it with the shower."

She took another stab at tugging the comb through a knot near the crown of her head and failed.

"Would you like me to give it a shot?" Cade asked quietly.

"Not if you don't want to," she answered, unable to keep the edge out of her voice.

"Well, and not if you don't want me to, either," was his seemingly mild reply.

She looked up at him, trying to make out the expression in his eyes and failing. "All right. Go ahead."

Shifting the baby onto the bed beside her, she gave Cade the comb, and he placed one knee on the mattress behind her. But he didn't begin, and Sara waited, her breath caught in her chest.

"It'll probably hurt less if I start with the ends and work

up," he muttered. "At least that's what works best when I'm combin' Destiny's tail and mane."

She felt him lift a back section of her hair and, taking short, light strokes, begin to unsnarl each tangle with infinite patience.

Both of them were silent for several minutes. Sara couldn't have said what Cade was thinking. As for herself, she was once again soothed by the gentleness in this man's large hands. She experienced not one yank or pull on her scalp. Just the tiny tug now and then of a knot finally combed loose.

"The phone's workin' again," Cade said abruptly.

Sara jerked. Her eyes had drifted closed. "That's good to know. Not that we need it at the moment. Everything seems to be under control."

"Yeah, well. Still, I gave Doc Barclay a heads-up to let him know about the baby. Come mornin', I'll get him on the line and let you speak to him. He'll have some questions about your progress, probably some good advice to follow, too, until he can get through on the roads and give you and the baby a thorough going-over."

"When will that be, do you think?"

"Couldn't say for sure, but I'm bettin' at least a few days." He lifted her hair from underneath, and his fingers grazed the back of her neck in a way that nearly made her twitch in another sort of reaction. "The storm's past, at least."

She hadn't even noticed the wind had finally quit its relentless whistling. Only now did she realize how truly lucky she was to have made it to Cade. No telling what would have happened to her and the baby had she gotten stuck in the blizzard.

She must have been terribly desperate to have taken such a chance. Or terribly certain Cade was the only one who could help her.

"I'm curious—how did you explain who I was to the doctor and Virgil?" Sara asked.

"I just told Doc that you'd come in from the storm needing help with deliverin' your baby. There wasn't exactly time to get into the particulars. I gave Virg a quick rundown 'fore I sent him to the bunkhouse to get some rest. He's pleased as punch to know you're family."

Another silence fell in the room as Sara tried to grasp the concept that yes, she was family to this man. His sister-in-law, to be specific. And the baby on her lap was his nephew.

It still didn't seem right, and she knew that was something she needed to come to terms with—in herself and with Cade.

"I was having a dream, just before you woke me," she blurted out. "There were…people I seemed to know, conversations that were familiar."

Cade paused in midstroke. "Such as?"

"A…a man who looked like you but wasn't you," she whispered. "He was going away, somewhere he'd be difficult to reach."

"Loren?"

"Y-yes, it must have been Loren."

He took a minute to absorb that before saying, his voice hushed, "I tried callin' him. In Albuquerque, just about an hour ago."

Her heart skipped a beat. "And?"

"All I got was an answering machine."

"At this time of the night?"

"Exactly. It's comin' up on five here, which would've made it 3:00 a.m. then in New Mexico." He gave another of those mirthless chuckles that sounded so bleak to her ears. "Maybe the next little trip you take to Dreamland, you could make a mental note to ask where he is and how the hell to get ahold of him."

She chose to ignore his sarcasm. "Are there friends of his…ours there that you might call and see if they know how to reach him?"

"Not likely. I didn't even know what part of the country he was livin' in till a few days ago."

"Oh, I forgot." He'd told her he hadn't heard from his brother in seven years. "What happened between you two, Cade?" she asked. "Or should I wait and see what I dream up?"

The short laugh that came from him this time was more wry.

"Trust Loren to pick a live one," he commented. He hesitated, then went on, "We had a fallin' out, as brothers are bound to. Except Loren lit a shuck, left the ranch 'fore we could square things. Being as how we've both got stubborn streaks a mile wide and more pride than the law allows, neither of us was willin' to make the first move, and the time for doin' so stretched longer and longer till it got embarrassing. I don't think either one of us ever intended to go on for so long."

His hands rested on her shoulders in pause, then he admitted, "For myself, if I'd've known that argument meant I wouldn't see my own brother for nearly seven years, I would never've let him step one foot off the ranch without settlin' the matter one way or the other."

Even without seeing his expression, Sara got the distinct impression Cade had made less of what happened than what actually had—and that he was taking on more of the blame for the estrangement from his brother than was his to own.

That impression, it occurred to her, came from her dream.

Placing her hand over Cade's, she turned her head, lifting her eyes to his. "There's something Loren said in my dream I didn't tell you, Cade."

His features froze. "And that'd be?"

"He told me if I needed anything, anything at all, I could count on you. And that you were the kind of man who never quit someone you loved—even after that person quit you."

Cade's gaze delved into hers, mining deeply as if to unearth her every secret thought or memory or desire, even those which she herself had no conscious knowledge of.

And what would he discover about her, should she give him entrance to her mind? Sara wondered. What would she?

With a shudder, she glanced away. *I must be very careful here,* she realized. Careful to keep her thoughts close. Careful to keep her heart close.

Because what she'd felt for the man in her dream who was supposed to be her husband had been anything but wifely, and paled drastically to what she felt for the man whose touch and very nearness roused in her the deepest of those kinds of feelings.

Were their strength for Cade truly because all she knew of any man was what she'd experienced in the last several hours with him? Somehow, she couldn't accept that possibility.

Yet she knew it didn't make those emotions any more right.

Especially when he took up his task again, placing the comb against the back of her head to take the first full stroke through her hair, from her crown to the ends. The next stroke was as long and full, tugging at her scalp and making it tingle deliciously. Tugging her back, for one moment, against him.

If ever a man *had* brushed her hair in that murky, unclear past of hers, Sara knew such an experience could not compare to the vivid here and now of this one at the hands of Cade McGivern.

It was heaven. It was hell. It was wrong.

Sara reached back, fingers closing over his and nearly wrenching the comb from his hand. "I can finish the rest. It won't take but a minute to b-braid up my hair, and I really should get a few minutes' sleep while I can before Baby C-Cade wakes up for his next feeding."

"Of course." Cade stepped away.

"Th-thank you, though," she belatedly remembered to say. Her hands shook, her voice shook, and when she caught the stricken expression on Cade's face as he headed for the door, she thought she would cry. Or worse, as the panic of before set itself to clawing at her once more.

She couldn't let him go this way. For some reason, somehow, she had to make it right before he left.

"Cade."

He turned at the doorway, and it took her breath away to realize how familiar his stance, his every move, were to her already.

"I just wanted to tell you again," she said, her voice barely audible to her own ears, "how grateful I am to you for being here for me and for my baby. For giving me, with your promise, the ability to go on. It was an act of purest selflessness, of pure faith. Truly, no matter what happens, I will never, ever forget it, because I know there's no way on earth I could ever forget that moment when my baby was born. And if *you're* needing something to believe in, you can believe that. Because I do, with all my heart."

He said nothing for a good minute, and it almost seemed he was marking the same realization about her that she'd just done of him. Or perhaps that was, again, more about her own hopes and wishes than anything else.

"I thank you for that," he finally said, "but it was nothin' really."

His voice was as cynical as ever.

She watched him walk out the door, her fear not allayed in the least. Yes, she must be very careful. Careful not to lose what this man had given her in that special moment. Because she couldn't go back to before.

Chapter Four

Funny how a simple change in perspective could turn the blizzard that had been a bane into a boon, Cade reflected a few days later as he and Destiny worked to locate cattle and bring them close to the mineral tubs and stock tanks. He'd spent yesterday and today riding out as far as he could to check the herd, leaving it to Virgil to stay close to home blading out the drifted-over ranch yard and lane so he could look in on Sara and the baby now and again.

Out on the range the snow had had little to drift against, with just a few wisps in spots that made the entire landscape look topped in an endless vista of meringue. The sun shone bright in the cloudless sky, but the air remained so clean and sharp and crisp it instantly froze any moisture in mouth or nostril.

Still, Cade didn't mind. The activity got him out of the house from sunup to sundown, and the exertion put another layer of exhaustion between him and his thoughts—about Sara.

He'd promised not to leave her, but there was just so close he trusted himself to get.

And they were coming up on another evening—alone.

Which was why exiting the stable he perked up at the sight of Doc Barclay's familiar dark-blue dually pickup lumbering up the road.

Cade went to greet him.

"So you got a genuine new year's baby in the house!" Doc called out his open window, looking like a modern-day Mark Twain with his wavy white hair, horn-rimmed glasses and bushy mustache.

"Not quite," Cade answered, tramping across the yard toward the doctor, his boots crunching on the packed snow. "If he'd've taken about a minute longer to be born, he would be, though. He and his mama seem to be doin' fine, but I appreciate your comin' out to give 'em a once-over."

Actually, Cade was relieved as hell that the doctor was here. Sara had been able to talk with Doc Barclay yesterday, and she'd had nothing of immediate concern to report from the conversation. Cade didn't want to leave anything to chance, however. He'd never forgive himself if he did. Wouldn't blame Loren, either, for not forgiving him—this time.

Because there was Sara's amnesia, too.

He got to the truck just as Doc was pulling out a worn and raggedy medical bag, along with a couple of brown paper grocery sacks. He handed them to Cade before removing his glasses to polish the fog off the lenses. "Figured you'd need some supplies till you could get into town."

Peering inside, Cade saw milk, bread, fresh fruit and vegetables—and a big box of diapers for newborns.

"Sara will sure be glad to see these," he said, adding as he heard footsteps behind him, "Or maybe I should say

I am. I swear, Virg has taken it on as a personal crusade to keep the young'un dry. I came downstairs this mornin' to find him rooting through my clean laundry for materials to make more diapers out of. I nearly lost my best pair of longies to the cause.''

"Well, if ya's fold 'em up proper when they come out of the wash insteada leavin' 'em throwed over the door, I never would've thought of 'em!'' the old hand retorted.

Doc laughed. "Well, they don't make much of a baby gift, but I thought they'd come in handy even if her kin showed up with a bunch of 'em. You know what the story is there yet?''

"Yes.'' The late-afternoon sun reflecting off the snow was so bright Cade felt his face might freeze in a permanent squint. "She's Loren's wife.''

"No! Loren's here and no one mentioned it?'' Doc glanced toward the house in surprise as they approached the back door. "Whyn't you tell me that and spare me a few days' worry? I got the impression you were havin' to deliver the baby by yourself, Cade. Your brother always had a knack for handlin' himself in an emergency.''

His gaze swung around the ranch yard. "Pret'near could take care of any veterinary need y'all had out here. I used to think he'd've made a pretty fair doctor if he hadn't had ranching so thoroughly in his blood. And it must be, if he'd drive in weather like it was on New Year's Eve to make sure his boy was born here on the family homestead, just like him and his daddy was, and his daddy afore him.''

The doctor beamed at them. "Y'all must be tickled to have him back where he belongs. I'm curious to know how he ever coulda left here in the first place.''

Cade had no immediate comment, making the moment more uncomfortable than it already was. Virg even took to shuffling his feet.

No one knew why Loren had left the ranch, for Cade

had kept the particulars to himself. Even Virg had only what amounted to sketchy details of the situation.

But the ranch hand knew the brothers better than anyone, and Cade assumed Virg had figured out what had happened, or close to it. For that reason, Cade knew he'd best have his wits about him if he was going to keep a lid on the real state of affairs.

Which, when it came right down to it, was the same as before with Marlene: nothing. As he'd told Sara, there was nothing between them beyond that brief moment they'd shared.

"Loren's not with her," Cade finally said. "But that's not the biggest news. I wanted to wait to tell you in person—Sara didn't know she was Loren's wife."

Doc fetched up short of the back door. "She what?"

"We pieced it together from a note Loren had written, sending her to my care while he apparently went off on some trip, and a letter I got from him just this week," Cade explained. "Here's the thing, though, Doc. Even though she knows now she's Sara McGivern, she still doesn't *know* it, not in the way you or I know who we are. Seems she lost her memory somewhere on the way to or from Albuquerque, where she and Loren live."

"Good Lord, Cade." Doc frankly stared. "Did she suffer some kind of head trauma?"

"Not that I can tell, although she'll rub her forehead now and then, like it hurts. She's held on to her learnin'—you know, reading, geography and the like. And she remembers bits and pieces of people and conversations." He felt his explanation fell far short of dispelling the doctor's confusion, because said out loud, the story sounded as improbable as it had yesterday when he'd given Virg the rundown. "But she seems to've forgotten near to everything having to do with her past. Includin' Loren."

"She's the sweetest li'l thing you'd ever want to meet,

Doc,'' Virg, for some reason, felt compelled to offer. "Eyes blue as cornflowers and a smile that'll like to break yer heart. And when it comes to Loren's baby, she's as devoted as a mother can be. No doubt about it, that boy is her whole world right now.''

Doc's eyebrows rose over the rims of his glasses. "Well, let's get on inside and see what we can do for them both. It sure sounds like it was one helluva New Year's, Cade.''

He shook his head slowly. "Dang if you don't have all the luck, startin' the new year off with a bang while the rest of us were shut up tighter 'n ticks in town.''

"I got *that* knack, for damn sure," Cade agreed grimly, stamping his feet as he followed the doctor inside, Virg trailing behind.

The three men entered the kitchen a few minutes later to find Sara stirring a pot on the stove.

"Sara! You shouldn't be doin' that!" Cade said, depositing the paper sacks on the counter and nearly snatching the spoon from her hand. What would Doc think, him letting his brother's wife slave over a stove within days of giving birth!

Of course, if he'd been here with her, as he'd promised he would be, then she wouldn't have had to.

"I was just heating up a can of soup," she protested. "I know, I've been putting away enough food to feed a camp of lumberjacks, but all of a sudden I was starving, and I wasn't sure when you and Virg would be coming in for supper.''

"What d'ya think I gave you that red bandanna for but to get Virg's attention when he's out in the yard?" he pointed out curtly.

He became immediately contrite when she looked up at him with stricken eyes. Immediately sorry, too, for not being more careful, for his move had put him close enough to her that the effect of those blue eyes on him was as powerful as it had been the first time, drawing him in, drawing him under with that tidelike force that wouldn't be denied, completely negating hours of effort he'd spent doing just that.

And setting a blaze up from his vitals that had the sweat popping out on his forehead, despite the cold lingering on his cheeks.

Heart pounding in his ears, Cade took a step back, and it did him no good to see Sara's gaze turn even more stricken—and hurt. But damn it, he had to keep some distance between them, for both their good!

Except the long and short of it was, that distance was of necessity growing wider and wider. At this pace, he'd be bunking in the stable with Destiny come nightfall.

"So you're the new mother," Doc said from behind him.

Cade swung around, his hand making a hurried journey over his face, as if to wipe away any trace of his thoughts. "Sorry, yes. Doc, this is Sara…Loren's wife."

"Oh!" Sara grasped the older man's hand in both of hers. "Doctor, I'm so glad you're here! I mean, I know we talked about the baby and he seems fine, thank goodness, but I won't rest easy till you've checked him over. I've just had this nagging sense he was born on the early side."

She shot Cade a quick look. "I—I don't know for sure, you see, when my due date was."

"That's what Cade was tellin' me," Doc replied calmly, taking her arm. "Well, let's take a look at both of you. And once it's heated, Cade can bring up a bowl of that soup on a tray for you to eat while I'm examining the baby. You put some of them carrot sticks with it, son, and pour her a big glass of that milk, too."

"You bet."

Cade watched them disappear around the corner before turning to fetch a bowl. He came practically nose to nose with Virgil.

"You wanna tell me what was goin' on here a second ago?" the hand asked.

Cade pushed past him to open the cupboard. "I don't know what your talkin' about, Virg."

"Bull loney. The tension was so thick 'tween you two I coulda sliced off a slab and fried it up in a skillet. It's been the same way since when I first come in and found you and Sara together."

Cade gave the older man a long look, counting to ten, before saying pointedly, "Now that I'm back, you might want to take a trip out to the barn to see how that mama cow I brought in with a couple of frozen teats is doin'." He reached into a drawer for a spoon. "Unless you think you've got the picture already, given your new occupation as a professional know-it-all."

"Using that rusty bobwire tongue of yours on me don't get you nowhere, and you know it."

When Cade silently continued to assemble a tray for Sara, Virg set a grizzled paw on the counter next to him, effectively boxing him in, even if Virg was a good half-foot shorter.

Cade raised his eyebrows in mild warning, but Virg wasn't budging an inch.

"I ain't accusing you of nothin', Cade," the hand said.

"Then what are you doin', Virg?" Cade asked, deadly quiet.

"I dunno." The older man blew a huff out of the sides of his mouth, raising the ends of his tobacco-stained mustache. "Y'know, I never asked what happened those years ago. Figured it was between you brothers. I got eyes in my head, though, and I've seen how you've taken care of this ranch for the past half-dozen years when I knew your heart weren't entirely in it. And when Loren finally does come home, he'll see that. Maybe he'll see a lot of things, if he hasn't already figured 'em out on his own.''

He shook his head. ''All I know is that whatever—or whoever—it was that came between you and Loren before, it weren't worth it. But now…''

His sentence trailed off, Virg obviously *not* knowing what exactly he was concerned about or how to express it. But he was right about one thing: Marlene Lane *hadn't* been worth setting brother against brother, and not because nothing had happened. That had always been the hell of it.

But now…now there was Sara—soft, sweet, seductive Sara with her big blue eyes and heartbreaking smile—to come between them.

Yet she wouldn't. Cade simply wouldn't let it happen.

He set one hand on the older man's shoulder. ''You're right, Virg. What came between Loren and me before wasn't worth it. And you *have* been here the past seven years to help me hold the ranch in trust so that if Loren returned he could take over what's always been his.''

Cade gave Virg's shoulder a squeeze, looking directly into the hand's faded brown eyes. ''I'm tellin' you nothing's changed in that aim, Virg.''

''Nothin'?''

''I got the chisel if you got the stone,'' Cade averred.

Yet even as he watched the relief flood Virg's eyes, he realized it was the second time in two days that he'd made a solemn, heartfelt vow. And that both vows went completely counter to the other.

Well, he had the chance right now to make good on at least one promise. Sara was hungry as a grizzly in springtime, and she needed to keep her strength up to nurse his brother's son.

When he entered the bedroom, Doc had apparently finished up examining both Sara and the baby, for he was perched on the edge of the bed admiring the little one in her arms.

"I gotta say, that's one healthy-lookin' baby there," he remarked, setting his clasped hands on one crossed knee. "You must live under some kind of lucky star, young lady."

"I must," she murmured, glancing gratefully at Cade as he set the tray on the nightstand next to her. "A lucky star that led me to the one person who could help me with my baby."

He kept his face carefully blank, but couldn't help pausing, struck as he was, yet again, by the peculiarity of this woman in his house, in his bedroom. In his bed.

Today she was dressed in a maternity smock of blue-and-black plaid flannel and a pair of black woolen leggings, clothes evidently from the small suitcase Virg had found in the trunk of her car when he'd dug it out and moved it yesterday morning. With her hair back in a braid and not a speck of makeup on her pale-white skin, she looked about twenty years old.

Cade wondered how old she actually was, and guessed that was another one of those things that would remain a mystery until she regained her memory—or until Loren showed up.

He didn't know which he least looked forward to.

"I didn't do much other than help nature take its course," he said bluntly. "Nothin' to get up a ticker-tape parade for, to be sure."

Sara tried to brush down the shock of downy black hair on the baby's crown, her gaze glowing. "Oh, I don't know about that. I sure think Baby Cade is worth at least that much of a celebration."

The doctor gave her a look over the top of his glasses. "Baby Cade, is it?"

"Yes. I named him after his uncle," she said with soft defiance, as she had the other night, and Cade wondered what Doc would make of it, if he would get the same impression Virg had. "I know Loren would approve. I *know* he would. I mean, what father wouldn't approve of naming his child after the man who brought him into this world?"

"None that I know of," Doc agreed. He turned to Cade. "Seems you handled the situation pretty well, son, Loren or no. I don't want to scare either of you, but there's any number of things that could have gone wrong, even when you're deliverin' a normal, full-term baby."

Leaning against the bedpost, Cade only shrugged, but the praise put a little of the shine back on his tarnished trust in his abilities.

"So Baby Cade's not premature?" Sara asked the doctor after she'd eaten half her soup and downed the entire glass of milk.

"Course I don't know for sure, but he looks close to full-term to me, from the size of him."

"Then…where did I get the idea he wasn't ready to be born?" She gazed down at her child in bewilderment. "It just seemed so…so direly important that he not come yet. I mean, I was so scared I nearly lost my mind…."

She must have realized, as both Cade and the doctor did, what she'd said.

"Well, let's talk about that for a sec," Doc said. "Your vitals are good, eyes are clear. I don't see any outward evidence of head trauma, but we won't know for sure till we can get you into Amarillo for a head CT and an EEG."

"Virg and I took a good look at her car after we dug it out," Cade provided, "and we didn't find any sign of an accident. Not even a dented bumper."

"And you haven't had any other disorientation, no seizures," Doc asked Sara. She shook her head.

The doctor pursed his lips, thinking. "Do you have any problem remembering what's happened since you got here?"

She shook her head again, and Cade noticed that the action didn't seem to cause her pain as it had before. "No. I could tell you minute by minute everything that's happened."

"But you don't remember much from before then."

"Right. I just seem to have blanked it out before a certain point."

The doctor flashed Cade a covert look of dubiousness, and he was hard-pressed not to give an equally skeptical glance in return.

Yet Sara must have sensed their doubt. "Look, I know it sounds improbable at best, but that's all I remember! Don't you think I'd tell you if I knew more?"

"Of course you would—" the doctor began placatingly.

"Don't you think I want to know more about what's going on with me?"

Her gaze shifted imploringly between the two of them, and Cade could see she was getting upset—just as she had before when he'd pressed her for information.

"Start at what you do remember then, Sara," he said matter-of-factly.

She clasped the baby close, as if afraid he'd be taken from her, even now. "Well, it's not like it was a definite moment. I just sort of became aware that I was driving. The wind was blowing hard. It seemed to be coming at me from every direction, buffeting the car and making it difficult to keep it on the narrow road."

"You weren't on the interstate at that point?" Cade asked.

"No. When I sort of 'came to,' I was on a side road. All I knew, or seemed to know, was that I had...someone to get to."

She ducked her head, and Cade knew it was to avoid looking at him—the someone she thought she'd been running to.

"Do you remember much else about what was goin' on with you when you realized you had amnesia?" Doc prompted.

"I remember…oh, I remember feelings more than what happened. Like the desperate fear that the baby was too early to be born yet, even though I wasn't having contractions."

She had closed her eyes and spoke as if in a trance. "No matter what, though, overriding my fears was the feeling that I'd be all right if I could just get *here*. But maybe…maybe that was because I had nothing else to go on, nothing else to hold on to but that one thought."

Cade was so caught up in her story it wasn't until a tear had slid down her cheek that he realized how difficult this effort was for Sara. Still, she pressed on, and he had to admire her for it. "Because I was fighting another feeling that, until I did get here, I was a-alone. So terribly…terribly alone." She swallowed painfully. "At times, I thought…it would consume me. And somehow I'd be lost forever."

Damn, Cade thought. It was the one thing she could have said to pull him in yet again. Her feelings of aloneness simply resounded in him, canyon-deep, as nothing else ever had or could.

Except that raging river of desire he'd experienced that ran as deeply and fiercely.

And that was why, even in full view of Doc, Cade couldn't have stopped himself from responding to her. He eased down on the opposite side of the bed and reached out to take Sara's hand in his in an attempt to reestablish that connection between them that had been so vital in pulling her through. In pulling them both through.

At the pressure of his fingers, her mouth trembled and she clung to his hand, but no more tears escaped from under her lids.

"Are you sayin' you didn't have a pocketbook or anything else in the car to tell you what was goin' on?" Doc asked.

She swallowed with difficulty. "No."

"Huh." He scratched his chin in puzzlement. "I'm just tryin' to feature how a woman would leave her house, much less start on a cross-state trip, without money or credit cards or ID."

Sara blinked open her eyes, then looked at him. "I didn't," she said abruptly. "Somehow, I do know that."

"Know what?" Cade asked.

"I had a purse at one point, and...then it was gone. No—stolen, and I didn't realize it till later." Her fingers clenched around his. "Th-that was part of what made me feel so desperate."

"But how could that be?" Cade thought about not pressing the subject when Sara was so obviously upset, but he had to know. "I mean, hang me for bein' an ignorant cowboy, Doc, but how can she know what happened with some things—like getting' her purse stolen, and not others?" Like her own husband?

"Well, that wouldn't be that unusual in some types of amnesia. Of course it's rare," Doc said slowly, "but sometimes amnesia doesn't have a physical cause."

"What do you mean?" Sara asked, more dread than ever in her voice.

"Meanin' sometimes somethin' happens in your life that's hard to get your head around, so you tuck it away for the time being. If that's what the situation is with you, Sara, the likelihood is your memory'll come back all at once, although it could also trickle back in bits and pieces.'' He hesitated. ''Or, in some very rare cases, not at all.''

''You mean she might never remember her past?'' Cade asked.

Chin down, Doc tugged on one end of his mustache ruminatively. ''Depending on the person, different events affect us differently. I knew a gal once who said she didn't remember the whole year after her mama and daddy got divorced when she was about eight. She just blocked it out, even though she was still goin' to school and for all appearances leadin' a normal life. She never did remember that period of time.''

The doctor glanced up at them both. ''Like I said, it's sorta like the mind has to put a particularly tryin' event away for a while until it can deal with it. The trouble is, in the process a person can lose a sense of everything else that's goin' on in their lives during that time.''

Again, Cade had to ask the question, squeezing Sara's hand even harder, regardless of the doctor's presence. ''Are you saying maybe somethin' happened to Sara that she couldn't deal with?''

But Doc had eyes only for Sara at this moment. ''Or happened to someone she cared for very much,'' he said gently.

At the doctor's words, Cade's stomach crashed to his toes. He stared at Sara. ''Loren?''

She stared back at him, and he could see in her eyes she was experiencing the same kind of mortal fear that was eating the life out of him even as he spoke his brother's name.

Fear—and guilt.

In shock, he dropped Sara's hand like a hot potato. ''What happened to Loren?'' he demanded.

Mutely, she shook her head, clutching her son close to her breast.

"What happened to my brother?"

"I don't know!"

The baby started to cry.

"Now, Cade," Doc said, "we can't know for sure that anything's happened—"

"You tell me, what's not to know?" he interrupted, springing to his feet and taking two steps away from them, his mind whirling. "What else would keep Loren from bein' here with his wife when his firstborn was comin' into the world than if something dire happened to him?"

He drove both hands through his hair. "And here I stand not doin' a thing, not a damned thing, to find out what that is!"

Suddenly, he wanted to be gone from there in the worst way, wanted to jump into his dually and drive straight through to Albuquerque, find his brother's house and break into it if he had to. Ransack it top to bottom, whatever it took to find Loren and prove to him…

Prove what to him? That he was the dutiful brother who never quit a person even after they'd quit him? Who'd practically made it his life's mission over the past seven years to show Loren that he could never, ever play his brother falsely?

Because look where it'd gotten him.

Cade pivoted and found Sara with his gaze. Yes, look where it had gotten him: even worse off than where he started. For he realized then, in a fool's rush of hindsight, that he should have seen this situation with Sara coming. After what happened with Marlene, he should have known, because, in another flash of recognition, Cade remembered—there *had* been signs of Marlene's attraction to him that he'd literally blocked from his mind: the way she'd brush up against him on her way past him in the hall. The flirty way she said his name when he answered the phone and she was on the other end of the line. How she ran her thumb and index finger up and down the long neck of her beer bottle while he and Loren played cards of an evening, all the while a come-hither gleam in her eye—and aimed straight at him.

That was why he'd been ridden with guilt when Loren had accused him of cheating with Marlene behind his back. Subconsciously, Cade had seen the signs of her attraction to him and ignored them or pretended they weren't there.

Or, even worse, had subconsciously been encouraging her.

Or was it simply his own lousy fate that he come between his brother and the woman he loved, again and again?

No! Cade thought vehemently. He was not at the mercy of some force, either from within or without. Where Sara was concerned, he did have control. Control over his feelings for her.

Except he obviously didn't. How else could he have justified letting himself waste precious hours that he could have been using to locate Loren, who might be God knew where and in what condition?

He came back to the present with a start as he realized Sara was voicing the very rationalization he'd been telling himself.

"Cade, whatever *has* happened, how could you be to blame? How could either of us be to blame?" she said desperately, holding out her hand to him, a gesture, it seemed to him, to reestablish that connection, just as he'd given her.

It was the last thing he wanted right now.

He made a short sound of pure disgust. "Oh, but I *do* blame myself. I should've got on the phone to Texas State Police to retrace your route and see if Loren was stuck out in that blizzard somewhere along the way."

"But in my dream, he was going on a different trip, not one with me."

"Yes, in your *dream*, which only God knows whether it was a real memory or just another symptom of your delusion."

Doc frowned at his sarcastic tone. "Now, see here, Cade—"

He held up a hand in apology. "All right. That doesn't change the fact that the least I could have done was get in touch with the authorities in Albuquerque the minute I found out you were Loren's wife, have them track him down. I mean, it *was* an emergency. Still is, with you obviously havin' gone through *some* kind of awful event!"

"Cade," Doc repeated. The infant started to cry in earnest, his face flushing and arms waving about, and Doc seemed to be wanting to set a calmer tone, for he came around the end of the bed to clap Cade affectionately on the shoulder. "Just take a minute to think about it rationally, son. You were stuck here in a blizzard, still are for all intents and purposes, with your hands full. A lot of things have been out of your control—"

"A lot aren't, too." Cade lowered his voice, but it tempered not a whit the force behind his words, as dead set as he had been the other night to state the unvarnished truth as he saw it. "I know, sometimes bad things happen you can't control, like a blizzard. A lot, though, you can prevent, or take some action to cut the damage. And I didn't."

"Well, if that's true, then it stands to reason there're a lot of *good* things that happen you can't control, too!"

This, to Cade's surprise, had come from Sara. Her blue eyes crackled with a conviction he'd never seen in her before. She'd always seemed to him to want nothing more than to avoid friction.

"Fine, I'll grant you that." Cade moved out from under

the doctor's arm to stand next to the bed. Sara had to crane her neck back to hold his gaze, but she never let hers waver. "But if a man isn't smart enough to take charge of the happenings, either way, that he *can* control in his life, then he deserves the kind of luck they bring with 'em."

"And just what is that supposed to mean?"

He could see the dread in her eyes at what his answer might be, but he was determined to be ruthlessly honest with her—and himself—to the last.

"There's a time for waitin', and there's a time for taking action," he explained. "Waitin' for things to take their natural course, for people—and I'm not necessarily talkin' about you here—to come to their senses. I've sure enough come to mine, even if it's taken me seven years. And my time for waitin' is through. From now on, even if I can't control a particular circumstance, I can at least by God not be a victim of it."

He saw a flush spread across her creamy skin, as she seemed yet again to hold her emotions in check.

But no, he was wrong.

"Well, all I know, Cade," she said, shifting her crying son to one arm while she grabbed up the bath towel she used as a nursing blanket, "is that there's no way you can convince me we didn't have every bit of the new year's fortune guiding us all when this baby was born, whether you wanted it to or not!"

Obviously out of patience with him, she flung the towel over her shoulder, draping it over the baby's head, before fumbling with her clothing underneath it. Too late she seemed to recall his and the doctor's presence in the room.

The towel covered her more than adequately, but Cade knew what she was remembering as her gaze collided with his.

And despite the doctor standing there, despite his seconds-old resolve, Cade was instantly immersed in the memory of Sara, her shirt parted and revealing her perfection in the soft glow of the bedside lamp, of the little one he'd taken from her body only a few moments before questing instinctively for the rose-colored nipple that would provide him all sustenance.

Of the look in her eyes, like twin flames of pure blue fire answering the heat rising up from deep within his soul that would not be denied.

Even if it betrayed his brother.

He wouldn't give in to it! He couldn't, and not just for himself or for Loren.

Yet Cade couldn't conceal the bleakness in his voice when he said, "Me, fortunate? You must be confusing me with my brother, Sara. Loren's the one with all the luck."

He turned to go. "Now if you'll excuse me, I've got some phone calls to make."

Chapter Five

After the grandfather clock's chime of twelve had come and gone, Sara finally gave up trying to sleep.

Throwing back the covers, she rose, feeling for her robe at the foot of the twin bed before going to the window to pull back the curtain and let the moonlight in, rather than turn on a lamp. It had been difficult to get the baby to sleep after his last feeding. The last thing she wanted to do was disturb him.

Still, she couldn't prevent herself from drifting over to the beautifully carved cradle Cade had brought in to place a hand on that small, downy head and listen for the reassuring sound of her son's breathing. Even with the doctor's assurance that the baby seemed to be full-term and was fit as a fiddle, she couldn't set aside that nagging worry of him being early—much too early.

Yet she could feel rather than hear the soft in-out, in-out of tiny sighs, even a little grunt of contentment. Her child was fine.

Giving a sigh herself, Sara straightened, wrapping the velour robe tighter around her, resigning herself to being up until the next feeding. Too bad *she* wasn't hungry. The kitchen was now right around the corner, as Cade and Virg had moved her into this room on the ground floor earlier in the evening. It had apparently once been a side parlor, but had been outfitted as a bedroom for Cade's grandfather when he'd grown stiff with arthritis, limiting his mobility. That had pretty much been the reason for moving her there, too—Cade felt she'd have it easier on the ground floor, where she wouldn't have to descend stairs to get to the kitchen if she wanted a bite. There was even a full bathroom conveniently around the corner that she had all to herself.

She glanced around at her new lodgings. The bed with its fifties-era maple headboard had been shoved against one wall to make the most of what space was available. A bookcase full of tattered Louis L'Amour and Will James novels sat kitty-corner to it. Backed into one corner was a worn wooden rocker. An equally worn but authentic-looking Indian rug kept the harshest chill of the wood floor from soaking into her soles.

Everything, right down to the snout on the stuffed creature—an armadillo, it came to her—who stared out at her from the top shelf of the bookcase, was covered with a layer of fine red dust.

Sara didn't need full use of her faculties to figure out there hadn't been a woman living on the ranch for several years.

Strangely, though, she felt right at home, even if she missed the familiarity of the bedroom where Baby Cade had been born. And where his uncle now slept.

Turning slowly, she brushed a lock of hair back from her eyes, unable to stop herself from remembering when Cade had done so—in that very bedroom above her.

Yes, *that* she remembered—and more. She hadn't been completely truthful with the doctor today. There *were* bits and pieces of…impressions, more than actual memories, that she hadn't told him or Cade about. Impressions of the man who must be Loren.

She'd dreamed of him again last night. A dream filled with busyness: things to do, details to see to, arrangements to be made. Only this time, she was the one preparing for a journey.

And, as she also hadn't revealed today, she felt she was leaving someplace or…someone. She'd been doing so with that same mingling of flip-side emotions as in her first dream, like she was a coin spinning in the air: regret mixing with relief. Yearning turning to retreat and back again. Dread going head-to-head with hope.

Shivering abruptly, Sara peered out at the stark, snow-covered landscape. The most disturbing episode by far had been when Cade had burst into the kitchen this afternoon to scold her for not taking better care of herself, for not calling on him to help her, and she'd had another flash of déjà vu—or something very like it. This time it wasn't an event that she'd experienced with Loren being played again. More, it was as if the situation between her and Cade was similar to one between her and that faceless, nameless *someone* she'd been leaving behind. Or trying to.

The creak of footfall on the stairs was like the crack of a whip in the silence, and Sara gasped in terror. Catching her breath, she realized who it must be. *Cade.*

Down the steps she heard him come, ever so slowly and quietly, but even a mouse would have caused the ancient floorboards to pop and snap.

At the bottom of the stairs he paused, and her breath suspended again as she waited for…for what? What did she want to happen? What didn't she want to take responsibility for letting happen—again?

But when the footsteps started up again, it was away from her bedroom and into the kitchen. Then...no sound at all.

Crossing her arms, Sara determinedly stayed put. He'd barely said a word to her since that scene in his bedroom earlier today, and those he had said to her at supper had been only because of Dr. Barclay's presence. Afterward, when the doctor had been making out the birth certificate for the baby, she'd been half-tempted to tell him to put the baby's name down as Homer or Buford or even Clementine, anything, just to see if she could get another rise out of Cade.

But getting a rise out of him wasn't her intent, hadn't been her intent when she'd spoken up this afternoon. She was beginning to see how it worked with him, however: challenge Cade, and he turned into that remote, cynical man she had come to dread encountering. Yet whenever she tried to push *herself* to go closer to the bottomless abyss that contained her memory somewhere within it, he was right there with her, changing back to the Cade who'd seen her through her baby's birth, taking her hand, giving her his all and holding back nothing.

So which would she encounter tonight if she ventured into the kitchen? And at what cost to herself?

When several minutes passed with no further sound, Sara couldn't stand it. She made her way down the hallway to the kitchen.

Clad only in jeans, Cade stood at the window over the sink, each hand crammed under the opposite arm as he stared out into the darkness beyond, much as she'd been doing. As if he were searching it for answers, too.

Or for someone—such as Loren.

"Couldn't sleep?" she asked.

He pivoted, his stance immediately guarded. It obviously wasn't from surprise. She hadn't bothered with being quiet.

"I didn't mean to disturb you," he said impassively.

"You didn't. I've been wide-awake for hours."

There was a little more emotion in his voice as he asked, "Is it the new room?"

"No. It's very nice. Very convenient, like you said." She spread her arms. "Witness my presence here right now."

He shrugged in depreciation as he had when Doc had given him credit for saving her child.

She didn't want to let this opportunity go by to do the same. "I meant to thank you, yet again, for all the special considerations and accommodations you've made for Baby Cade, and me."

"It's nothin'. Although it pretty much breaks every rule of the house, givin' you and the little mite such treatment."

He had yet to call the baby by the name she'd given it, she noticed. "Oh, and what are the house rules?"

"Strictly serve yourself." He gave a nod in three different directions. "Beans on the stove, beer in the fridge, library in the john."

She had to laugh. He had a way of putting things that delighted her. Almost as much as the definite thaw in the atmosphere, which heartened her even more.

Unfortunately, it wasn't to last.

"Mind if I have a seat?" she asked. "I don't feel like sleeping."

His eyebrows lowered. "Sara, you need your rest."

"It seems all I've done the past few days is rest," she answered tartly, moving deliberately to the square Formica-topped table in the middle of the room and taking a chair. "If it weren't for this frigid winter weather, I'd go outside for a little air right now."

"If it weren't for the frigid winter weather," Cade commented, as cool as ever, "you wouldn't even be here right now."

So. She had her answer. She concentrated on pleating one end of the belt on her robe. "That reminds me. I was watching the news show some footage of the blizzard. It's been declared one of the worst to hit the area in a decade."

Cade gave a mirthless chuckle. "This storm was nothing but wild and woolly Panhandle weather as usual. Why those media folk've got to make stuff out worse than it is, is beyond me."

"As I understood from the reports, people along the Gulf have had even worse problems with the weather front as it moved south. Apparently the flooding was pretty bad in Houston. People were stuck on their rooftops waiting to be evacuated."

"It's never taken more than a little bit of weather to stop traffic in Houston," he said. "Up here, life goes on."

Sara left off toying with her belt. "I'm only trying to provide you with some reassurance that this weather front really has been instrumental in keeping you from doing much to locate Loren."

"I appreciate the thought, but I can make my own assumptions." He scoured his hand over that springy chestnut-brown hair, making it stand up even more. "Although I do keep wonderin' how I could've waited to contact the police."

On reflex, Sara reached her hand across the table toward him. "Cade, really. You've got to stop blaming yourself."

He eyed her hand where it lay, palm up, as if it were a live wire. "Well, I gotta blame someone for not takin' immediate action," he said with the merest hint of his old sarcasm, which she had begun to hate. It usually meant he was withdrawing for good, as he'd done earlier today—when she'd challenged him.

It hit her then. "You blame *me,* don't you?" Sara said, astounded and furious at once. Well, her mind may not be returning right away, but she most definitely was getting back some of her spirit. "Don't you?"

True to form, his whole being turned remote. She thought he'd leave—but no, he simply said stubbornly, "Somethin' doesn't add up, that's all. I'm not sayin' it's your doing. Just…something's not right."

Once more he returned his vigil out the window as if it contained a crystal ball that would provide him the answers he sought—unless he wasn't looking for answers there so much as avoiding her.

Oh, she knew he didn't want to be here with her! It was practically in his every glance and movement. That awful, debilitating panic expanded in her like a balloon filled to its bursting point, and Sara sought to control it in the first way she could think of.

"I've remembered more about your brother," she blurted.

That brought him around, although warily as ever. He propped the heels of his hands on the counter in back of him, and with only the light over the stove to provide illumination, the pose accentuated every muscle in his chest and stomach. "What do you know?"

Sara buried her hands in her deep pockets so he wouldn't see them tense into fists as she negotiated the tightrope walk of revealing enough but not too much to him. "Like I said, I don't *know* anything for certain—only that in the images I've seen of Loren, never is he in trouble or even distressed. He's a little concerned is all. That's why he wrote your name and address on that scrap of paper—he knew you were the one to send me to if I needed someone in his absence. And since that thought was virtually the only one I held on to from the past, I've got to believe such images are real and that Loren's all right.''

Cade's gaze was probing, and it was all she could do not to drop her own to conceal her real thoughts from him. No, the danger that continued to hover in the back of her mind *wasn't* coming from Loren.

Finally he drawled, "You'll still forgive me if I don't take these 'images' you've seen on faith and keep doing some checkin' around myself.''

"Fine!'' Sara sat back in her chair in exasperation. "So what *have* you found out about Loren?'' she challenged.

His mouth thinned. "Not much, that's for damn sure.''

He shoved off from the counter, taking a step toward the table, seemed to rethink his direction, then pivoted and reached into a cupboard for a glass. "I talked to a detective in the missin' persons' division over in Albuquerque. He said normally they don't take any action to look for someone till they've been gone three days. I told him I didn't know but that Loren had been missing that long or longer. I gave him the gist of what you knew, what I knew, about what might have happened. So he's going to send some officers over to the address I gave him and have a look around, talk to the neighbors.''

He paused at the sink, one hand on the faucet as he stared yet again out into the vast darkness. "Who knows but that Loren's there and just...not able to come to the phone.''

"Cade, honestly,'' Sara said. "Let's try not to borrow worry.''

"I told you, that doesn't work for me.'' He cranked hard on the faucet. "Damn it, I *do* have a past with Loren I remember.''

Water gushed into the glass and spilled over. He lifted it, dripping, and drank deeply, then wiped his mouth on the back of his hand, gaze ever trained on that darkness beyond the window he seemed determined to own. "I wouldn't be doin' right by him not to use it to try and come up with some whys and wherefores," he said, "so don't expect me to."

"I *don't* expect you to!" Sara contradicted in pure frustration, hands clenching harder within the pockets of her robe, her nails biting into her palms. She wished he'd quit looking out that blasted window and turn around and look at her! She needed him to, actually, and soon, although she couldn't have said why.

"Cade." She hoped her voice didn't sound as desperate to him as it did to her. "I'm worried about Loren, too, believe it or not. But remember what you said to me when Baby Cade was taking so long to be born? About letting go of the past for the time being, try not to borrow trouble by worrying about the future, and put our efforts into the here and now? I don't know what's happened to Loren, but whatever has happened *has*. It's done. So let's just do what we can, and the real story is simply going to unfold as it unfolds."

He lifted one shoulder and let it fall. "Sorry, Sara. I can't do what you seem to be able to do and take it as it comes, and trust that it'll all come out right in the wash."

"Really, Cade, this is such a silly argument."

"*Really*. Well, it doesn't seem silly to me."

Her fists flew out of her pockets and slammed on the table. "What a stubborn man you are!"

"Just like my brother before me, which, of course, you will have forgotten."

Sara glared at that strong, stalwart, *stubborn* back of his. He may doubt the accuracy of her dreams, but she knew without a doubt she'd been experiencing a scene straight out of her past when the man who must be Loren had told her how his brother never gave up, even when sure defeat stared him in the eye.

Or was that simply her own projection of what she felt about Cade? Because of its own accord her gaze drifted to those wide, sturdy shoulders, and she was taken back to the night of her son's birth. She'd seen in Cade's eyes then how much he had not wanted her there, did not want this responsibility thrust upon him—and yet he'd more than risen to the occasion; he'd very likely saved Baby Cade's—and her life. And it had seemed to happen through sheer force of his will.

And now, through that same will, he seemed equally determined to deny that force.

Was *that* what Cade had meant today when he'd said something about controlling what happened to us, good or bad? Was it really possible to bend fate to one's will?

It seemed utterly impossible! No one could change what was meant to be any more than they could change what had already happened!

Oh, but you can sure play every kind of hell trying, can't you?

Sara stood abruptly, knocking the chair over behind her. Cade whirled at the sound.

"Sara, what is it?"

She felt clammy, as if the ghost of something—or someone—had passed through her. "I don't know. I just... Oh, Cade, what's going on with me?"

She peered at him as if through a tunnel, which made her feel suddenly claustrophobic. "I mean, something does tell me there's nothing wrong with Loren, but then...there's another part of me that's saying there *is* something terribly wrong! Before, I thought it was the baby, but he's fine, the doctor says he's fine. It's me who's not fine!"

As before, that clawing, gnawing fear took hold of her and, leaning her hands on the table as she squeezed her eyes shut, Sara fought it off as best she could. But it was an impossible task—how could she fight what was inside her, a part of her? How could she fight herself? Why should she have to?

And oh, she felt so alone! Heaven knew how she had wanted to avoid going to this place in her mind tonight, but somehow it had happened.

"Sara. *Sara.*" Dizzily, she strained to find Cade at the end of that tunnel. She was shaking all over, teeth chattering. If only he would reach out to her, touch her, as he had before, then she knew she'd be all right. In the past few days, though—even in the past few hours—something had changed in Cade. He wouldn't touch her again, she knew of a sudden, and it was because of that strength of will of his, so strong it had seemed the only force strong enough on earth to save her baby. To save her.

She simply couldn't live without him!

The darkness sucked her down deeper, a pit of pure terror and chaos, and still she stood alone, fought it alone, eyes wide-open but unable to see, mouth agape with no sound, no voice, no hope...

And then strong hands were upon her, gripping her by her upper arms, holding her up, supporting her, as Cade called her name. Yes, he was here for her, as he said he'd be. Nothing had changed. He wouldn't let her fall backward into that bottomless pit, not Cade.

Yet when her vision had cleared infinitesimally, she saw not that will of iron in Cade's ravaged features, but a man desperately torn—all because of her.

It was wrong, what she wanted from him, for it was more than just his support. More than just a touch. Still it seemed beyond her power not to want that precious connection with him again, even if it did tear them both apart.

No, she couldn't go to that place in her mind, but what sort of impasse waited for her back there that she'd run from, as if for her life, rather than face it?

And what kind of woman did that make her?

She covered her face with her hands. "Oh, *Cade.*"

"Here, sit back down while I get you some water."

He stooped to right her chair and she slumped into it, her fingers twining and untwining on the tabletop, her thoughts still awhirl and heart aching. Then he was there again, pressing a glass into her hands. She gulped down half the water in two swallows.

It helped. She became aware of Cade crouching at her side, concern written into every line of his face.

"I didn't tell you, but I called Loren's number again," he said, low. "All I got was the answering machine, but I let him know that you and the baby are safe and well and taken care of." He swallowed with difficulty. "I—I didn't mention your amnesia yet. I didn't want him to worry…you know, if it still matters—"

He broke off, obviously trying to give her the assurances she needed, the assurances they both needed, that they were doing the most that they could be expected to at this moment for her husband, his brother.

Heart full to bursting, Sara choked out, "It does matter, Cade…to me."

Their gazes connected as the moment between them held and lingered. Oh, how badly she wanted to reach out and make the bond burgeoning between them real! She knew she dare not, for with that gesture she'd lose what he had given to her that first night, and had renewed just now, that gift of trust in a force, whether heavenly or fateful or whatever, that she'd felt forsaken by in her slumbering memory.

He was right, though, in that they couldn't remain in that place forever. The past they shared connected them even more strongly than the present. And so it stood to reason that until she remembered the past they hadn't shared—the past she'd forgotten—it would forever keep them apart.

And she'd lose Cade instead, not through the vagaries of her memory, but because she had not shown the same strength of mind as he'd shown her.

She owed him that much.

"Would you…would you tell me about Loren, Cade?" Sara made herself ask before she lost her courage.

His expression became immediately skeptical. "Why?"

"I was talking to Dr. Barclay before he left, and he said something called reality orientation might help me to get my memory back, such as hearing familiar music or looking at photos of Loren, th-that kind of thing."

"But are you sure you want to stir yourself up even more than you are already?"

"Not at all." She knotted her fingers together to keep them from trembling. "I'm simply trying to do the right thing here, too," she whispered.

He cleared his throat, lashes dropping slightly. "I don't have any photos of Loren, is all."

"You have memories of him, though."

"That I do." He shifted on his haunches. "All right." He glanced around, his gaze lighting on the deck of cards on the table Virgil had gotten out earlier to pass the time by teaching her to play poker.

Cade picked them up as he took the chair opposite hers. "How about a game of poker while we talk?"

"Now?" she asked, surprised. "I know Virgil said even if I learned how to play from Loren, I'd need to keep my skills sharp if I was going to survive in this family. But just how much do you McGiverns play?"

"Right about this time of winter when there's not much to do? It's an ongoing thing." He shuffled expertly. "And Virg's right. You really do need to sharpen your game if you're gonna survive in this family. We McGiverns—of which you're one—are a competitive lot. Granddad was the best. Used to pop out his glass eye and polish it on his sleeve, all the while with a face blank as a stone wall. Tell me that didn't blow your concentration all up to be damned.''

Sara dubiously watched as with one hand he cut the cards, then cut them again.

''Look, Sara,'' he continued, obviously interpreting her look, ''it just seems to me that if we're gonna be diggin' into some of the past about Loren, and doin' so in a frontal attack tends to make you as agitated as a short dog in long grass, then having the side distraction of a poker game might occupy enough of your mind to keep you from feelin' quite so desperate. You know?''

When still she hesitated, he slid the cards across the table toward her, his hand remaining atop them. ''You can deal first. I even shuffled for you.''

She could see what he meant. Such a tactic would also turn the pressure down between them, too.

She tried to remember what the ranch hand had taught her. ''All I know how to play is five card draw.''

Rather clumsily, she dealt the cards. ''So are you as tough a competitor as your grandfather?'' she asked.

''As far as the kind of sport I am, I guess I'd have to say fair to middlin'. Not a sore loser, but if I win, I'll say it myself—I have a bad tendency to gloat. It's not a pretty sight.''

Sara couldn't imagine it as he sat across from her shirtless and unshaven, his hair tousled. He looked as if he'd just come from bed, which he had.

She became abruptly aware that she herself wore only her robe and nightie. Beneath it lay her unbound breasts, tender and sensitized from nursing. And between them, the thin gold band on its chain around her neck.

Maybe this exercise was doomed from the start.

"I really do want to hear about Loren," she reminded him as much as herself.

"You got it," he said firmly.

She picked her cards up. It was all she could do to keep a bland face. She had two tens, two fives and a three. If she discarded the three, all she needed was a ten or five to make a full house, if she remembered her hands right. If she didn't get any of those cards, though, she still had two pair, which was a pretty good hand.

"You want to know who the competitive one was in the family, it's Loren," Cade said, studying his own hand. "He'd set his mind on somethin', and there'd be no getting him to change it."

"How do you mean?" she asked, trying to keep the excitement out of her voice. Maybe she had a bit of the McGivern competitiveness in her, after all.

He rearranged his cards. "Only that he could take a notion into his head that the moon was made of Swiss cheese and even with evidence to the contrary starin' him in the face, he'd still contradict you."

Sounds like someone else I know, Sara reflected but thought better of saying as Cade went on.

"Once, when he was fourteen or so, he decided to take up breakin' horses. Mind you, this was a kid who was all angles, with limbs like a daddy longlegs. I've seen newborn colts that looked less gangly. Two cards, if you please."

She dealt him two. "Why would being gangly be a problem riding horses?"

"T'isn't, not *riding* horses. But I'm talkin' about climbing on a green horse that's never known the feel of someone on its back. Getting bucked off comes with the territory, and it's as important to know how to get thrown as it is to stay on. You gotta be able to tuck in tight and roll or you'll not only break a bone but get stomped on.

Anyway, Loren climbed aboard his very first one and two seconds later hit the dirt in a perfect four-point landin'. Not only that but he could only lay there, stars dancin' around his head, so that sure enough, the horse stomped him a good one right in the kidney.''

"Ouch," Sara said with a wince of empathy.

"You said it. After about half a dozen more such wrecks, Granddad finally told him we were a cattle outfit and he couldn't be spared out on the range in order for him to try and kill himself at breaking horses, even though I was being allowed to spend every waking hour in the corral.''

He gave a short cough. "Loren didn't have much to complain about, though," he said loyally, "I'd've traded some of my horse sense for his way with cows—or girls, for that matter. When it came to handlin' *them*, I was the one sittin' on the fence wonderin' what the hell was goin' on.''

The confession seemed spontaneous, coming from Cade almost without thinking, for his mouth curved downward as he made a show of studying his cards.

"I guess I didn't realize you are so close in age," Sara said. Trying to be helpful, she added, "That would explain some of the rivalry going on between you two."

"You gonna take any cards or should I call?" he asked abruptly.

"Oh!" She'd been so engrossed in the conversation she nearly forgot about the game. "Yes, dealer takes one."

She discarded the three and drew one card for herself. It was a ten.

"Full house, tens and fives," Sara crowed exultantly, laying the cards down. Leaning forward on her crossed forearms, she couldn't keep from treating him to a roguish smile. "The saying, I believe, is read 'em and weep."

But he seemed not to even register her hand as Cade's

gaze fixed on her mouth, then practically jerk away. "Hold on just a second there, pilgrim. I got four of a kind."

Sara stared as he spread his cards on the table: four twos, and a three.

"Darn!" She tamped down her disappointment, determined not to be a sore loser, either. "Well, go ahead, give it to me. I can take it."

Cade paid undue attention to gathering up the cards. "Give what to you?"

"I thought you gloated when you won."

"That I do—when it's fair 'n' square."

Sara shot up straight. "Wait a minute—you mean you stacked the deck in your favor? But that's cheating!"

He cocked an eyebrow at her. "I prefer to call it a little lesson in how to make your own luck."

Her jaw dropped. Then she laughed, and the lingering vestiges of her fear disappeared like mist from a mountaintop.

Slouching in his chair, Cade considered her, his lower lip jutting out pensively, his eyes narrowed appraisingly, and she thought he looked like nothing so much as a tiger assessing its prey.

"If it *was* a matter of rivalry 'tween brothers," he continued ruefully as if there'd been no pause, "I don't know why it mattered so much to Loren. Like I said, he was a whiz with everything cow-related. Every year at the county fair he'd draw the honors for his prize heifers. I'd come scraggling in at the bottom of the field, and my heifer was getting the same top groceries his was."

She'd noticed that he spoke of his brother mostly in the past tense and wondered why, when he was so set on bringing Loren alive to her.

"Well," Sara provided helpfully, "if you're both as competitive as you say you are, and with the closeness in age, don't you think it's inevitable you'd have a rivalry between you for just about anything that either of you both want even a little?''

"Inevitable—you mean as in that way of just lettin' things happen without us having any control over them?'' He pushed himself to his feet, and she was aware that somehow, suddenly, he was once again on the verge of heading out the door. And leaving her alone, once again.

"No!'' On sheer reflex, she came to her feet, too. She tried to hold in check her words, her thoughts, her emotions, lest they impel him away. But she couldn't, for she was getting a sense of what Cade's life had been like for the past seven years since Loren had left. It seemed to her Cade had put a lot of effort himself into not leaving, as if the competition between brothers continued...and the loyalty which made him never give up on someone had in some way turned, as wine sours into vinegar, to that stubbornness she'd been treated to time and again.

"I simply meant inevitable as in the way of human nature! I mean really, Cade. What stories would Loren tell me about you if he got the chance?''

He planted his hands on the table, bending closer. "Are you rememberin' *anything*?'' he asked.

No. The answer was on her lips as she gazed across at him, whiskey-brown eyes glowing like molten gold, the sinew and brawn over arm, shoulder and chest stretched taut with the urgency of holding his own emotions in check. His thick, chestnut hair begged for a hand to smooth through it, to soothe over this soul, so long alone itself.

No, how could she remember anything of the past when the here and now that was Cade McGivern kept reaching out to her, holding her here? *Nothing* about Loren stirred her innermost feelings—not of happiness, or even fear or sadness. Or love.

Whereas with Cade...oh, he frightened and fascinated her in such opposing ways, like that coin spinning in the air. She was almost forced to respond to him as quickly, from the very bottom of her heart.

As he had responded to her at first. Had it only been a few days ago? How she wanted to go back to that moment when her baby was born, when it had seemed as if all the forces in the universe had brought the two of them together to do what neither of them could have done alone.

She couldn't go back to that night, even if she could neither go back to before it—to when she had not known this man.

Something of her thoughts must have shown on her face, for Cade's gaze darkened and turned liquid. Then his eyes shifted lower of a sudden, and as if in slow motion, Sara lifted her hand to her throat. For she knew what he looked at: that thin, gold band hanging upon a chain around her neck.

Yet another action had already been set into motion as Sara swayed forward as if drawn by a tide. And Cade never hesitated, moved by the same force as he, too, tilted toward her...

From her room came a cry that started out wavering and becoming an all-out wail before either of them could move. With a shake of his head, Cade straightened.

"It's the baby," he said inanely.

"Y-yes. I'd better see what's wrong."

Turning, Sara fled down the hall, her heart drumming and guilt nipping at her heels. Flicking on the hall light before hurrying into the room, she scooped Baby Cade up and into her arms, where he continued at full blast.

"Sweetheart, what is it?" she asked, cuddling him against her, his sobs wetting her neck and sending another stab of guilt through her.

"It must've been us talkin' so loud," Cade said, hovering behind her. She hadn't been aware he'd followed her. "I'm sorry, Sara."

"I don't think it's that. We were clear down the hall."
She checked his diaper. "He's not wet."

"Could he be hungry?"

"I fed him not an hour ago."

"Maybe it's a little gas, like last night."

"But I've been making sure to burp him regularly." She
held the baby against her shoulder, swaying and patting
his back, just in case. It didn't seem to help.

She hated this part of mothering, not knowing what was
wrong with her child or how to make things better, and
not knowing what to do to find out.

The story of my life, she thought with uncharacteristic
rancor. Cade was apparently rubbing off on her.

"You don't have to stay," she said stiffly, now anxious
to have him away and not a witness to her shortcomings.
"I can handle it."

"He might just be a little colicky," Cade observed, not
budging an inch toward the door.

Sara stopped in her tracks. "What's that?"

He scraped the edge of an index finger across his shadowed jawline. "It's sorta like scours in a calf. Sometimes,
a mama cow'll eat a certain kind of forage that agitates
her gut. And if it doesn't agree with her, chances are it
won't agree with her calf."

Her hand stilled on her son's back. "You think Baby
Cade's crying because of something I ate? Like what?"

"Who knows? Although if I had to lay a wager, I'm
guessing it was Virg's badass chili you packed away at
dinner like you were afraid Pancho Villa was riding up
from the Rio Grande."

"Cade!" Sara exclaimed in dismay. "Why didn't you
tell me the baby could get colic from what I ate?"

"Don't blame me," he drawled, the glint returning to
his eyes. "If you'll be for rememberin', I don't know what
you know and what you don't."

She could have cheerfully wrung his neck! Even if he had a point, she was in no mood to give it to him.

With a huff, she returned to her pacing. Yet after several minutes with no letting up on the baby's part, Cade said, "Here, let me take a turn."

Somewhat sulkily, Sara handed him the baby. Let *him* try to soothe the infant!

"Hush now. You're all right," Cade murmured in low, rumbling tones. "What's the fuss about? Y'all'd think we were holdin' something out on you. Is it the new digs? They're the best in the house, but if they don't suit, they don't suit and that's all there is to it. Right, darlin'?"

Her heart thumped as he called her by that name, but then she realized he was talking to Baby Cade.

Wait a second, Sara thought. Darlin'—that was his name for *her*.

Yet he said it again, asking the baby, "What's it you want, darlin'? Whatever it is, it's yours."

He cradled the baby's head in one palm, the child's bottom in the other, holding the newborn before him as he bent over the little one, and Sara was abruptly taken back to when he'd first held her son in those large, capable hands, to when he'd been the Cade who'd given himself over to her and her needs.

So what would he do, if not for her, then for her child? she wondered, crossing her arms.

"I've found that singing helps calm him," Sara said innocently.

Cade's face went slack. "Singin'?"

She hid her smile with a little cough. "Yes."

"Like…what?" he asked in total bafflement.

She leaned a shoulder against the doorjamb. "Well, the only lullaby I could *remember* was 'Twinkle, Twinkle, Little Star.' He really likes it."

He slanted her a quelling glance. Unfortunately, Baby

Cade was still squalling, harder than ever, and showing no signs of stopping.

Cade cleared his throat—and started singing. "'Twinkle, twinkle, little star, how I wonder what you are...'"

He had a fine baritone, but Baby Cade was oblivious to its quality. In fact, Cade's singing only made him howl even louder, his face screwed up in a prune, his tiny fists waving about in fury.

Cade momentarily left off singing to mutter the observance, "Dang if he doesn't look like a tomato that's sprouted black hair."

To her horror, Sara felt a bubble of laughter start in her chest and fight its way upward. Setting one forearm across her middle, she propped her elbow on her wrist and pressed her knuckles against her lips to keep from coming out with a giggle.

Cade, however, evidently caught the glimmer she was unable to erase from the bland look she gave him.

"What's so all-fire amusing? I might not have the kind of voice that makes the ladies throw their underwear up on the stage, but I'm not that bad. You sure he likes singin'?"

"It always works for me." She waved him on, trying to keep a straight face. "Keep going. It might take a while."

He gamely crooned another few verses, to no avail. Baby Cade only cried harder, which made Cade sing that much louder, which only made her want to laugh even more.

He broke off again, simply staring at the squalling infant in his hands. "Jeez, Sara, is this normal? He's gonna blow a tonsil any minute. And just what is so damned funny?"

She clapped her hand over her mouth, but her laughter spilled out from between her fingers. "You! Both of you.

You've obviously met your match in your nephew, Cade McGivern.''

He gave her a glance of supreme tolerance. "It's that stupid kiddy song you got me singin' him. I'd beller like an orphan calf, too, if I had to go to sleep to that hooey.''

He hitched the baby up on his shoulder. "What's needed here is a lullaby just for him.''

Sara extended her hand. "Be my guest.''

He thought a moment, then started singing a song that was lilting and lyric and did seem ready-made for Baby Cade. Or for Big Cade, apparently, for it was about a young cowboy who lived on the range, his horse and cattle his only companions.

And it sounded…familiar to Sara, as well. She listened closely, catching the drift of lyrics—of December snows and the songs you sang as you took to the highway, of moonlight ladies and homes in the sky—over the sound of the baby's cries.

Yet the infant, to her amazement, *was* quieting, making only little snuffling noises into the crook of Cade's neck by the time he ended on "Rock-a-bye, sweet Baby Cade.''

Her breath caught. It was the first time he had called her son by his name—by *Cade's* name. Yes, there was a difference from the other lullaby and this one. This song was one Cade obviously knew and loved, for he gave himself over to it.

And in the process, he also did as she'd wondered whether he would, and gave himself over, completely, to making her baby happy.

So she hadn't been wrong before about what she'd experienced with him the night Baby Cade was born, when he'd seen how much she needed him, what she needed from him, and he had given his all to her. Or was it simply that do-or-die determination of his that allowed no room for defeat, even when it meant coming up with a song especially for this child, her "sweet Baby Cade."

But…there wasn't actually a song by that name, was there?

"I know," Sara said excitedly, "that's a James Taylor song, isn't it? 'Sweet Baby James.'"

She sang the chorus herself, the words coming to her spontaneously, as if up from a deep well, as well as another image, a new one: of swinging gently in a hammock, the stars glittering above her in the night sky—and contentment surrounding her like a warm, much beloved blanket.

Tears welled in her eyes as relief rocked through her, though she couldn't have said why. Perhaps it was because she feared as her memory returned it would reveal to her bad things—things she didn't want to know, about her life and even about herself.

But maybe now, she thought, it wouldn't necessarily happen that way. Of *course* there would have been good things to remember, such as songs, and enthusiasms, and good feelings for the people she had loved, still did love and always would.…

As if coming to from a faint, her vision sharpened and cleared, and when it did, it was resting on Cade standing in front of her, her son dwarfed in his hands as he supported the newborn against his shoulder.

"So you remember this song?" he asked tersely.

She focused on him. His own expression seemed anything but happy. "Yes—I remember singing it, or hearing it sung. Why, was it a favorite of Loren's?"

"Couldn't say, but it's been a favorite of mine from way back." He gently patted the baby, who was by now nearly asleep. "The tape was in the cassette player of the pickup when he took off in it."

He crossed to the cradle and eased the baby into it. He straightened slowly and turned to take in the whole of her as she stood at the doorway. His scrutiny sent another of those abrupt flushes sweeping over her.

"Th-thank you, Cade," she murmured, trying to fill the silence, "for helping me with Baby Cade."

"It's nothin'," he answered with his usual depreciation of his efforts. "After all, I did give you my word, but even if I hadn't, I have the responsibility right now to take care of my brother's wife and son. And I *always* live up to my responsibilities."

She reared back as if slapped in the face. "You mean as you feel I haven't?"

He said nothing but headed for the door. Sara budged not an inch to let him past her. "Is that what you mean?" she persisted. "Because I think I'm doing the best I can under the circumstances."

"Yeah? Then why doesn't it make sense?" he snapped, his voice pitched low.

She stared up at him in the dim light from the hallway. "What doesn't make sense?"

"Why can you remember some things and not others? Why can't you remember my brother?" His brooding gaze pierced her. "What—or who—were you tryin' to leave behind in Oklahoma City?"

Shock ripped through her. "Why do you think I was trying to leave something there?"

"I guess because I just don't buy how you woke up, or came to, or however the hell you choose to explain your amnesia, with the one thought that you had to get to me for everything to be right with you."

He took a step closer, and she flattened herself against the doorjamb to keep from coming into contact with him. Yes, that was what she wanted, she couldn't deny it, but not this way.

"You didn't even know me, and I sure as shootin' didn't know you," he continued, a note of desperation in his voice, "but that didn't stop you in the least from latching on to me, justifyin' it with that silly notion of yours that it was fate or destiny that brought you here."

"It's not silly!" Sara heard how desperate she herself sounded. "All right, maybe there's something else going on with me, but when I first woke up in your bed—in your house, I mean—I really did believe I'd been sent to you because this was where I belonged. But when you didn't know me, that's when the labor pains first struck. And so why else had I been guided to you other than because you were supposed to help deliver my baby? It *was* destiny, Cade, and you can't make me believe any different!"

"So you call runnin' from your responsibilities destiny?"

"I *am* living up to my responsibilities!" she declared, tears threatening in the back of her eyes. "I am! I would have done anything, *anything* to make sure his child was brought safely into this world!"

"I'm not talking about the baby!"

Before she could register what was happening, he'd raised his hand, and she thought he meant to curl his fingers about the back of her neck and pull her close to…to do what? Instead, he reached for the chain around her throat. With one swift tug, he broke it.

Grabbing her wrist, he dropped the chain and the ring it held into her palm. "You're lookin' for ways to remember Loren? You can start by wearing his ring. And while you're at it, maybe it'll help you recall what it is that destiny's made happen that you don't have the nerve to face, so much that you've blocked out all memory of it— or should I say him?"

He struck another blow, dead on, and God help her, Sara fought back this time. There was just no way she was going to go back to that place that seemed to wreak such an unholy fear in her. Not this way, without someone to support her. Not without Cade to support her.

Oh, but how had he become the one she needed to defend herself against?

"*I've* blocked Loren out of my memory?" she asked. "What about you?" She flung out an arm, making a circle of the room. "You said it yourself. I haven't seen a single picture of your brother! Why is that, Cade? You think I don't see how much it pains you to be here with me? What don't I know about the two of you that might not be because I'm forgetting it?"

He stared at her, his slack expression reflecting the fact that she'd taken the wind right out of him. She got no satisfaction from doing so; if anything, it hurt her as much as him, for they were both in the same boat here. And both rowing like crazy to keep the inevitable from happening.

It was too late, though, at least for her. She'd already tumbled headfirst over the waterfall. She couldn't go back.

The baby hiccuped, then started to cry. And still they stood chest to chest, neither willing—or was it able?—to move, as if a magnetic force bound them together.

She had to, though, and soon. Baby Cade needed her.

It was the only force stronger right now. Still, it took everything in her to break eye contact with Cade.

Sara pivoted and stepped to the cradle, lifting out Baby Cade and trying to kiss away his tears, stifling back her own.

"Hush, now. Mama's here," she crooned, her voice rough. "I'm not going anywhere. I'm here, sweetheart."

She turned to find Cade still lingered in the doorway.

"You don't have to stay any longer," she said, this time meaning it with all her heart. "In fact, you're hereby released from any promises you made to either me or your nephew. You're free to leave."

He looked as bleak as she'd ever seen him. "Well, as luck *would* have it, Sara, I've got nowhere else to go."

With that, he turned and left, footsteps echoing in the silence.

She opened her clenched hand. The ring glowed in the ambient light from the hallway. Shaking, Sara shifted the quieting infant to one arm and slid the gold band onto her left ring finger.

It brought her no comfort, but neither did it cause her pain. Just...sadness. A sadness she knew she could not escape.

No, such tactics obviously hadn't worked before in that murky past of hers. They wouldn't now.

"But I'm not the only one," she whispered, lips pressed to her child's velvety crown as she lifted him close. "Just because you stay, Cade McGivern, doesn't mean you're still not facing up to something, too."

Chapter Six

Sara walked with peglike steps on the packed snow, arms out to keep her balance in the too large snow boots Virgil had dug out from who-knew-where and insisted she wear if she had her mind set on venturing out into the cold.

Which she had. She'd come down with a powerful case of cabin fever, and now that she had a willing baby-sitter, she was anxious to take in some well-deserved air.

She filled her lungs with the sharp, invigorating stuff before blowing it out, improved by the experience. Maybe it would clear her head, as well. Last night had been hard on her, and not merely because she'd lost so much sleep. Yesterday's repeated confrontations with Cade had worn her out and were wearing her down, as were the ups and downs of emotions such conflict wrought on her. She'd awoken this morning determined not to let them—or Cade—get the better of her.

Or these infernal boots, which her feet didn't fill by half.

They were like walking in clown shoes, and probably just as funny looking. At least they'd keep her feet warm as she took in the scenery, such as it was.

The day was cold and clear, the sky a rich blue, made all the more blue by its contrast to the pristine snow that went on without relief for as far as the eye could see. The frigid breeze, when it was up, nearly robbed her of her breath, but she wasn't about to turn around and head back for the ranch house.

Stepping carefully on the unevenly plowed ground, Sara rounded the corner of the barn—and jumped, nearly losing her balance, when she came face-to-face with Cade.

"Oh!" She leaned her hand against the side of the barn for support. "I didn't know you were back from town."

In fact, she wouldn't have ventured outside if she'd known he was anywhere around, and experienced a moment of disappointment. She simply needed not to get into a confrontation with him, which they inevitably did.

He seemed as put out by her presence. "I'd picked up some extra mineral tubs and unloaded them, and didn't feel like goin' back inside yet," he explained.

Yes, he'd been hoping to avoid her, too.

So this is what we've come to, she thought with regret.

He could have remained outside for quite a while, too, the way he was dressed in a chocolate-brown suede jacket, its wool lining peeking out at the collar, his hands protected by thick leather gloves. On his head he wore a black cowboy hat that succeeded, somehow, in shading his face just right, so the lines of nose, cheekbone and jaw were finely drawn, and the amber in his eyes glowed with a new depth as he looked pensively down at her.

She became abruptly aware of what she looked like in her own hat, a men's knit balaclava, again from a collection Virg had in stock, complete with earflaps so that only her face, which was undoubtedly cold-reddened, showed.

Her nose was probably Christmas-bulb bright, too. The chill was making it run like a drippy faucet.

Feeling even more awkward and unattractive, Sara dropped her chin, fumbling for the tissue in her pocket. That's when she noticed behind him the glossy red-brown horse he held on a lead. It nickered gently, exhibiting none of its owner's caution as it bumped Cade aside to stretch an inquiring nose toward her, nostrils flaring.

Immediately captivated, Sara extended her mittened hand for inspection. "Is this the horse you mentioned once? What did you say his name was?"

"This here's Destiny," Cade volunteered.

Reaching out, she stroked her mitten down the splash of white on his broad nose. "Destiny?" She arched an eyebrow.

"I didn't name him, but I have to admit it fits." Cade himself seemed unable to resist giving the horse's long neck a pat or two as he gazed at him fondly. "Destiny's gonna make my reputation."

She sniffed, remembering her original intent, and rooted around in her pocket for the tissue. She couldn't find it.

"Your reputation—as a rancher?" she asked, sniffing again and wondering if she'd have to resort to using her sleeve. Talk about being unattractive.

"Nope. As a horse trainer." Apparently noticing her predicament, Cade pulled a clean, neatly folded bandanna from his back pocket and handed it to her. "Come spring I was aimin' to take him around to some of the shows in my spare time, give people a gander at what I've taught him, and see if I could sign on a few clients."

"Well, he's beautiful just to look at," she said, daubing at her drippy nose. "It must be magnificent to see him perform."

She could tell she'd pleased him. "I was just gonna put him through a few paces in the corral," Cade told her.

"Oh, can I watch?"

He shrugged as if it concerned him not the least. "Sure."

She fell into step beside him as he continued toward the wood-fenced corral on the other side of the ranch yard near what must have been the stable. Sara concentrated on walking in the boots, still loose on her heels even with three pairs of socks on, becoming aware after a moment that Cade watched her.

"You must have been pretty desperate to get out of the house if you had to resort to wearing Virg's hat and boots," he commented.

"I *was* feeling hemmed in. Not that I don't adore every minute with Baby Cade," she added hastily.

"Well, I imagine the isolation out here on the ranch is durned hard on a body if you're not used to it."

She picked her way over a deep tire track in the snow. "How did *you* get used to it?"

Cade squinted against the glare of the sun. "So was it Virg or was it you who trussed you up like a Thanksgivin' turkey?"

Wondering why he didn't answer her question, she responded to his readily enough. "That would be Virgil. He must have packed twenty layers of clothes onto me. He didn't want me to get cold, although I feel like I'll perish from heat any minute."

He opened the gate into the corral. "Well, you'll cool off soon enough sittin' up on this here top fence rail."

Sara shaded her eyes against the late-afternoon sun. "Actually, I'm going to move over to the far side so I can see better."

She trudged across the corral in those ridiculous boots and, grasping the top railing in both hands, struggled to climb up and sit on it, knowing she looked like a toddler trying to clamber onto a step stool.

"Here, let me give you a hand," Cade said from behind her in that muted voice of the first night when he'd volunteered to comb her hair. Not really wanting to help, but making the gentlemanly gesture.

"I can do it," Sara huffed crossly. With a grunt, she hauled herself up and managed to turn around and sit, but not without almost falling off backward into a drift of snow.

"See?" she said brightly, hoping he wouldn't realize how ungainly and unattractive she felt—or wonder why it mattered to her if she wasn't.

But he was back to his remote self, she could see. "Suit yourself."

She could have cried with regret. How could things between them go so sour so quickly?

Yet it wasn't to remain so, as Cade swung fluidly into the saddle. And the performance began.

Her mood did another of those flip-flops as Sara watched, rapt. Even without a background in horsemanship, she knew she was seeing a rare sight as Cade and the horse loped in a circle around the corral first one direction, then slowing to a steady walk before stopping smoothly and, with a graceful turn, reversing their direction, all without Cade saying a word or seemingly signaling the gelding in any way.

She forgot everything—her chapped cheeks, runny nose and absurd clothes—as the picture they made filled her vision, Cade sitting tall and relaxed in the saddle, his dark clothing and coloring perfectly complementing the glossy chestnut.

Horse and rider were a thing of sheer beauty, a study in movement, timing and undiluted talent. And love. More than anything else, Sara saw how much Cade loved this horse and loved riding it, giving himself over completely to it in a way that she knew instinctively made all the difference in the world in Destiny's performance.

But then, she'd seen that ability in Cade before.

When he successfully got Destiny to sidestep over a railroad tic first in one direction then the other with nary a hesitation, Sara couldn't restrain herself and burst into applause.

"Cade, that was wonderful!" she enthused with all sincerity. "I can certainly see why you want to take Destiny out and show off what you've taught him."

He actually gave her an aw-shucks grin that made her heart thump, it was so open and unguarded. "Watch," he said. "I only taught him this a few days ago."

Sitting up straight in the saddle, Cade said, "Destiny."

The gelding rolled his ears backward, listening.

"Destiny, I want you to back up three steps."

Sara watched as, with no visible prompting from Cade, the horse took one, two, three steps back, and stopped.

Her jaw dropped. "How did you do that? You didn't move a muscle."

He leaned forward to stroke the horse's neck. "Don't need to, when you've got Destiny doin' the arithmetic."

"I know—you taught him how to take just three steps back and that's it," she called out, playing the skeptic for once.

Cade's lifted eyebrows shifted the brim of his hat up an inch. "Did I? How many steps would *you* like him to take, then?"

"Okay, how about…seven."

He gestured with a lift of the reins. "Don't tell me, tell Destiny."

Sara couldn't resist the challenge. She stood up, balancing her feet on the lower railing and hanging on behind her with her mittened hands.

"Destiny," she commanded in sonorous tones, "I want you to take seven steps back."

The gelding reared his head, then dropped it, as if giving a nod. Cade was still as a carved totem pole on Destiny's back. The horse lifted a hoof—then took one, two, three steps back...a pause...four, five, six back...another pause, then one more step. And stopped.

If it'd been warm enough for insects, a fly would have flown straight into her mouth. "How did you do that?" Sara demanded, sitting back down with a thump. "It's like you and Destiny are fused together. You move together like one. I've never seen anything like that before."

"Course, you don't know but that you have seen somethin' like it before," Cade drawled as he rode over to her, "but I'll take the compliment, anyway. You should see him cut a contrary steer out of a bunch of cattle. Now there, he just plain shines."

He reached down to rub Destiny's neck. "Yup, what this is, is natural-born talent. I've never seen an animal more quick to learn or eager to please. He's sure enough cut proud."

As usual, he'd depreciated the matter, placing credit elsewhere, yet she could see in his eyes she'd again said something not only right, but something that had touched him deeply. All she'd given him was an appreciation of him for who he was and what he'd accomplished.

Cut proud. She wasn't quite sure what that meant, but it certainly described both horse and rider.

"So how does one learn to handle horses the way you do?" she asked, studying her clasped hands and being very careful not to spoil the moment. She wanted nothing less than to see it end.

"Horses have always been somethin' I've just...known." Cade dismounted and looped Destiny's reins around the railing, resting his forearms next to them—next to her. "It's hard to explain. When I come up on somethin' I want Destiny to learn, I figure out, without even beginnin' to know how, how I ought to go about it."

"But you must have a clue as to how you know."

He rubbed his gloved hands together ruminatively. "Well, I've studied on it and talked to some horse trainers about it. I guess in layman's terms you just sort of ask the horse to do something by fixing it up and letting him find it. You make the wrong thing difficult to do, and the right thing easy. And you make sure you feel it yourself, all the way through your body on down to your toes."

Sara was completely lost. "What do you mean?"

"Like when I wanted him to back up, I shifted back on the saddle just enough so Destiny wanted to step backward to keep the balance the same. I kept leanin' back till he'd taken seven steps, then I shifted forward again, and he stopped tryin' to correct the balance."

"But I didn't see you move at all!" Sara persisted, aware she was back to challenging him. Although he didn't seem to mind her questions on this subject, perhaps because it was one he knew implicitly—and had the greatest confidence in.

"I don't have to do much." He half turned toward her, his elbow propped on the railing, his expression intent. "It's mostly about lettin' go and just thinking and feeling the movement as it comes. I feel the horse's movements in my own body, and Destiny feels mine in his."

Sara frowned. "I still don't understand how you made that trick happen."

"Best as I can explain it is, with horses, you don't *make* anything happen. Like I said, it's how he deals with the choices he's been given, makin' him feel he's the one in control."

She still must have looked severely befuddled because he smiled up at her. She'd seen his smile before, but it struck her anew how it changed his aspect entirely, and one could see, of a sudden, what a handsome man he was.

Handsome—and irresistible. But she had to resist him.

"I guess it would make as much sense as tryin' to read Greek upside down and backward to someone who didn't have a natural talent for it," he allowed. He peered out across the frosted landscape. "Like how ranching has been for me—takin' all of my attention and then some just to keep on top of it."

"Really?" From her perch, she had a good view of the well-kept-up ranch yard and buildings. "If you ask me, it looks like you've got more than a handle on things."

His gaze remained fastened on the horizon, but Sara got a sense that once again she'd given him some validation that he'd long gone without, because in the next moment he went on quietly, "I know ranchin' well enough, been doin' fine at it for years. But I've always felt like my ranching abilities only go so far, that I can finesse it up to a limit, and then the finer points escape me."

He gestured, a sweeping movement with his open hand. "That…knowing with one glance over a bunch of cattle if there's any that're sick. Or whether a mama cow is fixin' to drop her calf in the next day. Like Loren could."

Cade glanced up at her. "Now, there's a natural-born talent. My brother could spot a steer brushed up in a stand of tamarack I'd ridden by ten times. I sure enough got the horse sense, but when it came to knowin' critters of the bovine kind, Loren got the nod."

She wanted to ask him why he persisted in speaking of his brother in the past tense when he was so determined to keep him alive both in his mind and hers, but she was reluctant to recall any part of last night's scene. Yet she couldn't prevent herself from inquiring, "Then why isn't Loren ranching and you training horses for a living?"

"I thought at one point he wouldn't be able to stay

away, but he must have found another calling, even more powerful than ranchin' had been for him," he said, deftly avoiding her question. "In any case, I don't intend to wait any longer to follow mine. As soon as matters get settled with you and the young'un, and y'all are back in Albuquerque where you belong, I'll be sellin' off part of the herd, maybe rent a section or so out, so I can be on the road as much as I can showing Destiny."

"But what if Loren does want to get back into ranching, if not now, then sometime in the future?" Sara asked, her throat tightening up of a sudden.

His gold-brown gaze roamed her features. "He's welcome to come back. But I can't go on planning my future around that possibility. Horses like Destiny don't come along but once in a lifetime, and I'd be a fool to waste this chance. Destiny—*your* kind of destiny—has already taken me for a ride. Now that I'm back in the saddle, so to speak, I fully intend to hold on to the reins."

Their faces were close enough their breaths mingled and swirled in a cloud between them. "This time, nothin' is gonna stand in my way. I can't let it."

A quiet finality had entered his voice during the last part, and for some reason she felt as if he were trying still to make her understand something that was beyond her ken.

And she wanted to understand! It was too important not to.

"What happened between you and Loren, Cade?" Sara asked, needing to know the truth, even if it cost her. "And something did happen, didn't it? I know you mentioned before that there'd been a falling out, but it had to be over something big to tear two brothers apart. Otherwise, why would that letter be the first contact you'd had with him in seven years?"

At her questions, he looked away. "It's not for me to say, Sara. If Loren's already told you, then you'll find out when either he or your memory comes back. And if he doesn't…if he didn't tell you, then he'll have had his reasons, which I'm guessing are that it's all water under the bridge—now that he has you.''

She was more confused than ever. ''But it's obviously *not* water under the bridge with you, Cade.''

''Yes, it is,'' he contradicted in a low voice. ''It has to be, Sara.''

He turned to untie Destiny's reins from the fence, evidently in preparation for leaving—again.

For a moment, Sara sat in silence trying to make sense of it all. His words had been characteristic of the determination and stubbornness he used like a scythe to cut through any argument to the contrary. But his tone was not. It was desperate. He was desperate…desperate for her to believe. Or perhaps *he* was desperate to believe—that he was in charge of his fate, could set its wheels in motion as he chose.

Or bring them to a grinding, screeching halt.

But he couldn't! Sara knew it with a certainty she hadn't had last night. He couldn't—and neither could she, any more than either of them could have stopped Baby Cade from being born. And that was what *she* needed to make him understand.

''Cade, wait,'' Sara said, reaching out to grab the arm of his coat to detain him. Too late, however, she remembered her precarious position on the fence rail, so that when she missed his sleeve, she lost her balance. For a few seconds she windmilled furiously, but the effort was for naught.

Sara pitched straight backward into a three-foot drift of snow.

It completely engulfed her, going down her back and up her front, into her eyes and muffling her hearing. She struggled to sit up and only sank down deeper.

From far away it seemed she could hear Cade shouting her name. Sara flailed her arms, trying to catch a breath and inhaling only snow.

Then, abruptly, she was being hauled up and out of the drift and into Cade's arms.

"Sara, are you all right?" Madly, he brushed the snow out of her face, dislodging her cap so it fell to the ground. Her hair spilled out in a cascade.

"I think—" she coughed. "—I think so."

"Did you hurt anything—your back? Your head?"

He stooped, peering into her eyes. She could see the fear in his, and was abruptly plunged into a memory.

It wasn't from her forgotten past, though. Suddenly, it was New Year's Eve again, with the blizzard raging outside, the two of them cocooned in his bedroom as if suspended in time, bound there together, where all that mattered was saving a baby who was determined to be born at that moment whether either of them wanted him to be or not.

That was then, though; this was now. This time, she had a choice. A choice of whether to connect—or turn away.

"I'm f-fine," she stammered.

"You sure? You sound like you might've got the wind knocked out of you."

She shook her head. "No. The snow cushioned my fall. I was surprised more than anything."

Sara glanced over her shoulder at the indentation in the drift and gave a nervous laugh. "Goodness. Doesn't exactly look like a snow angel, does it?"

"A snow elephant is more like it," Cade observed. "I mean, you really hit bottom, there."

Sara slanted him a sidelong glance from under her lashes. *"Really?"*

One side of his mouth dented in, while the other side puckered toward the middle, as if he were trying not to laugh. "Sure did. 'Cept how you looked buried in that drift, with those boots cocked up in the air—now that had horse opera comic relief written all over it."

That decided it. She made as if to bend over and brush off the hem of her coat, but when she straightened she came up with a mitten full of snow, which she deftly ground into his face.

Momentarily stunned, Cade gasped, sputtered for air, and came back raring for action. Sara was already running in the opposite direction, though. Over her shoulder she saw him stoop to scoop snow into his glove before taking off in pursuit.

Hers was a lost cause, she knew, hampered as she was by her long coat and Virgil's Bozo-size boots. She'd barely rounded the corner when Cade seized her by the waist. In one swift move, he swung her about, and before Sara knew it she had her back up against the side of the stable. And Cade pressed up against her, a fistful of snow held aloft.

He lifted one eyebrow. "Too bad you didn't give me a chance to warn you, but when it comes to snowball fights, I definitely got that talent in the family."

"Oh, yeah?" Sara gasped, struggling to get away before he chose to make use of his snowball. "Well, all the talent in the world won't help get you out of the dangerous waters you're in now, telling a new mother she's as big as an elephant."

"Oh, is that what this is about?"

"Yes!" Sara squirmed, still trying to get away, but she may as well have been a mouse under a cat's paw. "I'm fed up to here with your tactless comments about how much I eat and what I look like!"

He did another of those slow perusals that somehow made her whole body blush.

"Trust me, darlin'," he said in that thoroughly provocative drawl of his, "you've got a long ways to go before you can stand on the street corner in Sagebrush and sell shade.''

Darlin'. At last, he'd called *her* darlin', and in that instant Sara realized just how much she'd wanted him to, had missed him doing so.

They were both in dangerous waters here. Both with a choice to make. Or did they? Because as for herself, Sara knew she couldn't go back. The choice had already been made for her.

As a result, she found herself being dangerously honest.

''Even without remembering Loren, I don't think you'd have to do anything so drastic as make a trade with him for his way with women,'' she whispered, her heart in her throat.

''I was sixteen when I wanted that, Sara,'' he said, his voice as low, with a particular thrum of warning in it.

And now? What did he want now, and what would he give in trade to make it his?

''I'm simply telling you,'' she admonished softly, ''your brother's not the only one with all the skills—or luck.''

He didn't respond, for she could see that at her words, his lashes had dropped as his eyes homed in on her mouth.

Involuntarily, Sara wet her lips.

The moment held for what seemed like an eternity in which time both suspended completely and raced past with the speed of light.

Then Cade lifted his eyes again to hit her with that molten gaze of his that was, amazingly, filled with the same promise as it'd been during her little one's birth.

''Damn, your eyes are blue,'' he muttered, almost angrily.

As if that magnetic force bound them, their faces came an inch closer, and then apart two as the tension intensified, then closer three, gazes still locked, and holding…mere millimeters now…and holding…achingly, agonizingly holding…

And then his mouth was upon hers, a shock of unfamiliar contact and coldness. But only in the first instant, before he pressed and parted her lips and filled her with the hot, lush velvet of his tongue.

And oh, it felt right! So right it almost brought her to tears. As if they were two halves of a soul that had come together again for the first time in centuries. As if destined to. It *wasn't* all her wishful thinking. It wasn't.

Sara made a low sound of satisfaction deep in her throat, which Cade answered with his own, capturing her closer, sharing breath as he urged the kiss deeper as if seeking to surpass what was already edging into sublime, yet knowing nothing of how not to quest further.

Happiness welled up in her unbidden, like water from a hidden spring, for a miracle had happened. He'd become the Cade of before, the man who'd held nothing back from her, who, with great passion, had made her a promise to take care of and keep her and her baby as his own for as long as they needed him.

Yes, the promise…and the passion.

Heated desire spread through her abdomen, pooling down low and making her still-swollen womb contract within her. Her breasts, too, heavy with milk, seemed sensitized even through the layers of clothing as Cade's arm tightened around her, pressing her that much closer still.

He seemed to realize the constraints hindering them, for he released her only long enough to tear off his gloves before taking her face between her hands and fusing his mouth with hers again. His thumbs caressed her jawline, back and forth, then drifted down her throat—oh, blessed touch!—to the edge of her collar, to dip just underneath it to where her pulse beat wildly.

Whimpering for want of touching him the same way,

Sara spent precious seconds struggling with her mittens, finally yanking them off and letting them fall to the ground. Yet her urgency left her of a sudden as she drew away slightly, mouth throbbing and vision hazy except for the warm whiskey of Cade's eyes. Slowly, she reached up and lifted his hat from his head, tossing it carelessly aside.

Then, equally slowly, equally deliberately, she wove her hands into his hair and tugged him down to her to lose herself in him again.

And lose herself she did, completely. How could she not when he held nothing back? Neither of them did, as caress turned to crush, and clasp to clutch.

They were frenzied, she realized. Desperate. These were stolen moments. And stealing was wrong.

Sanity returned, but hung only by a thread. *Oh, what kind of woman was she?*

"Cade, wait," Sara cried, drawing away.

He groaned.

"Cade, this is too dangerous…what if someone sees us?"

To her surprise, he didn't let go of her but dragged her down on top of him into another soft, deep snowdrift.

She gasped at the feel of that hard, lean body against hers, and heaven help her, Sara couldn't prevent herself from letting Cade tow her under again, into the insulating snow and the unbelievable sensation of his kiss.

Truly, they were wrapped in a cocoon, with all thought and time suspended. Nothing of the past mattered; the future had yet to be written. All that was real, all that mattered was the present. It was all that would ever matter….

Yet they weren't trapped in a blizzard, with no one and nothing to depend upon but each other. Then, she'd had to let the knowns in her life take precedence over the unknowns. They had both had to.

Now, though, they knew. And they each had obligations, if not a choice.

With a dry sob, Sara broke the kiss, burying her face against his neck.

Wordlessly, he pressed his palm to the back of her head, and she felt him swallow painfully again and again as he held her. Held them both.

Finally, she lifted her head. "Oh, Cade, what are we going to do—"

"No, don't say it," he interrupted, pressing three fingers to her lips. "Don't say anything either of us would regret."

"But we can't keep ignoring what's happened between us, hoping it'll go away!"

"Nothing's happened!"

He sat up, bringing her with him, then pushed himself to his feet before extending a hand to help her up, too. Sara watched numbly as he collected hats and gloves and mittens, slapping them against his thigh to shake the snow loose, all very much with the look of a man who needed to do something right now, where only seconds ago it had seemed enough to simply be.

He handed her belongings to her without looking at her, and she thought she'd cry.

She held it in, though just barely.

"Cade," Sara finally said when it became clear he wasn't about to speak. "Please. Can't we at least talk about it?"

"Why?" He turned on her. With the sun shining directly in his eyes, they looked bloodshot, and a flush painted the hollows of his cheeks. "What good will talking do when it can't go anywhere? It's got to stop right here, right now, don't you see that?"

He drove his fingers through his hair, dislodging the snow, and when he placed his hat on his head she could see his hand was shaking. "You're my brother's wife, Sara! And by God, we *both* need to remember that!"

"You think I don't know that? Cade—" She swallowed back the tears in her throat "—I wish I could remember Loren, truly I do. I keep looking for him in our baby's features. But I don't see him there!"

Dropping her chin, Sara squeezed her eyes shut, as if one last time hoping to see—or not see—with a certainty what she knew in her heart to be true. "And when I do see him, in those vague dreams of mine, I don't feel for him…what a wife should feel for her husband. And something tells me I never did."

The silence was unnatural, lacking any sound of bird or animal or other signs of life. Even the incessant wind had dwindled to nothing.

"What're you saying, Sara?" Cade finally asked, as deathly quiet.

She shook her head miserably, her eyes still shut. It helped, right now, to have the ability to close out part of the world. She couldn't do that forever, though. "I don't know. Who knows why I'm repressing my memory of Loren, if that's what's going on inside my head?"

Finally, she opened her eyes and found him. "But that doesn't change this—this bond between us. And I can't just make it go away because it's wrong. Right *or* wrong, I can't go back to before."

"You've got to, Sara," Cade repeated desperately.

She shook her head slowly, her eyes never leaving his. "I'm truly sorry, Cade, but I can't, any more than you can. Call it destiny or fate or the luck of the draw, it doesn't change what is, and that is I love—"

"No!" Taking a step forward, he gripped her upper arms, practically hovering over her. Sara faced him resolutely, not knowing whether he meant to try to make them both, with characteristic determination, continue to deny the truth, or to embrace it—and her. Either way, she wouldn't back down.

A whole spectrum of emotions crossed his expressive eyes, from guilt to hope to anguish to relief. She simply stared back at him, her own naked, honest emotion in her eyes.

"Sorry to interrupt."

They both jumped at the sound of Virgil's voice. He stood at the entrance of the corral, wearing no coat or hat. Just a scowl of censure on his face.

Cade dropped his hands and stepped away.

On reflex, Sara said, "You weren't interrupting anything, Virgil."

"That a fact?" Virgil said skeptically.

"It is," Cade answered for her. "Sara fell off the fence into a drift, and I was helpin' her get dusted off."

His face had flushed an even deeper red, but he met his ranch hand's eyes steadily, as if daring Virgil to challenge him.

Fingers shoved mightily into his front jeans pockets, the hand looked not in the least convinced, but he didn't contradict Cade, either.

Shame, insidious and devouring, skulked through her. Oh, was Cade right? Because right or wrong, *this* certainly couldn't continue—she couldn't deceive good-hearted, honest men like Virgil, and she couldn't ask Cade to.

Most of all, neither of them could deceive Loren. It would eat them both alive, but most of all Cade. She couldn't do that to him, either.

No, she'd never be able to deny the bond between herself and Cade, but he was right in that it could go nowhere. Not as long as she was married to his brother. And she *was* married to him, no matter what she felt or didn't feel for Loren.

Oh, could fate be so perverse, she wondered bitterly, as

to have given her this kind of undeniable love for Cade, only to make her forever deny it?

It wasn't fair! Would she have to let Cade go—too?

Her breath abruptly left her as her mind started to go into a spontaneous spin. She didn't know if she could. *Not Cade.* But she had to, if she truly wanted what was best for him. And she did, more than anything.

Let him go. Just let him go. You've got to. Yet the very suggestion that she might put her on shaky ground, so that she felt herself slipping into despair again, into that place in her mind that was foggy and murky and muddy and oh, so terribly frightening.

Real denial rose up in her. *No!* She wouldn't let it happen.

Then you'll lose him for sure....

The strength of that inescapable truth tugged her inexorably down into a whirling, swirling tidal pool—

Then she felt Cade's hand gripping her elbow, bringing her back, supporting her yet again. Or perhaps sending her a warning.

For as her vision cleared, she saw what he must have: the real portent, which was framed in Virgil's expression and confirmed with his next words. "I thought it best to come find you straightaway," he said.

Sara's hand flew to her throat as all air definitely left her lungs. "Oh, is it the baby?"

"The babe's fine," Virgil assured her gruffly. "No, it's the phone call you've been waiting for."

It wasn't clear whether the hand meant her or Cade, but it was clear who the call was about.

Their gazes collided.

"*Loren,*" Cade breathed.

Chapter Seven

Cade was over the fence in an instant and halfway across the corral before he remembered Sara. He came back to help her around the corral, his hand on her elbow to hurry her, but her long coat and those damned boots hampered her gait and slowed them both down.

It was next door to impossible for him to check his impatience—and fear.

"Virg, you'll stable Destiny for me, won't you?" he asked on his way by.

The hand nodded, his face as stony as Cade had ever seen it.

He flat didn't have the courage to ask Virgil the real question on his mind, whether it was Loren calling or one of the detectives from Albuquerque with news of his brother. He tried to believe either would be better than this ceaseless not knowing that was wearing him down like sandpaper on soapstone, but the attempt was futile.

So what *did* he wish for? What *could* he wish for that didn't betray his brother further and place the blame squarely, directly on him?

Beside him, Sara stumbled. Cade caught her before she fell, yet that didn't prevent him from urging her on at an even faster pace. It was those stupid boots of Virg's. He'd half a mind to burn them behind the barn first chance he got.

"Cade, wait!"

Coming up short, he glanced down at her with barely concealed frustration.

"I…need to catch my breath," she panted, holding her side.

He'd forgotten she had given birth only a few days ago. Right now, that seemed like it had happened in the distant past.

She leaned upon his arm, and he saw only then how pale she'd become. Perspiration sheened her forehead.

What a self-absorbed jerk he was! He wasn't the only one fighting panic. "God, Sara, I'm sorry."

"Give me a minute, please. Just one minute."

Funny she should say that. One minute. That had been all he would have asked for once—a minute on either side of Loren's entrance into the stable to find him and Marlene in what his brother had believed to be a state of unbridled passion.

And now? What if Virgil had interrupted Sara and him a minute or so earlier, before he had known the ecstasy of Sara's lips under his, the bliss of her whole being melding with his?

He glanced down at her, and found she stared up at him with those bluest of blue eyes. Even clouded with worry, they reminded him of stars star sapphires. He'd seen that kind of stone once, and the name had put him in mind then, as it did now looking at Sara, of someone having stolen them from the heavens.

No, he couldn't do it. Right or wrong, he couldn't go back to not knowing that singular pleasure of holding Sara in his arms, even if it haunted him for the rest of his life. Which he was betting it would.

"Ready?" he said, not ungently.

She nodded, straightening. "Yes."

He took her elbow again, this time walking at a slower pace. Finally, they reached the back door. The warmth of the house hit him like a furnace as he entered, Sara close behind him, but he couldn't be bothered to stop and remove boots or coat or hat. Cade strode straight to the phone in the hallway and picked up the receiver, his hand shaking.

"Hello?"

"Cade? Is that you?"

He sagged against the wall as relief, blessedly pure, rocked through him, and he said a brief prayer of thanks for that, if nothing else. "Loren. Yes, it's me. Are you all right?"

"I'm fine, just fine."

He sounded fine. His voice cracking, Cade said, "We were sure worried about you."

"Sorry about that. Believe me, it was no fun on this end, either. Been holed up in an airport in Cancun for the past few days trying like hell to get a flight or even a phone call out. That storm system took out electricity in every town on the Mexican coast, is what we were told. But we're doin' great now that we're back in the good ol' U.S. of A. The big question is, how's Sara?"

Cade's gaze shot to hers as she stood beside him, herself still in her outdoor clothes and snow melting in her hair. "She's fine, too. So—so's the baby."

"Yeah, we got your message soon as we got in." That

was the second time Loren had referred to "we." Had he been traveling with co-workers on business? To Cancun?

And Loren continued to do it as he said, "Sorry we weren't here to get it in person. I take it you got my letter?"

"Y-yes, I did." Feeling like he'd die of heatstroke in the next second, Cade unbuttoned his coat one-handedly and shucked it, tossing it over the stair railing. "And your note, sending Sara to me—to here."

"Thank God I thought to do that. Decided not to try to outrun a blizzard, did she?"

"Uh, yeah." He realized Loren might want to hear the story from his wife and turned, about to offer the receiver to Sara, only to find she had disappeared. Where did she go? He'd have thought she'd be frantic to talk to her beloved husband.

Except Sara didn't feel that way about Loren.

In any case, it was apparent his brother had no idea she was even there on the ranch as he went on. "I hope she didn't mind having her baby born at Sagebrush's small-town clinic instead of a proper hospital. Where's Doc been putting her up?"

Cade took a deep breath and decided to just say it. "Loren, the baby was born here. And Doc wasn't able to make it, on account of the blizzard." He did hesitate over the last piece of information. "I had to deliver the baby myself."

It was almost as if Loren had hung up, the ensuing silence at the other end of the line was so complete, and in an instant Cade was back to being the brother with less experience, less natural-born instinct when it came to knowing how to handle a sticky situation, be it with a cow or a woman.

Then Loren exclaimed, "My God, Cade, how did you do it? I mean, the baby wasn't due for another six weeks.

Even thinkin' Doc was doin' the honors, it gave us both shivers.''

Who was this ''we'' he kept talking about? Sara and him? But Sara was here!

Or at least she had been. Where had she disappeared to? he wondered, his confusion growing, along with that sense of alarm he'd encountered the first time he'd laid eyes on her.

''But Doc Barclay said the baby was full-term, or close to it,'' Cade said distractedly, stretching the telephone cord to try to see into the living room.

''Really?'' Again there was a silence on the other end of the line, and it became apparent to Cade this time that Loren had muffled the receiver and seemed to be talking to someone in the room with him. ''Well, that's sure strange. Her doctor in Oklahoma City seemed pretty sure she wasn't due for another month and a half.''

His confusion only compounded. ''Sara's doctor was in Oklahoma City—not Albuquerque?''

''Sure, although we'd already made plans to line her up with a good doctor here as soon as she arrived. Believe me, Cade, I'd never have let her try to make a trip, even if it was only a ten-hour one, so close to her due date if I'd known. Damn it! How in the world could things have gone so confoundedly wrong?''

Wrong…wrong…wrong… The word echoed in Cade's head, and he slumped against the wall, thumb and forefinger pressing into his eye sockets, as the weight of his sentence sounded as deeply within him. He should have known he wasn't to get off so easily. Not that Loren knew what had transpired between him and Sara—for Cade vowed then and there that he would never know—only that he would have to find some way to live with the knowledge of what he had done.

And that was fall in love with his brother's wife. He

may be able to deny it to Sara, but he was no longer able to deny it to himself.

"Aw, hell, what am I sayin', 'cause they didn't, did they?"

Cade shook his head, still bent against his hand. "What?"

"Things didn't go wrong, did they? It all ended up just fine, thanks to you, Cade." Loren's voice grew rough. "Really, there's no way either Sara or I could ever thank you enough. I should've known, I guess. You always come through when a body needs you to, no matter what. I told Sara that, you know."

"I—I know," Cade said as roughly, the regret and the guilt growing apace as he wondered how under God's heaven he was going to be able to come through this time.

Then, something at that moment made him lift his head. Sara stood at the end of the hallway. She'd divested herself of her coat and boots, and held her dark-haired baby cradled against her. Her own dark hair, black as night, swirled around her shoulders, and with those eyes of starshine, she looked almost otherworldly. And as much out of his reach.

"I—I needed to have our baby in my arms when I first talked to him," she said. A shaft of light reflected the gold of her wedding band as she pressed her hand to the back of her child's head.

Reflected in her eyes were the guilt and regret that were tearing him apart. Tearing them both apart.

Yet he could see she was concerned for him, too—concerned that he also find a way within himself to set matters right with his brother and be at peace.

Strangely, he had already gotten what he needed from Loren.

"You—" He cleared his throat, full of emotion, his gaze resting on the woman who filled it so completely.

"You don't have to thank me, Loren. Just seein' Sara and the baby safe and well—that's all that matters."

And with those words, Cade knew he gave in to the inevitable, accepting what had happened for what it was. Sara and the baby's health and happiness *were* all that mattered, had been all that had mattered the night he'd been born. And if he'd had to give away a part of himself that he now was unable to take back, then so be it.

Besides, to try to do so would be to deny his very existence, especially when he saw Sara's blue eyes fill with tears, making them look for sure like sapphires on the starriest of nights.

Barely realizing it, Cade prayed for a miracle with the last particle of hope in his soul.

"Considering what Sara's had to deal with in the past six months, I'm sure she feels the same," Loren said. "She's had kind of a rough time of it. Did she tell you what she's been through?"

"Not exactly," Cade hedged as Sara came toward him.

"What do you mean?" his brother asked.

"Maybe she should tell you herself," he said, starting to hand her the phone. But she was already shaking her head, indicating that she wanted him to, which made sense, he realized. He was the one who actually "knew" Loren.

"I don't know how to say this 'cept just to say it, Loren. Sara has amnesia."

"Amnesia? You mean she doesn't know who she is?"

"That's right. It took a while for us to figure it out here, what with your letter spellin' her name with an *H* on the end and leaving it off on the note you gave her with my info on it."

"There's no *H* in her— Wait a minute." There was another muffling of the receiver before Loren came on the line again. "So was she in an accident? Is she all right?"

"'Cept for the amnesia, Doc says she's fit as can be, so

no worries so far as that goes. He did say, though, that the memory loss could be caused by her goin' through some emotionally traumatic event that she's had to block from her mind."

Sara had arrived at his side, and it took everything in him not to reach out to her. He'd gotten used to touching her that quickly. "That's why we thought something had happened to you."

Swallowing hard, he made himself go on. "Loren, she doesn't remember you."

"What about Sara? Does she remember her?"

"Does she remember...who?"

Loren actually laughed. "I'm sorry, Cade. It'd help if I quit confusin' us both. I usually call 'em by their middle names when I'm talkin' about them in the same conversation or when they're in the same room. I'm askin' if Sara Jane—Sara without the *H*—remembers her cousin Sarah Ann—Sarah *with* the *H*. Sarah Ann McGivern. My wife."

Every bit of blood in his body drained to his toes. Or at least it seemed that way, because he'd become light-headed of a sudden, his sight going black around the edges, so that when he stared down at Sara, all he could see was her face—that hopeful, trusting face that had never stopped, couldn't stop, believing that all would work out in the end.

His own face must have looked a fright, for instead of him reaching out for her, Sara reached out to him, grasping his forearm as he held the phone.

"You mean my Sara...I mean, the Sara who's here, who gave birth, isn't your wife?" Cade asked through numb lips. "This isn't your baby?"

At his question, Sara's own face drained of color, her grip on his arm tightening. His free hand shot out to support her and the baby, so that they stood locked together.

"Good grief, Cade, is that what you thought?" Loren asked. "No, my wife and I have been in Mexico the past week on a delayed honeymoon before *our* baby is born in five months. We'd planned to be back by the time Sara Jane had driven to Albuquerque, but a ration of bad luck and a monster weather system took care of that."

Heaven forgive him, but Cade could have cared less about his brother's travel plans right then. "So if not you, then who—who *is* Sara married to?"

Again silence fell on the other end of the line, this one reverberating with shock. "Good Lord, Cade," Loren breathed. "Of course, neither of you know."

"Know what?" Cade almost shouted. Sara clung to him, the baby between them, and it took all of his strength to keep them both upright at this moment as he tried, once again, to alter his thinking—to alter his world—in which this woman had begun to figure so greatly. *"Know what?"*

"Her husband…he's…" He cut himself off in another of those damnable sidebars on the other end, but he was back on again within a few seconds. "Look, Cade, the news isn't good, I'll tell you that, but it's not the kind of thing that should be explained over the phone, especially with Sara Jane already in some kind of shock. It's only about five hours to your place from Albuquerque. I'm lookin' at Sarah, and she's as dead on her feet as I am, but neither of us is gonna rest easy until we get there. If you can stand another couple of guests, we'll be on the road as soon as I hang up."

Cade knew he had no choice but to answer yes. It took him three tries to get the phone back in its cradle because he was holding on to Sara and the baby with all his might.

Once he did, he wrapped his other arm around her, lending her all the support he could, gathering as much as he could from her as he tried to sort it out in his head.

Sara had a husband—a husband who was not Loren, the

man she'd just claimed not to love as one. So she'd been right—they'd both been right—in their feeling that something wasn't matching up, although in Sara's case it was her "knowing" that she didn't feel such love for Loren, just as she'd simply "known" he was not in trouble.

But what about Sara's real husband? From the way Loren had made it sound, something *had* happened to him, but how? When? And why couldn't Sara remember anything about him or the love *they'd* shared?

Or had she been trying to do exactly that when this baby was born, and he had thwarted the effort by stepping into the breach in her memory, and instead pulled her back to him?

On that thought, the alarm ringing in Cade's head sounded its warning even more, a thousand ringing bells and noisy sirens reverberating in every corner of his soul, for this time its message was loud and clear.

With dread in his heart, Cade looked down at Sara. Her eyes were filled with that crushing aloneness, as devastating to his self-control as ever. Like always, he was as helpless not to respond to her—even if it meant losing a part of himself.

And acknowledging such a fate was the most devastating to Cade of all.

The half-dozen hours until Loren and his wife arrived seemed like a century to Cade. The irony wasn't lost on him, given how a day ago he'd almost been praying for more time...time alone with Sara.

It helped to keep busy while he waited. He opened the furnace vents in the front bedroom, put clean sheets on one of the single beds there, then put clean sheets on his own. He'd already decided to give his bed to Loren and his wife—it seemed too bizarre yet even to think of her by her name—and to take a bed in the room that had been his and Loren's when they were growing up. As a married couple, they'd want to sleep in the double bed. Had the most right to.

Taking a broom to some of the worst of the dust bunnies floating around the wood floor, Cade couldn't help but remember how he and his brother had slept, dressed, talked and feuded away most of their boyhood in this dinky ten-by-twelve room.

He shook his head. How they'd managed not to kill each other was still a mystery to him. Of course, there was barely enough floor space to turn around, much less do any serious fighting. Not that they'd done a lot, he thought in retrospect, but as close as they'd been in age, in addition to close quarters they'd endured in this room, some amount of sibling rivalry had probably been inevitable.

But that had been Sara's insightful observation, hadn't it?

Sara. He could barely think about her. Couldn't *not* think about her and what she must be dealing with. To his surprise, she'd been calm when he'd repeated his and Loren's conversation to her, holding back only the part about the news not being good about her husband. But Cade had detected that fear in her, and it had taken everything in him not to override her wishes when she'd asked quietly to be left alone. As much as what she'd known before, believing she was Loren's wife, hadn't made sense, it still beat going back to square one, having to reorient herself to a whole new identity. And trying to figure out a whole new set of feelings—for a man she still didn't know, or know what happened to him.

So what *had* happened to her husband? What kept him from being with her now, had kept him from being with her on that fateful New Year's Eve? Guilt gnawed a plate-size hole in his gut as Cade went back and forth between hope and dread. And what would he hope for, if he did?

He couldn't seem to find an answer to that one. No logical scenario he came up with boded well for Sara, and in none of them did he come off looking too good, either.

Because the fact of the matter was, he'd already done enough damage by letting her fall in love with him. And if that meant she must now deal with even more turmoil in her life as she tried to come to terms with what she felt for the man who'd fathered her baby, he couldn't help feeling that the blame for it rested smack-dab on him.

Cade attacked a cobwebby corner of the ceiling with particular vehemence. Oh, he knew he didn't have the ability to change the course of events that were beyond his control. He knew also, though, that the human mind was a powerful thing to be reckoned with. The evidence of that was Sara herself and how she'd blocked from her brain whatever tragedy she literally couldn't comprehend.

Or was that the doing of her heart, not being able to accept the loss of so great a love that life as it stood held little meaning without it?

Now there was a thought that had the ability to make him lose *his* mind with hopelessness.

And so he tried to avoid guessing games, to keep his mind both occupied and blank at the same time. He dared do nothing else, almost in self-defense, for if he'd learned anything in the past seven years, it was that fate had a way of putting a wicked twist on any wish, even passing, he might come up with.

Best just to play a waiting game, he thought, mentally adding, *which has pretty much been par for the course for the past seven years.*

At nine in the evening he made his way downstairs, after stocking the newly spick-and-span bathroom with clean towels, to find fresh coffee on the burner and a short note from Virgil saying he'd headed back to the bunkhouse to get a shower in before Loren and his wife arrived.

Cade filed another regret behind the others. He could have counted on one hand the number of times in his life the old ranch hand had seen the necessity of putting pen to paper. But after Sara had gone off to her room, he'd given Virgil the rundown in the kitchen on his phone conversation. Arms crossed as he leaned back against the edge of the counter, the hand had listened to the whole story before asking what he could do to help get ready for Loren's arrival. Cade had suggested a few of his own outdoors chores that would need doing since he had to get the house ready, and Virgil had headed outside to tend to them without a word of judgment nor condemnation regarding the scene in the ranch yard this afternoon. There wouldn't be, Cade knew. And that was the biggest condemnation of all.

Suddenly restless as a dog with a fresh crop of flea bites, he took a wander around the house, trying to see the place from Loren's perspective of a seven-year absence, and failing. He had grown too used to this house and ranch to be able to see it from an outsider's eyes. Not that Loren was an outsider, only that what had once been more both of theirs together was now more Cade's alone. And yet he'd never felt so dispossessed in his life.

Somehow, he ended up at the door to Sara's room. Much as he should, he couldn't stay away.

She certainly made a peaceful picture, sitting there in Granddad's old rocker, the baby tucked into one arm, his head hidden beneath the nursing blanket. She'd put her hair back and changed into the blue corduroy jumper that she'd arrived in a few short days ago.

She seemed not to register his presence but continued staring sightlessly out the window, apparently deep in thought.

"Well, the house is as clean as it's going to get, given we only had time enough to more or less rearrange the dust," he commented. "They should be here anytime, I'm thinkin'."

"Yes," she said, rocking gently. She seemed far away, in her own world, and shutting out the one in which he stood.

Could he blame her? So much was still a mystery, and a damned frightening one, at that. It worried him, though, this daze she'd been in since Loren's call. Along with her amnesia, it seemed a dangerous combination.

"I bet your cousin'll be glad to see you," he said in what seemed a hugely lame attempt to be helpful.

This time, she said nothing, her grasp on the here and now seeming as fragile as ever.

It scared the death out of him.

To hell with getting invited in, even if she was nursing. Cade stepped into the room, taking a seat on the old cedar chest at the foot of the bed and directly in her line of vision. He wanted, badly, to pull her into his arms, reestablish the bond between them that had seen her through, seen them both through, time and again. But he dare not touch her. He just didn't think it'd do either of them any good right now, and might in fact muddy the situation even more.

But God, he needed to hold her!

At least his action seemed to bring her out of her fog, for she gave a slow blink. "Oh. Cade. Did you want something?"

"No. No." He swallowed and made himself go on. "Just to tell you that…well, I'm sorry for all the things I said. You know, about you not bein' a good wife to Loren. It's pretty clear findin' out you weren't married to him was a big shock. I—I blame myself, for tryin' to play Sherlock Holmes, putting clues together and obviously comin' up with the wrong answer."

"*Cade.*" She seemed to come out of her funk a little

more as she extended her hand. Yet she let it drop before reaching him, evidently thinking better of such a gesture, too. ''I don't blame you.''

''But it must be damned difficult now to adjust to thinkin' about what might have happened to your real husband—''

Cade clamped his jaw shut. Would somebody take him out and just shoot his sorry hide? He didn't come in here to make things worse for her! It seemed, though, that filling that role was his lot for the moment.

Gritting his teeth against that sort of doomsday thinking, he set off on a more positive tack. ''Still, no matter what news Loren and your cousin have, it already isn't as bad as it could be, you know? I mean, they both obviously care about you a lot. From what I could tell, you were on your way to go make your life near them, and that's somethin' to feel hopeful about, don't you think?''

''I—I suppose.'' She dropped her chin, her brow furrowing as she idly caressed one of the baby's tiny feet. ''But these are still people I don't know, Cade. They're strangers to me.''

''Not completely. You said that you saw Loren in your dreams or whatever those were,'' he persisted.

''Yes, but I also knew that what I felt for him wasn't the kind of emotion that would have caused me to lose my memory—or would be enough to help me regain it.''

Dropping her head, she rubbed her forehead, and he realized it was the first time he'd seen her do that since right before the baby was born.

''I'm not trying to be perverse, Cade, honest I'm not,'' she continued slowly. ''But can you see what I've been dealing with?''

Her tone was the same as that first evening, too, a plea for understanding. ''Like now—you tell me I have a cousin named Sarah McGivern, and I believe you, but it's as foreign to me as the concept was of *me* being Sara McGivern. Soon they're going to walk through that door and tell me I'm supposed to be someone else—that I'm supposed to feel all those feelings I didn't feel for Loren for another man who's going to be a complete stranger to me, too.''

Disconsolately, she let her hand drop to her lap. ''It just seems like such a—a failure on my part,'' she said softly, ''not being able to deal with the events in my life, so much that I'd block out what's happened and the people who meant something to me. But I'm so afraid, Cade—afraid of discovering what it was I couldn't live with. The fear, when I get even a little close, is indescribable. I'm scared, too, to stay this way, not knowing. Maybe never knowing. And that I'll go on indefinitely in this unreal existence, in between living my life and someone else's. In between loving you, and loving someone else.''

Her voice dropped to a whisper. ''Because that's the one thing that hasn't changed, Cade. Just because we know now Loren's not my husband, I still can't make myself stop loving you.''

He let go of her hand and sat back, his upper lip firmly gripped between his teeth to keep from giving in to that rush of emotion again. It seemed a useless action, because she was right. Whatever the reason, however it had come about, in that darkest of nights and fiercest of storms, they had forged a bond between them that was now unbreakable. He had given his word; she had given her trust. There was no going back to the way it was before, no matter what.

But what, really, would happen when Loren and her cousin showed up? Would the sight of them and the truth they brought with them trigger Sara's memory? And once she remembered, how *would* that change her feelings for him?

The mere thought set his own fears raging out of control. But they couldn't stay this way forever, either, with neither of them knowing.

Because it occurred to Cade then that perhaps it was only in facing yourself and your own true nature that you could begin to understand the forces, both within and without, that were at play in your life. No, neither of them—nor anyone, for that matter—had a choice in what happened to them, but everyone had control over how they dealt with those events.

But how to make Sara understand that? How to convince her to keep pushing ahead through the fear, especially now when she stood back at the beginning of not knowing who she was or where she belonged?

And if he didn't try to do the same himself, then was he shirking his responsibility—to her, and to himself?

"Look, Sara," Cade said, rather desperately, "you know how you argued with me that we can't control the good things that happen to us any more than we can control the bad things?"

She perked up a little at his question. "Y-yes."

"Well, I'm willin' to concede that point to you. You're right. But I'm thinking sometimes it's hard to tell when you're in the situation whether somethin's gonna turn out good or bad. Except a lot of how it *does* turn out is in choosin' how you deal with it."

She gave him a blank look, and he had to wonder if it was because she didn't understand or a result of that trance she seemed caught in. "What do you mean?"

"It's like when this baby of yours was tryin' to be born. At the time, it didn't seem to you like it was a good thing, especially if he was early. And especially if you were gonna have to deliver him alone." Needing to, badly, he took the baby's other velvety soft foot between his thumb and forefinger, stroking it gently. "But we were both de-

termined the situation was gonna work out for the good.
And damn if he was sure enough ready to be born. And
you didn't have to do it alone.''

She said nothing for a long time before, thankfully, he
saw in her eyes the understanding he'd wanted so much
for her to have.

"So what do we do now, in this moment?" she asked,
her voice hushed—and hopeful.

It was damned hard not to give in to that hope. It would
be stringing them both along, though, and keep them from
facing up to the real truth—that more often than not the
events in our lives *didn't* work out for the better.

And not everyone lived happily ever after.

"Well," Cade said, his voice as hushed, "how about
we do like we did the night Baby Cade here was born?"
He gave the infant's foot a gentle shake. "Y'know—try
for now to let go of what's past, let what's to be, be. And
put all our efforts in the here and now."

Yet uttered now, after all that had transpired between
them for which they both *did* have a past, the platitude
seemed highly inadequate.

Well, it was the best he could do right now, the most
he could offer her. The most he dare offer her.

It seemed he'd have no chance to do anything different,
anyway, as the windows rattled in their frames with the
back door being thrown open, thrusting Cade and Sara
both headlong into the moment.

"Cade?" He heard his brother's voice. "Sara Jane?
We're here!"

Cade started to rise but was arrested by the sight of
Sara's face. At the sound of his brother's voice, she'd gone
paler than ever. Her head actually reared back, as if she'd
heard the most shocking of news, and Cade realized only
then how truly frightened she was. Almost as much as
when she'd learned he didn't know who she was that first

night, and he'd seen that soul-shattering forsakenness in her eyes.

And it was there now, fighting its way past the trancelike numbness.

For once he didn't leap immediately to her aid. Because the idea flashed through his brain that she just might *need* to go to that terrible place in her mind, if not now, then sometime, if she were ever to confront her fate and what it meant to her future. And that every time he jumped to her aid, he locked her more securely to this time and place. More securely to him.

Talk about *really* taking control of a situation.

Yet now...now, in this moment, with her whole world set to shatter all over again, he simply couldn't let her feel as alone as that, no matter what.

Sitting back down again, Cade clasped Sara's hand between both of his, trying to prevent her from going to that place her mind seemed determined to take her away to, whether it be the recesses of her memory or into another cavern of oblivion where she might forget even more of her life instead of remembering it.

He didn't want her to go to either of those places, at least not until they'd heard what Loren and his wife had to say. Because however slim, there still might be a chance, maybe not for him, but for her...

"Sara. *Sara.*" She looked at him, distracted and dazed at once. He grasped her hand even more tightly in both of his, feeling almost as if he *were* pulling her back from the brink of some terrible danger. "Sara, listen to me. I know you still don't know what's happened to you. But you're not alone, and I'm not just talkin' about because your cousin's here. I made you a promise the night Baby Cade was born. I mean to keep it for as long as you need me to."

He wondered if she'd even heard him, she sat so still,

as if in the eye of a hurricane, and sure destruction all around her. Finally, she shook her head, her gaze dropping to their twined hands, then lifting to focus on him. Tears pooled in her eyes.

"Oh, *Cade*," she said achingly. There was a world of emotion in those words, and he felt every bit of it resonate within him.

"Cade?" Loren called impatiently. "Where the hell is everybody?"

They jerked apart.

"Go," Sara urged. "You haven't seen your brother in seven years."

"You'll be all right?"

"Y-yes." She nodded, wiping her cheeks with a shaking hand. "I'll just see to the baby and then I'll be out."

With a final squeeze of her hand, he left her, closing the door behind him, feeling drained and shaky himself.

Then he turned to see Loren.

From either end of the hallway, he and his brother just stood and took in the first sight they'd had of each other in seven years. Cade had long envisioned this moment, through many a weary day on the range, many a sleepless night in bed. And in none of his imaginings had he known the strength of sentiment that now poured through him, surprising him with its intensity and genuineness.

And it came to him in a flash of knowledge that, at least between brothers, no amends would ever need to be made. Oh, sure, there would be explanations and apologies, maybe even a few accusing words exchanged. But where once Cade may have felt he'd have trouble if not being forgiven than in forgiving, he didn't any more. Any lasting blame on either side, he knew now, was as water under the bridge.

And that, if nothing else, was something this whole occurrence had produced for which he'd be forever thankful.

Loren grinned, then took a step toward him. Cade found his feet would move, too, and in half a dozen strides they caught each other in a bear hug that involved much slapping of hands on backs and laughing out loud and maybe even a tear or two.

"You haven't changed a bit," Loren said, taking him by the shoulders and giving him a once-over. "Still look to be in that hardworkin' cowboy form I'd thought would've gone to seed at least a little by now."

Cade felt himself grinning like a fool. "Pretty amazin', isn't it, considerin' mine and Virg's steady diet of steak washed down with beer."

He looked his brother over, too, stunned into blurting out, "But you, Loren...you've definitely changed. A lot."

"Blunt as ever, aren't you, Cade? I hope I've at least changed for the better!"

Truth be told, he had. The once lean, lanky kid of twenty-four had filled out some, and from the looks of his hair and clothes, he'd grown even more citified. And more...sure of himself. Sure of who he was and what his purpose was in life.

And Cade could see at least part of the reason why as Loren let go of his arm and turned, beckoning behind him. "I've been wanting you to meet someone for a long time."

A tall woman came shyly forward, her gloves and woolen hat held before her in her hands. She had short, red-gold hair and soft green eyes and a smile that stretched a mile wide.

Loren put his arm around her shoulders as pride fairly shone from him. "This is Sarah, my wife."

"Cade." Her voice was low and sweet. "I've heard so much about you."

"That so?" He slanted Loren a baleful glance.

"All good," his brother assured him on a laugh.

Feeling awkward as a duck out of water, Cade held out

a hand, but Sarah would have none of it. She put her arms around him in a warm hug, kissing him on the cheek.

"Loren told me what you did for Sara and her baby," she whispered against his ear. "I'll never forget that for as long as I live. Never."

Strange, he thought, that she should say almost the exact words Sara had.

"It was nothin'," Cade mumbled, sure he was turning turkey red.

She pulled away, her green eyes filled with worry. "And I understand she's got another challenge ahead of her."

He nodded. "It's not gonna be easy on her."

She pressed her lips together, and he could tell she was trying not to cry. "At least she has that precious baby to help remind her of—"

"Hello."

Looking beyond his shoulder, Loren's wife gave a small gasp, her hand going to her mouth.

Cade pivoted. Sara had come out into the hallway and stood with her hand on the doorknob of hers and the baby's bedroom as if she were of a mind to flee back inside, shut herself away physically as well as mentally. Protectiveness surged in him, and he felt for a moment he'd have done anything to spare her this trial.

He didn't dare move, though—or pray—either way.

Then his lungs filled with relief as she dropped her hand and, squaring her shoulders, slowly approached the three people, two of them perfect strangers, who watched her from the other end of the hall.

Sarah Ann wasn't about to let her make such a difficult journey alone. She rushed to meet her cousin, arms open, but something in Sara's face must have stopped her from embracing her, for she came up sharp in front of the shorter woman.

"That's right, you don't know me." She pressed her palm to her chest. "I'm—I'm your cousin, Sarah Ann."

His Sara extended her hand. "I'm happy to meet you—and sorry not to know you."

Sarah Ann gave a soft laugh that turned into a stifled sob. "Oh, you poor darling! What you've been through."

Sara held her head high, and pride threatened to overflow in Cade's chest. Maybe he'd been wrong, and she had a lot more emotional fortitude than he gave her credit for.

As for himself, though, his stomach had turned to fire.

"I don't feel poor but very fortunate, actually," Sara said. "I have a wonderful baby." Her gaze touched on Loren, who stood beside Cade. "And now I have a cousin, and a cousin-in-law, I didn't know about."

She faced Sarah Ann stalwartly. "But I need to know now, Sarah. Who is my husband?"

Sarah Ann glanced back quickly at Loren, who gave her a nod of encouragement. "Your husband…was Greg Childress, dear."

Hearing the name at last gave Cade a feeling of that unreality Sara must have been experiencing. *Greg Childress.* Sara's husband. Her baby's father.

Yet he could see the name still meant nothing to Sara. "Was?" she asked calmly.

"Dear, dear Sara," her cousin murmured, her voice breaking. "Greg died in a car accident, six months ago. You'd only just learned you were going to be parents."

So, here at last was confirmation of the terrible, horrible event that Sara hadn't been able to live with. They'd both dreaded such, but at her cousin's words, Cade knew he never could have imagined the kind of desolateness that eclipsed his soul at that moment.

For Sara stood as still as death itself, her eyes growing larger and rounder than he'd ever seen them, as if she'd happened upon a scene of shattering devastation. But then, such an incident truly had occurred: the utter destruction of her heart with the loss of her husband.

And Cade understood then, with completeness, that no, there was no chance, not for either of them.

Still, it took everything in him, every last particle, not to go to her, wrap her in his arms and shield her eyes—shield both their eyes—from having to confront the destruction—and the crushing aloneness.

Her cousin had no such hesitation, for welcome or not, she put her arms around the slighter woman, hugging her as if she'd never let her go.

"We wondered if you'd die, too, from grief," she said. "I think it was only the expectation of that baby of yours that kept you hanging on."

Chapter Eight

Sara felt made of wood. Her body, enclosed in her cousin's embrace, seemed like a column, her legs two posts of support. Even if she'd tried with all her might, she couldn't have found it in her to return Sarah's hug, because she didn't think her arms would bend. Nothing would on her body. She was stiff—and lifeless. Especially her face, which seemed carved in an expressionless mask. An impermeable one, too, with nothing further being allowed to filter into her brain while she continued to fight with all her might to stay in this moment, moving neither backward nor forward. For some reason, doing so had become vital to her. Almost a matter of life and death.

At the thought, the panic and fear she'd been fighting struck again in a killer blow, nearly causing her to lose all the breath in her body, all perspective in her mind....

The next thing Sara knew, she was sitting in an armchair in the living room, a glass of water in her hands. She stared fuzzily at it, wondering where it had come from. Had she fainted?

But no—no one was acting overly concerned. Across from her on the sofa were her cousin and her husband. Loren, who *had* turned out to be the man in her dreams, was talking rather animatedly to her. Sarah Ann was cooing over a baby in her arms, and Sara realized with a start that it was hers.

Maybe she'd actually blanked out, as Dr. Barclay had said his friend had done, losing a year out of her life she never recovered memory of. The possibility that she might have done the same, even for a few moments, gave rise to another wave of panic in Sara. It was much too close to the scene on the side of the road in which she'd come to the slow realization that she didn't know who she was or where she'd come from.

What if this time she lost her memory of her baby? Or Cade?

She couldn't! But she seemed to be growing less and less resistant to stopping the inevitable. Less able to know which choice to grab hold of—and which to turn away from.

Yet she wasn't alone this time. She did have her baby. And Cade. Or did she?

Frantically, Sara glanced around for the man who was her strongest link to whatever past she had right now.

Her heart settled not at all as she found him standing at the coved entrance to the living room, one shoulder against the wall, his gaze trained watchfully on her.

For that distance had returned to shadow his eyes. There were plenty of places left to sit, even with Virgil occupying the other armchair on the far side of the fireplace, but he seemed to be taking pains to keep in the background.

Yes, Cade was and would be there for her, as he said, but she realized that it could only go so far.

Because she had an identity now: Sara Jane Childress. Had a husband, Greg, whom she had apparently loved to such distraction his death had shattered both her heart and her mind.

But such a thing still seemed completely unreal, she wanted to tell him. The name meant nothing to her. At least when she'd heard Loren's, she had felt a glimmer of recognition, however faint. With Greg, though…nothing. Nothing at all.

And what kind of woman did that make her?

Feeling as if she were still fighting her way through a fog of confusion, Sara tried to focus on what Loren was saying.

"Y'see, the plan was for me to drive to Oklahoma City and help you arrange for the movers, then drive back to Albuquerque on the twenty-seventh in time to catch the plane to Mexico with Sarah Ann here," he said, giving his wife's shoulders a squeeze. "Then, once you'd tied up the rest of your affairs and seen the movers off, you were going to leave from Oklahoma on New Year's Eve Day, timing *your* arrival to coincide with ours back in Albuquerque."

His handsome face, so much like Cade's and yet completely different, clouded over with remorse. "It's only about a ten-hour drive, easily doable in a day, and interstate the whole way. Your doctor in O.K.C. had given you the go-ahead, told us that even with some of the risks, getting you moved closer to us ASAP was gonna be the best thing for you, seeing how your emotional state was so changeable…."

He held a hand out to her in appeal. "I—I swear I thought you'd be fine, Sara."

"Of course you did," she murmured, ducking her head to take a sip of water, needing it running through her and reminding her to stay in the moment. "I don't blame you or anyone else for what happened."

"So why was she drivin' your car?" Cade asked, his own expression unfathomable.

"Hers didn't seem to me in the best shape for highway drivin'. It was a little compact, older model, perfectly fine for getting around in the city." He looked across at Sara. "You told me it was yours and Greg's second vehicle. I guess your good car was the one he'd been driving when…uh, I mean… Oh, shoot, I'm sorry, Sara."

At his gaff, he reddened, and his wife put a hand on his knee, squeezing it in a silent sign of loyalty and understanding that made Sara feel suddenly more cold and alone than ever.

"In any case," Sarah Ann smoothly continued for her husband, "Loren just didn't think your car fit for you to take on a road trip. There was no time to sell it and buy another, so he decided to drive it back to New Mexico himself, and leave ours for you to drive."

"I was also thinkin' about the weather," Loren added helpfully. "I mean, the real snow doesn't usually come through the Panhandle until January or February, but obviously we can get some pretty ugly weather in these parts before that. God, when I think of you out on the highway and that storm rolling in…"

He ran his hand through his hair distractedly in a gesture reminiscent of Cade. "Jeez, Sara, I'm sorry. I thought I'd given you some cautions and what to watch the forecast for before you took off—"

"But for some reason I took off anyway," she finished for him, the affection she'd felt for him in her dream coming back to her, and she drew on its comfort. "Really, Loren, I don't blame you for that, either. I—I must have had my reasons."

Although it was anyone's guess as to what those reasons

were. She could see Loren and Sarah Ann looking at her expectantly, as if she could pull the answers out of a hat like a rabbit.

"So that's why Sara had your car," Cade spoke up. "And probably why I kept smelling your sandalwood cologne around her. It was about all we had to go on, figuring things out."

Loren nodded thoughtfully. "Yeah, I guess I can see how you might've thought Sara Jane was Sarah Ann."

Cade scratched one cheek with a decidedly studied air. "But why wouldn't she have any other belongings other than the overnight bag Virgil found in the trunk?" he asked. The information he was prompting Loren for occurred to her when he continued, "I mean, you'd think Sara would have been carrying a purse or billfold of some kind."

"Oh, dang, where's my head?" Loren said with a snap of his fingers, turning back to Sara again. "I guess I am runnin' on fumes. Right after I got off the phone with Cade, the owner of some little café off of I-70 called. Seems a waste removal truck was pickin' up a Dumpster outside and they found a purse behind it with your stuff in it."

He made a face. "I'm sorry to say the guy told me whatever cash you might've had was gone, I'm betting the credit cards, too. He called the number on your I.D. and got the message forwarding your calls to my number. I told him we'd try to pick it up in the next few days."

"So my purse *was* stolen," Sara said slowly, not sure what to think about discovering she'd been right in that detail, at least.

"You already remembered that happening, Sara?" her cousin asked with the same anticipation.

"No. I remembered only my purse being gone, and that it had been stolen, but not how or when."

"But I didn't tell you the rest of it," Loren said excitedly, drawing her attention back to him. "The owner said he remembered a pregnant woman comin' into the café 'round one or so New Year's Eve Day to get some change to use the phone, but she didn't stay to eat. He said she seemed in a real hurry, pretty agitated. Could it've been because you'd been mugged or held up? I mean, I know Doc said he didn't find any evidence of head trauma, but maybe you *did* suffer some kind of physical blow that caused your amnesia."

Yet again, they both looked at her expectantly, but Sara could only shake her head. "I-It could have happened something like that, but nothing makes me feel as if it did."

"What about after that?" Loren asked. "Do you remember who you called or why?"

She shrugged helplessly, her fingers clenching around the water glass. "I wish I knew, but I don't. As Cade said, we've had little to go on but a few sketchy clues here and there."

Sara shot a confirming glance at him. But he no longer was looking at her. In fact, he seemed to be avoiding her even more completely all of a sudden.

Why? What had changed?

"Wait. I've got an idea." Loren sat forward intensely. "You and Cade've both said you had next to nothing to go on to figure out who you were or why you'd lost your memory. So maybe what's holding you up from remembering more is having something familiar, like the contents of your purse, to jog your memory. I mean, if your I.D. was still in it, your billfold probably is, too, which means any photos you had would be there. Do you know if you had any in your purse?"

"I don't know."

"Photos of you and Greg, I mean?"

"I don't know!" Sara clenched the glass tighter, until she thought she'd break it or her fingers. "I'm sorry. I don't know why I've got this hit-and-miss way of knowing some things that happened and not others. Believe me, it's almost driven Cade crazy trying to figure out how it happened if not why—"

Sara broke off, thoughts reeling. Yes, she was doing the same thing with Loren and Sarah as she'd done with Cade, being very careful to stay away from exploring too deeply why she'd gotten amnesia in the first place.

That wasn't her fault, though! The few times she had, she'd felt like she'd die of fear! She'd have done anything, anything not to go there.

Almost on reflex, she again sought Cade out with her gaze. He stood very still, head down and fingers tucked pensively into the front pockets of his jeans.

Sara rubbed the ache that had come to her head, feeling suddenly as if she'd keel over from weariness in the next second. "I'm sorry, but would you mind if I took the baby and went to bed? I—I'm very tired, all of the sudden."

"No, not at all!" Sarah Ann said quickly, gathering the infant to her as she came to her feet, her husband following suit. "We're sorry for keeping you up so late."

She burbled nonsense to Baby Cade right up to the moment she turned him over to Sara, who took him with a kind of desperate relief, holding on to him for dear life.

"Th-there's just so much to think about, so much to absorb, you see," she stammered in weak explanation. "All I want right now is to put it away for a while, put it out of my mind—"

She broke off, heartsick.

She saw a silent message pass between her cousin and Loren. "Now that we're here," Sarah Ann said, "we'll have plenty of opportunities to piece together the chain of events."

"Yes, don't worry, Sara," Loren agreed fervently. "No matter what happened, you're safe and sound now, right?" He slowly wagged his head back and forth in amazement, his eyes, as expectant as ever, on his brother. "What a stroke of luck that even with your amnesia you were able to find Cade."

For once, Sara herself couldn't look at him, would do anything not to, as the most awful fear yet sprouted in her. But just as Loren spoke, the tall, mahogany grandfather clock in the corner sounded another kind of stroke. No one said a word as it struck twelve chimes in all, the last echoing in the room—and in her head, it seemed, for she couldn't help remembering the moment she had first heard its peal.

"A stroke of luck, too, that Cade was here for you," Sarah Ann murmured, almost in echo of her thoughts.

"And I'll never forget that," Sara felt compelled to vow as, tugged inexorably by that magnetic force, she lifted her gaze to meet Cade's. She knew immediately his thoughts had gone to that same moment when they'd raced against time to see her child safely into the world. How far into the past it seemed now! And getting farther away every second that went by. The connection was waning even now, much as the clock's last chime—and would continue to, to nothing, if she let it.

That, she understood, was the real choice she had to make.

But she simply couldn't go back to before! Sara begged Cade with her gaze. She couldn't! Something else would die inside her.

Yet there was no moving forward with any part of her life, until she had. She couldn't cheat herself out of the past, for she'd be cheating those she loved out of a real future. She'd known it last night. Until she remembered the past they hadn't shared—the past she'd forgotten—it would forever keep them from forging ahead. Even with this news about her husband, that fact hadn't changed.

"It was...nothing," Cade quietly said.

And Sara knew then that the clock had started ticking on a different kind of race, though no less one of life—and death.

Bong...bong...bong...bong...bong...

Wearily, Sara leaned her head back in the rocking chair. She was beginning to hate that stupid clock. It pointedly marked off the passing hours of her life, telling her now that, though she'd finished nursing Baby Cade at three, she was still up and wide-awake a uselessly spent two hours later.

Holding her breath, Sara tried for the tenth time that hour to mentally delve through the miasma of fog and try and see through it and into the deepest recesses of her mind.

You're Sara Jane Childress, she called into that dusky, murky hollow. *Your husband is Greg Childress. Remember?*

No! The denial rose in the back of her throat.

No, he was...

Her breath came out in a wheeze. She couldn't do it. She couldn't go there, not this way, alone and desperate.

And she was now so very, very alone.

"Sara Jane."

Sara's gasp came out as a sob of sheer terror. Her eyes flew open, her fear escalating three-fold as she wondered what they'd encounter.

A shadow moved, and she saw it was her cousin who stood in the doorway, a white nightgown flowing around her.

Life-giving air rushed back into her lungs. "Sarah! It's you. I didn't know..."

Sarah Ann came swiftly into the room to kneel beside the rocking chair, her hand on Sara's arm. "Sara, forgive me for startling you! When I saw you sitting in this chair, I thought you were awake. I had no idea you didn't hear me come downstairs."

"I—I was awake." She slid a shaking hand across her forehead, slick with cold perspiration. Her head had begun to throb again. "I couldn't sleep."

"Neither could I," her cousin confessed softly.

Baby Cade started to fuss, and on reflex, Sara started to rise to go to him.

Sarah Ann pressed her back. "Here, let me." She bent over the cradle and lifted the infant against her shoulder, hushing and shushing him in tender tones.

"He might need to nurse again," Sara said when Baby Cade continued to whimper. She felt for the switch to the lamp on the table beside her, and turned it on, its soft glow warming the room and chasing away the rest of her fear. Or at least keeping it at bay—for now. "He didn't seem as interested in it as usual the last feeding. Let me try again."

Her cousin made a sound of regret at having to hand the baby over. Sara tucked him into the crook of her arm, her other hand automatically reaching for the buttons on her nightie. She stopped short in midgesture, though, in a sudden bout of shyness.

"Would you like me to leave?" Sarah Ann asked gently.

"N-no." Sara felt herself color. "I don't use a nursing blanket if Cade or Virgil aren't around, is all."

"Whatever you feel comfortable with. I know I'm still practically a stranger to you."

"Stay—please," Sara found herself saying impulsively. "I'd like you to."

"I'd like to." She perched on the edge of the narrow bed, hands on either side of her and elbows locked.

Sara found her shyness had left her once she started Baby Cade nursing. She simply hadn't the same reaction to her cousin as she had to Cade being in the room. In fact, it seemed the most natural thing in the world for Sarah Ann to share this experience with her.

It was nice, she decided. Nice to have another woman around. Another woman to confide in, as much as she felt able to.

"I named him after Cade," she confessed into the quiet of the room.

"I wondered what you'd decided to call him—if anything yet." Sarah Ann traced the worn pattern in the rug with her toe. "You didn't mention it, and I didn't want to pry by asking."

"Yes, well, at the time, it seemed the right thing to do." She ventured a look at her cousin. "It still does."

"Of course it does." Her eyes glowed as they lingered on the babe in Sara's arms. "I'm just so grateful you're both safe. We do have Cade to thank for that, don't we?"

"Y-yes."

"He seems just as Loren described him—loyal, reliable. A little reserved, but is that just until you get to know him?"

She ducked her head. *Oh, yes.* "He's been wonderful—with the baby, I mean."

"Well, and who could resist such a darling? He's utterly sweet, you know," Sarah Ann said.

"That he is, isn't he? Sweet Baby Cade." She couldn't resist stroking the back of one finger down his satiny cheek as she rocked, the song Cade had so tenderly sung to him rising spontaneously to her lips.

She'd hummed only a few bars when her cousin asked abruptly, "How do you know that song?"

Sara glanced up to find the other woman studying her intently. "It's a favorite of Cade's. He introduced Baby Cade to it just last night."

Her features relaxed. "Oh, of course. That makes sense."

"Why?"

"It's one of Loren's favorites, too." Sarah Ann gave a little laugh, shaking her head. "It's just that, when you and Greg told us you were pregnant, we sent you the CD as a gift. I thought for a second you might have remembered that. My wishful thinking, wasn't it?"

Sara didn't answer. "I understand you're to be congratulated, too," she said in a deft change of subject.

"Yes. My due date is May 29." In her loose gown, Sarah Ann barely looked pregnant, but when she pressed her palm to her abdomen, Sara could see the rounded mound of her tummy. "So far everything's proceeding normally, but it's been such a comfort to me knowing Loren's a paramedic. He'd know what to do if there were any trouble."

Her other hand joined the first, cradling her precious burden in a gesture so familiar to Sara. "But even then, who's to know what'll happen when my time comes? I can't imagine anything more gut-wrenchingly frightening than needing someone to be there for you and some act of God keeping them away."

She turned her head as if to peruse the paltry selection of books in the bookcase, but Sara could tell she was trying to hide her tears. She knew why she was crying, too.

"Sarah." The other woman turned back to her with a furtive brush of her fingers across her cheek. "You mustn't think that anything's going to happen to either you or Loren, or to your baby. Please. I'd hate for you worry another minute about it on account of whatever fate has befallen me."

Sarah Ann smiled tremulously. "Even if you don't remember it, you're still the strong, courageous, compassionate Sara Jane I've always known," she said with fierce conviction. "That hasn't changed a bit."

Tears started in her own eyes. "You don't know the good it does me to hear you say that," Sara murmured, extending one hand, palm down, which her cousin reached out to clasp warmly. "To know that I might have been that kind of person. To have a history, and family."

Yes, she *had* had a good life. And she had been the kind of woman who met the bad life doled out with courage. Suddenly, Sara was anxious to know these things again deep in her heart.

"So do we have other family?" she asked.

"I'm sad to say, no, not to speak of."

"Oh." She was disappointed.

"You and I are actually third cousins, the closest family each of us has. Our great-grandmother was a Sarah, too," Sarah Ann explained. "And from what I know of Greg, he was in the same boat as you."

"We were?" Sara asked, startled at her cousin's use of the familiar phrase, one she'd used so recently about her and Cade.

Sarah Ann, however, interpreted her stunned tone for a different reason. "I'm sorry, Sara. I didn't mean to bring up—"

The other woman ducked her chin, lips compressed, then went on in a muted voice. "It's just that…you told me once that you believed destiny must have brought you and Greg together, because you both knew what it was like to be alone in the world."

She took a deep breath, trying to find within herself that brave woman Sarah Ann had spoken of. "Tell me about him, Sarah."

Her cousin nodded. "I'm sorry to say I didn't get much

of a chance to know him very well, what with you living in Oklahoma and me in Albuquerque,'' she said, curling one leg under her. ''In fact, you and I have only had the opportunity to see each other a few times a year, at the most, in the past ten since graduating from high school. And even less lately. I've been working as a licensed practical nurse at one of Albuquerque's hospitals and going to school for my R.N. in the evenings, and you and Greg were pretty involved in getting your graphic design business up and running.''

''We had a—a graphic design business?'' She didn't want to embarrass herself by admitting she hadn't a clue what graphic design was. Although…as if by spontaneous suggestion, she did have a sense of the kind of person it might take to do such work: part writer, to take an idea and give it a voice, part marketer to make the message count, part artist to make it catch the public's eye…

''Yes, and a pretty successful one, too,'' Sarah Ann continued. ''Oh, it was just the two of you still, and you worked from a home office, but from what I understand, you were able to make a pretty good living at it.''

She tilted her head to one side. ''As I recall, that's how you met. You and Greg were both working for a communications firm in Oklahoma City. Once you got married, though, you decided to pursue your dream of building your own business. You were quite good, too, both of you. You sent me some samples of brochures and even some catalogs you'd done on the computer. I'm no expert, of course, but I thought they were very well done,'' she finished warmly.

Sara barely heard her. ''So *that's* what I did for a living,'' she murmured, gladness causing her throat to tighten with the threat of more tears. Yes, it was a relief to discover she had talents and enthusiasms and goals in life. Yet they'd also been goals she'd shared with her husband.

Dreams they had dreamed together. Precious hopes they had whispered to each other in the deepest, most secret part of the night.

"Why do you think I must have forgotten Greg, Sarah?" she asked with sudden urgency.

Her cousin sighed. "I don't know, dear. But you *were* pretty devastated by his death. When he died in that auto accident...you were frantic with grief, Sara. I wondered if it'd kill you, too."

Sara shook her head, making it start to hurt again. "You said that before, but that was months ago! Why would I lose my memory when I did? What happened?"

Sarah Ann leaned forward, taking her hand again, and Sara was glad for the contact while still on the verge of rejecting it. "I don't mention it to upset you, dear, just to provide background that might help you understand, even if you don't remember yet, what your state of mind might have been."

Her eyes shone with tears of empathy. "You were...inconsolable when I talked to you on the phone right after the accident. It happened less than a mile from your home. And you kept saying something about how you'd had an argument—a silly argument, you said, and how Greg had left the house that evening before you had a chance to make up with each other."

Sara withdrew her hand. "I said that? A...*silly* argument?"

"Yes. Why, are you remembering something?"

She was, but not from her forgotten past. *Really, Cade, this is such a silly argument.*

Really. It's not silly to me.

Sara rose abruptly, the baby still nursing as she paced aimlessly to the door. What was going on with her? Things were getting jumbled in her mind, the past mixing with the present, the bad with the good, as it had before in those flip-side emotions she'd experienced.

Maybe that's what she needed to do—concentrate on the good memories, ground herself in them first before moving to the bad.

Her cousin spoke. "I didn't want to bring this out when we first got here, but…'' She got up and left the room, only to return a second later with her handbag. Sitting back down on the bed, she searched through it, coming up with a billfold. She opened it and handed it to Sara. "It was taken on your wedding day.''

Sara studied the photo as she sank down on the bed next to her cousin, Baby Cade still at her breast.

Two people stood in front of a church altar, a woman in a white veil and dress, next to a tall man in a black tuxedo.

She brought the photo closer. The man had medium-brown hair and a mustache, and deep-set eyes she couldn't tell the color of. But she could make out the expression in them, easily: wildly joyous, deliriously happy. And lucky beyond belief.

Still, she got no sense of this man—who he'd been or what she'd felt for him. But the biggest shock to Sara was seeing the same happiness shining in the eyes of the woman next to him.

The woman was her.

Rather than grounding her, the sight of the photo made the whole situation seem even more unreal to her. It simply didn't seem possible that she could have felt such powerful feelings for this man. Contentedness, yes. Partnership, sure. But how could she have felt the sort of deep, committed love that fairly radiated from the couple in the picture?

Yet she must have! So why couldn't she remember him?

With anxious eyes, she scrutinized her son. His eyes

were squeezed shut in fierce concentration, tiny mouth working like a suction pump, as she tried to find something of the man in the photo in her child and failed. In fact, the baby seemed suddenly unreal to her, too—that he had been hoped for and conceived and anticipated with this man, her husband, whom she had no recollection of.

But this was her son! He was as much a part of her as Greg Childress. And she had wanted this baby, so much she'd have done anything to see him safely born.

Then again, there had been that dream just after his birth, and those aching feelings of confusion of wanting him, while still not wanting him to be born....

Her head felt as if it would pound off her shoulders at any moment.

"Loren didn't mention this, Sara," her cousin spoke up, "but your movers had also left a message on our machine that your belongings were set to be delivered to our house at the end of the week. I'm thinking you'll find a lot of clues there...a lot of reminders of your life with Greg."

She turned her head. Sarah Ann barely appeared at the end of that tunneled vision of hers, and that's how she knew that she was withdrawing into that frightening limbo again. She seemed helpless to stop herself. It was simply too painful, too confusing, otherwise. Especially without the life force of Cade McGivern to pull her back, without the promise he'd made to her in that most desperate of moments...the moment of truth...

Yes. Sara closed her eyes as calm surrounded her through the pain. Yes, there it was, its strains coming from far away at first, then becoming louder as the words resonated in her body: *Wherever both of you came from, you and your baby, you're here now—in my house, in my bed, right where you need to be. For now, you belong here, with me. And I won't let you down.*

No, she may not have Cade to pull her back, but she

did have the gift he'd given her when Baby Cade was born, that of trusting in a force—call it heavenly or fateful or whatever—in which she'd somehow lost faith in that slumbering memory of hers.

Its promise rose up in her, surrounded her. How could she have forgotten it, even for a second?

Baby Cade grunted, breaking his mouth's suction on her nipple. He gave a squeak of dismay, the forerunner to an all-out wail, that drew Sara's attention.

Of course, here was the other force in her life with whom she shared a powerful connection. The one for whom she'd have done anything not to lose. And she hadn't lost him. Somehow, she'd pulled him through, pulled them both through, to safety. She had not failed. She must remember that, too.

"Dr. Barclay did mention that one of the w-ways I might recover my memory was to surround myself with familiar things and people," Sara made herself say as she concentrated on guiding the infant back to nurse. "Maybe when I take a look at some of my graphic design work, that'll come back to me, too."

She swallowed painfully, fear rising in her at the very prospect of tackling even that much, yet she continued determinedly, "I may have forgotten my past, but that doesn't change the fact that I need to see to my future— mine and the baby's."

"Oh, but you mustn't worry about what's to become of you," Sarah Ann said fervently, putting an arm around Sara's shoulders. "You were moving to Albuquerque to be with us always, and that hasn't changed."

With her free hand, she tried to curl Baby Cade's thatch of black hair over her finger, failing miserably. "You know, we talked, you and I, of it being a sign of fate that I became pregnant when you were. A sign that we were meant to be closer to each other and share this experience.'' She paused. ''Loren and I had a long heart-to-heart about that very subject on the way here from Albuquerque. We both feel the same about things—about family. And you're about the only family I have left in this world, Sara. Loren has Cade, and that's about it for him, too. We don't want to be apart from those we love most in this life.''

Wiping away a tear, she hugged Sara's shoulders even tighter. ''If your losing Greg showed me anything, it's that life is too short, too precious, to waste a moment not being with those you love,'' she said with conviction. ''You belong with us now, Sara dear.''

Sara could only stare at her cousin for a long moment before she blinked.

''Th-thank you, Sarah,'' she said. She noticed that her headache had abated somewhat, leaving her drained. ''I—I actually think I could sleep now, if you wouldn't mind…?''

Sarah Ann released her. ''Heavens, no! I need to get a little sleep in myself, which I think I'll be able to, too, now that we've had this talk.''

After her cousin left, however, Sara didn't go to sleep. Instead she lay huddled on her bed, her body cocooned around her child as over his head she stared at the photo of the man who had been her husband, and the woman who'd been herself, until dawn crept silently into the room, bathing it in a rose-colored light, that first promise of the new day.

It was the same kind of light that radiated from both faces in the photo, promising more than a new day. It spoke of a bred-in-the-bone belief in the future—*their* future—and in signs that augured happiness for themselves and those they loved, so much so that there was no room for contemplation of anything different.

Yes, now she knew: *that* was the kind of woman she was.

Chapter Nine

"Damn," Cade murmured into the chill air of the unheated mud porch. He straightened slowly from pulling on his boots, mentally shoring himself up.

Two female voices mingled just beyond the back door, their timbre and pitch sounding like musical bells. Especially Sara's.

She glanced up at him as she came through the door, her cousin close behind her. Her cheeks were flushed from cold or excitement, he couldn't tell which, making her eyes stand out in her face like two pieces of clear blue sky.

"Oh! Cade," Sara said, rather surprised. But then, he'd been somewhat avoiding her for the past few days. She clasped the handle of the baby's carrier in both hands like a picnic basket, a crib blanket draped over it to protect the baby from the cold.

"Here, let me," Cade said quickly, recovering his manners. He reached for the carrier, and his fingers brushed hers.

She blushed an even brighter red. He wished to hell he knew what it meant.

"I was just headin' out to the barn," he mumbled.

"Oh, wait and see what we bought first, Cade," Sarah Ann said eagerly, her own arms loaded down with shopping bags. He hadn't much choice but to follow the two women into the warm kitchen. There, Cade set the carrier on the table.

Sara folded back the blanket's edge, exposing Baby Cade's face with a "Here you go, sweetheart."

The look of wonder that sprang to the infant's eyes at the magical appearance of three adults peering down at him was so comical they all laughed.

Again, Cade's and Sara's gazes collided, then skittered away.

He felt the strain between the two of them all the way down to his toenails, making him wish abruptly that it was again just Sara and himself on the ranch and the rest of the world held at bay. As difficult as that time had been, somehow they'd managed to get to what was important. Now, however, Loren and his wife's presence, although they'd answered some questions, only succeeded in muddying things in Cade's mind.

Not that it wasn't nice to have them here. They'd been great, especially for Sara, driving her to Amarillo yesterday for the tests Doc had advised. Being as how the both of them had experience with medical matters—least ways more than him—they were, of course, the logical choice to help Sara in that department, just as it made sense for Sarah Ann to take over spelling Sara with Baby Cade and being a companion to her.

Like now, as Sarah Ann pulled a tiny light blue romper from one of the sacks and held it up for his inspection.

"Isn't it darling?" she exclaimed.

Sara caressed the romper's footie as if she couldn't resist. "The dry goods store in Sagebrush had a bunch of baby things like this, all at great prices," she said.

Her voice held the kind awe one usually associated with discovering oil in her backyard. But he guessed that such delight as the two women were showing over the find could only be appreciated by those of the feminine persuasion—and distinctly left out those of the masculine kind.

At the thought, he flat couldn't stay there in the kitchen any longer. He didn't know why. All he knew was that it would kill him, for sure.

With a muttered "Looks like y'all don't need me anymore," Cade left the kitchen.

But once outside, with the brisk, clean air to clear his head as he strode toward the barn, he sure enough got the picture. He was jealous as hell. He'd tried not to be, fought like the devil to be charitable, to be happy for Sara that now she had people to care for her and be company to her as he couldn't.

And he was happy for her, deep down. If anything, seeing how well cared for she would be confirmed in his mind that she and the baby would be fine once everyone left here for their life together in Albuquerque.

The merest thought of that day nearly made him sick to his stomach. The loneliness would eat him alive. But what else could he expect? he wondered, as he yanked open the barn door with a bit more effort than needed. His fate had been sealed long before Sara and Baby Cade had come to the ranch.

At least now he had the comfort of knowing he'd done his part in seeing to hers and the baby's long-term happiness.

Cold comfort it would be, though, once they left.

Which was why a half hour later when he heard a friendly "Like a hand?" from behind him, Cade wasn't in a more receptive mood for help or much else, mostly because he'd bet it was the "much else" that Loren had followed him out here to dispense some of.

Regardless, Cade turned and said amiably enough, "Fact is, I could use two that didn't feel like they were gonna break off in the next minute."

The space heater he'd rigged up so he could get a little repair work done on his tractor only put out the kind of BTUs that held the worst of the cold at bay: enough to keep his fingers from turning completely to icicles, but falling short of thawing them out entirely.

Loren gave a rueful chuckle of commiseration as he ambled over, his own hands deep within the pockets of his down jacket.

"I forgot how cold it can get here in the Panhandle. That blizzard sure looks to've been a doozy. What'd you get, a foot of snow?"

Cade adjusted the shop light on its hook and stooped to retrieve the wrench. "Yup."

He gave a grunt of satisfaction as the bolt he'd been working at came loose. Brief as it was, the exchange was the most conversation the two brothers had had since Loren had arrived three days ago, but that was mostly on account of Loren and Sarah Ann seeing to Sara's needs—and himself, again, continuing to see to the welfare of the ranch.

"I haven't had a chance to ride out and take a look at the herd yet," Loren said, bringing Cade out of his thoughts. "Kinda itchin' to, I have to admit." He dropped his chin. "Didn't realize how much I missed the place until I got here. It makes me wonder how I could've left in the first place."

Cade concentrated on turning the tractor's bent shaft, getting a load of grease all over his hands in the process.

"Well, Virg is gonna be heading out to the east section tomorrow, if you're of a mind to go along."

Loren made a sound, and Cade glanced up at him. His brother stood lock-kneed, staring down at him with an exasperated expression. "I was hopin' you'd do the honors, Cade."

"Oh." He wiped his hands on a rag. "Sure. Whenever you'd like. I'm at your disposal."

Making another sound, this one definitely a huff of disgust, Loren took a turn around the interior of the barn, finally coming back to stand next to Cade, who'd turned back to his work.

"Look, Cade," his brother began, "I'm not sure how else to bring this up, but, well, I know I sort of hinted in my letter about maybe comin' back to the ranch to work and live."

That sure enough got Cade's attention. He sat back on his heels. "You did?" He'd thought that was just his own wishful thinking!

"Well, sure. What'd you think I meant when I said that about my kids having the chance to know their uncle?"

Cade shrugged. "I'm sure I didn't know what to think, Loren. It was the first I'd heard from you in seven years. Who knew the man you'd become during that time, what your priorities were—or where your loyalties lay?"

So. It seemed there *was* a bit of old business that needed to be gotten out of the way. He didn't like it, didn't like the bitter tinge to his words, but there it was.

To his credit, Loren didn't bat an eye. "You're right. You couldn't've known what was goin' on with me all those years."

Fingers still crammed into his pockets, he leaned against the tractor wheel. "Mostly it's what's happened in the past year or so that's made the difference, though. I got married to Sarah Ann. Sara Jane lost her husband right around when they found out they were gonna be parents. Then when Sarah Ann became pregnant...well, I guess I had one of those moments of truth you get in life, and everything suddenly seems crystal clear. You know, like when you get your throwin' rope in a tangle. One minute you're sure you'll never find the sense in all the snarls, and in the next the way out comes clear to you, so pretty soon you're turning it around your hand in nice even loops.''

He toed at a piece of hay on the cement flooring, his expression as serious as Cade had ever seen it. "And what I saw in that moment is just how damned important family is. Bein' with family is important. And I'd like us all to be a real family again—maybe even for the first time— here on the ranch.''

Planting his hands on his thighs, Cade stood with a cracking of joints. "If you're askin' me for permission to move you and Sarah Ann back to the ranch, Loren, I guess I don't feel that's my decision.''

His brother pushed himself upright. "Wh— Sure it is, Cade!''

"Granddad always meant for you to take over runnin' the place, y'know.'' And for Cade to make his mark in another arena.

"Yeah, but you're the one who's got the most say of what goes on here at the ranch after keepin' it going almost single-handedly for seven years,'' Loren protested. "And've made a damn fine job of it, from what I understand.''

He pointed in the general vicinity of the bunkhouse. "Virg's told me. The herd is in great shape, and you've never had to gather up cattle to sell to make it through the winter. You've kept the heifers producin', from what I understand, and the calf crop as uniform as you can get it.''

Loren shook his head in amazement. "Believe me,

Cade, that sort of ranch management is a real accomplishment—especially when I know your heart's been elsewhere. Hell, I kinda even thought…well, Virg told me, too, that you'd bought yourself a fine new gelding you've been trainin' up. I always knew you had an ambition to build a business training horses. I figured if I came back to take up some of the slack, you'd have the time to go after that dream without the ranch sufferin' a bit for it."

His voice turned rough. "It's the least I can do, seein' how you kept the faith, so to speak, for seven whole years."

Cade didn't know what to say. Couldn't say anything for a few moments as his throat worked and his thoughts whirled in confusion. Until just now, he hadn't realized, really, exactly how much his brother's opinion meant to him. Oh, despite all his fine compliments, Cade knew he'd never be the rancher Loren was; it wasn't about that anymore. No, what he had needed more from Loren was that special recognition of his efforts: for not quitting him or the ranch all through the seven years he'd been gone.

And now that Cade had that recognition, he discovered it was all that he needed, much as Sara's happiness was all he'd needed, to make every bit of heartache he'd gone through or might still go through worth it.

"In that case," he said as roughly, "I'd be pleased to have you and Sarah come to live on the ranch, Loren."

He stuck out his hand, and instead found himself engulfed in a hug that did him a world of good. Yes, there was something about knowing you'd stepped up and met a challenge, not only in an emergency but over the long haul, that sure enough gave a man something to be proud of.

When Loren finally pulled away, he wore the same old smile from way back, when they'd been two kids with so much to prove, mostly to themselves, and he knew his brother was experiencing the same feeling.

Cade tilted his head, indicating the broken tractor. "Just so long as you know, I've got seven years built up of doin' the nastiest, dirtiest chores around the place. You've got some catchin' up to do."

Loren laughed. "Now *that* really is the least I can do for takin' off like a jackrabbit and not even sending word of where I was or what I was doing." He sobered. "If it helps, I never had a day I wasn't sorry for doing that. I'm not proud of it. Believe me, I've spent a lot of time feeling ashamed about what happened with Marlene. Sorry, too, for accusin' you of something you'd never've done in a million years."

Cade's stomach did a full three-sixty. He knew Loren was talking about Marlene. He *knew* it. And yet guilt had still taken him on a roller-coaster ride.

That's why he also knew he'd have to come clean here and now with Loren—about everything. It was the only way he had a chance with his brother to set the past to rest and move forward, however that happened.

"Loren, there's somethin' I need to tell you," he said abruptly.

"Lord, you sound so serious, Cade," his brother said, eyes curious.

"Yeah, well." He cleared his throat. "First, I need to own up to some things about—about Marlene. Not that there was anything between the two of us," he said hastily. "There wasn't. The thing is, I didn't realize it until just a few days ago, but there *were*…oh, hell, signs of some kind of an attraction, I guess you could call it."

"You mean the way she'd sashay up to you when we'd come into the Lone Star Tap and give you a big ol' hug hello, even though she'd seen you not two hours before here at the ranch?"

Cade's jaw went slack. "You—you knew?"

"Knew? Not so's to have a conscious thought about it. But shoot, Cade, I'm not gonna beat myself up anymore for not recognizin' what was as plain as the nose on my face."

"Which was…?" Cade asked, almost mad with curiosity himself.

With a sigh, Loren took a seat on a hay bale. He squinted sideways up at Cade from under the brim of his hat. "You knew Marlene went with me, when I left here."

Cade nodded, himself settling one hip on the edge of the wooden workbench. "I figured you went ahead and got married, too."

"That we did. Fact is, I couldn't wait to get the ring on her finger, even after catching the two of you in a compromisin' position, no matter how y'all got there."

He leaned forward on his elbows, hands clasped between his knees as the nearby space heater *tick-tick-ticked.* "Of course, things went downhill from there. The only reason we decided to put down stakes in Albuquerque was because she had some relatives there. I started right in trainin' to be a paramedic so I could support us, so it was about a year before the blinders started to wear off.

"Honest," his brother continued, "I don't bear her any ill will—at least not now. I even talked to her just a few months ago and she's happily married."

He laughed again, a short bark aimed at himself this time. Dropping his head between his shoulders, he wagged it slowly back and forth. "Believe it or not, I don't think I really accepted it even after we'd split up. Truth be told, I was pretty bitter for a long time."

Loren lifted his chin and met Cade's gaze. "Then I met Sarah Ann. I swear, Cade, I took one look at her and suddenly everything that had happened up to then in my life fell into place. I just *knew*, then and there, I was right where I needed to be, however roundabout the journey I'd taken to get there.''

He spread his hands, the look on his face that of a man who'd witnessed a miracle. ''She's like…the other half of me. I can't imagine what I did without her before we met, even though I'm smart enough to realize that I wouldn't have recognized that at twenty-four, or twenty-five or even twenty-six. I had some growin' to do, and I don't just mean putting twenty pounds on my skinny-assed frame. I needed those years before Sarah to learn what it was to really love someone and have them love you, and how that's not somethin' you can make happen, any more than you can stop it from happening.''

Shock fired a path up Cade's spine, like a burning fuse heading for a charge of dynamite. Those were Sara's words, almost exactly!

He must have been looking at Loren pretty dementedly, for a flush crept up his brother's neck. ''Aw hell, listen to me, rambling on like a lovesick fool,'' he said.

He slapped his thighs, standing. ''You had something else you wanted to tell me?''

Now it was Cade who found himself flushing in confusion. How in hell now was he going to be able to tell Loren the rest of what he'd intended—that, believing Sara was his brother's wife, Cade had still fallen in love with her, and let her fall in love with him, in that inevitable way Loren had just described? Because as filled with trust as his brother was that such kismet between two people was for the good, would Loren see what happened between him and Sara that way?

In the final analysis, though, why did Loren need to know at all? Cade thought desperately. He hadn't actually betrayed his brother's trust in him, hadn't, in all truth, betrayed anyone's trust in him—including Sara's. At least not yet.

Avoiding his brother's gaze, he crouched in front of the space heater, holding his frozen hands out to the warmth. "Actually, I was just wonderin'—if y'all come back here to live, what'll happen to Sara?"

"Why, she'll be living here, too, we hope."

"It's not a problem," Cade declared, cranking like the devil on another infernal bolt. "Why should it be? You're right. We're all just one big happy family now. Of course we'd all want to be together, now that fate's allowed us this particular blessin'."

"Cade." Loren put his hand over Cade's, stilling it. "I am right, aren't I, about you and Sara Jane havin' a certain affection for each other?"

To put it mildly. Cade squeezed his eyes shut. "What if there is?" He flat couldn't keep the challenge out of his voice.

"Why, I think that's great! Sara Jane is a wonderful woman, and any man'd be lucky to win her. Why wouldn't you think so?"

Cade swore impatiently. "She's got a husband."

"No, she doesn't—"

"A husband she doesn't remember!" He turned on his brother. "A husband she loved so much she couldn't stand contemplatin' life without him—and so she hitched her feelings to the first man who came along after she wiped all memory of that husband from her mind. And I let it happen, Loren!" Cade gazed at his brother, stricken. "No, let's be truthful here—I *made* it happen, couldn't stop myself from doing it, even when I believed she was your wife."

His confession reverberated in the cavernous barn. Loren let go of his hand, and Cade's arm fell to his side as he dropped the wrench with a clatter and faced his brother squarely. He'd have liked to avoid this particular moment of reckoning, but it was best it had finally arrived, no matter what the consequences were. It would have eaten him alive, otherwise.

"So," Loren said quietly, "you and Sara Jane thought she was my wife, and still the feelings between you grew."

He paused, eyes shadowed under the brim of his Stetson hat, and as the seconds ticked by, Cade saw the rest of his life flash before his eyes—a life without Loren, without family. Without Sara. And God help him, in that instant, he'd have done anything to avoid such a fate.

"Yes," he answered without equivocation.

"Well," his brother said dryly, "she's obviously *not* my wife, so unless you tell me next you've got designs on Sarah Ann, then I've got no beef with you, Cade."

"You don't?" Cade asked, flabbergasted, wondering how he'd once again been able to avoid disaster. "I mean, even after what happened with Marlene…"

Loren groaned. "Have you not heard a word I've said?"

He bent to pick up the wrench. "Steady the drive shaft for me," he instructed Cade.

Still in a state of disbelief, Cade gripped the tractor's shaft, close to the bolt, as Loren yanked on it with both hands on the wrench.

"It's what I've been tellin' you, Cade," he said in between grunts of effort, "if I hadn't left the ranch with Marlene and moved to Albuquerque, I never would've become a paramedic and had to work with the nurses at the hospital. And I'd never have met Sarah. In my mind, how we got together couldn't have happened any other way— just like it couldn't have happened any other way for you and Sara Jane."

The bolt came loose. Loren stepped over to set it and the wrench on the workbench as Cade concentrated unduly on cleaning his thoroughly greasy palms with the shop rag.

"The thing is," Cade finally said in a muted voice, "while I sure enough can't change what's already happened between us, I don't see the good to be had in letting feelings between us grow. Not when Sara's obviously so grieved by the loss of her husband she's shut out the memory of him rather than face life without him."

His brother held out his hand for the rag, which Cade tossed to him. "It's your choice, of course," Loren said. "You gotta do what you think is best. Whatever actions you take, though, just remember—you're not alone any longer."

At the phrase, Cade shot Loren a probing glance. "Meanin'?"

"Meanin' whether you want it or not, you've got the responsibility of others' happiness to think of now, too."

With that, Loren left him to wrestle not only with the broken tractor but with his thoughts.

And wrestle with them Cade did. No, he couldn't change the chain of events leading up to now. But as he'd told Sara the evening she'd learned of her real fate, they still had a choice in how to deal with those events. That was good to remember.

Loren was right, however, in that such choices would have their own consequences, which would ripple outward from the center to affect the people around him who cared for him, and for whom he so greatly cared. Look at how Loren's choices had affected Cade's life, bringing Sara into it, for better or worse. He also knew, however, the choices he had made that had affected Loren—and Sara. For better or worse.

By the time he left the barn for the comfort of a hot shower and warm bed, Cade still didn't know what to do. All he'd been able to come up with was that, whatever it was, he had to do what was right for Sara and her baby and their future happiness. And he had to believe. As long as he kept that in the forefront of his mind, it'd all come out right for everyone in the end.

This time, though, he didn't dare let himself even contemplate the hope that he might be a part of that future.

"Hey."

Sara looked up from the computer screen. Cade leaned against the doorjamb of her bedroom in that way he had, hip shot and wide shoulders hunched just a bit, the fingers of one hand tucked into the front pockets of his jeans, the other ruminatively scrubbing that spiky chestnut hair of his.

She wondered if his mere presence would ever cease to thrill her.

"Hey," she said softly, trying not to be quite so glad to see him here in her room for the first time in ten days. Ever since they'd discovered the truth about her identity, he'd been noticeably distant from her, both physically and emotionally. And as wary as ever.

Sure, at first she'd taken the withdrawal of his support pretty hard, but now she understood why. She was feeling more than a little wary herself, but in her case it was *of* herself. Something told her it went the same way with Cade. She didn't know about him, but it wore her out having to be so watchful of her own subconscious and what it might spring on her next.

"You look pretty busy there," Cade said with a nod toward her computer.

She maneuvered the mouse around on its pad, pointing and clicking to close the current window. "I've been trying to see how much of my graphic design skills I remember."

He shoved off of the doorjamb. "How's it goin'?"

She worried her lower lip between her teeth. "Truthfully? Not too well. I've been reviewing some of the work I've already done for clients, and while I do get a sense of why I put a bit of text where I did or gave it the emphasis I did, the thought of trying to start from scratch on an idea from the conceptual stage…frankly, it terrifies me.''

Fingers still stuck in his pockets, Cade bent on a level with her to peer at the computer screen. He shook his head. ''Wish I could be of more help.''

''I'm not especially looking for someone to bail me out,'' Sara said with some impatience.

He cut her a sidelong glance. ''That's good, 'cause what I know about computers you could fit on the head of a tack and still have room for a flea hoedown.''

Where usually Cade's figures of speech brought a smile to her face, Sara couldn't find one in her this afternoon. She pushed her chair away from the makeshift desk Loren had set her computer up on, bumping Cade in the knee. Where the small bedroom had been a little cramped before, now even with just her computer and a few other items she had the movers ship from storage, it was so crowded it threatened that dreaded claustrophobia of before.

She couldn't let it affect her.

''I'm sorry, Cade,'' she said, meaning both bumping him and her impatience. She seemed to be apologizing so much these days. Actually, it was the frustration of this endless not remembering that was getting to her. Plus her head hadn't stopped hurting for a week, ever since Loren and her cousin had arrived, which was when things had changed between her and Cade.

She'd have taken that as a sign she was getting closer to recovering her past if it didn't make her nearly weep with sheer hopelessness.

Cade gave a shrug of absolution. ''Maybe it'll take really getting back in the saddle again, so to speak, to give you the oomph you need. Y'know, have a real project to work on that'll challenge you.''

''Well, it seems that might be a ways in the offing.''

She indicated the file boxes stacked in one corner. "From what I can tell, I retained only the few clients I could work with from a distance. It looks as if I must have been planning to build up my business in Albuquerque, but now that I'm going to be living here, at least for the time being, I'm not sure how to proceed."

She stared resolutely at the computer screen. "But I need to find a way to support myself and the baby. I need to start making a future for us, even without knowing what the past is. Sarah and Loren have been so supportive, saying this is my home now. Loren said he knows some businesspeople in Amarillo who might need some graphic design work done, or at least could get me an interview with some firms there."

Cade scrutinized her. "What if you get a job where you have to do the conceptual stuff you've been findin' so scary?"

"Then I'll either soldier on through and do it or I won't," Sara retorted. "I can't worry about that right now."

Cade straightened, lower lip jutted out in thought. After a few moments he said gently, "Sara. We need to talk."

Both her heart and her head started pounding at his words. "Talk? About what?"

He glanced around at the cramped quarters, not answering her question. From the kitchen came the sound of Sarah Ann "getting her nesting instinct out of her system," as she put it, by baking bread while she cleaned out cupboards. Sara had heard Loren tell her a few hours ago that he and Virgil were going out to replace a T-post on some fence in the east section and wouldn't be back until suppertime.

"Take a walk outside with me?" Cade asked. Then, with a lift of his eyebrow he added, "I only make the offer 'cause it's a pretty safe bet those new snow boots I spied on the mud porch are yours, and you won't be forced to clop around like a Shetland pony in a Clydesdale's shoes.

Now that Sara laughed at, hoping both the jest and gesture meant she was wrong about the portent she'd heard in his voice.

They fetched their coats from the mud porch, Sara asking her cousin on her way through the kitchen to listen for the baby, and were soon outside in the cold, clear air.

Sara drew it in deeply, feeling her head clear a bit as they strolled down the ranch lane, its surface still snow-packed. She wondered suddenly if the snow would ever melt, the ground turn from brown to green. It just seemed she'd lived all her life with this cold, stark landscape surrounding her, and it occurred to her that, actually, she had. At least, the life she could remember. Perhaps when the spring thaw came it would thaw her mind, frozen in some sort of suspended animation, as well.

Would that it were that simple, Sara thought ruefully, something telling her it wasn't going to be. She needed to continue, however, to have the faith and trust that such a transformation wouldn't devastate her, either.

"This was a good idea," she told Cade. "Thanks for suggesting it."

She thought she'd get his usual, depreciating, "It's nothing," but instead he responded with a quiet, "You're welcome."

Another good sign, she figured, enough of one so that she could screw up her courage and ask, "You wanted to talk?"

Walking beside her, shoulders hunched in his brown suede jacket and Stetson pulled low on his brow, he looked distinctly glacial himself. "Yes—about a couple of things."

Eyes narrowed, he gazed off into the distance. "Y'know, I haven't been completely truthful with you,

Sara, because I *can* understand how or why a person might block things from their mind—just completely forget, or choose to forget—something happening that you didn't want to face up to, or—or recognize in others.''

He hesitated, then admitted, ''Or yourself.''

''You can?'' she asked, surprised—and heartened again by his changed perspective. Oh, maybe he did mean to end this awful distance between them!

''Sure. And I also said before it was up to Loren to tell you this, but seein' as how you're not his wife, I guess it's not exactly privileged information anymore.''

His ears had turned red, and Sara didn't think it was because of the cold. ''I'm not of a mind to get into much detail,'' he said, ''but seven years ago Loren was engaged to a woman, not your cousin. Her name was Marlene Lane, someone he'd met in Amarillo, which is where all the cowboys went to do their serious drinkin'. And girl chasin'. Anyway, Loren fell for Marlene like a ton of bricks. First woman he ever really loved, he told me then. They'd hardly dated a month before they got engaged, and he had her out to the ranch meet his kin. Meanin' me.''

They had reached the end of the lane, and Cade turned around almost automatically. Sara followed suit, curious. This certainly wasn't the discussion she'd thought he had in mind when he asked to talk to her.

''Anyway, from the first Marlene flirted with me, kind of low-key stuff like throwing me meaningful looks when Loren's head was turned. Then it got to be even when he was lookin'. I'm sure it sounds pretty ignorant, but I just thought she was bein' friendly. Or I chose to see it that way.

''One day, I was out in the stable, and in she comes, big smile on her face and an innocent look in her eye. She sits herself down on a bale of hay and says seeing as how Loren had to ride out to the north section to help Virg with a bunch of cows that broke through a hole in the fence, she had an idea to use this time get to know her future brother-in-law a bit better. I said sure, whatever, even asked if she wanted to see how to rig up a leather halter. So she came on over to where I was working, and started leanin' on me, hand on my shoulder, askin' me why was I doin' this or that. Then she made to hand me a pair of needle-nosed pliers and got a smear of edge dye on the front of her blouse—''

Blushing, Cade made a swipe over his left pectoral. ''Right here. I started stammerin' and apologizin' and trying to rub the dye off with a rag, if you can believe it. And she was acting all dismayed, sayin' how this was her best blouse and she didn't know what she'd do if I couldn't get the stain off of it, all the while stepping closer as I kept backing up till the back of my legs hit that hay bale and I sort of fell back on it, her on top of me.''

He closed his eyes, jaw clenched. ''Man, I was so *stupid*. But I knew what was happening, deep down. And deep down, Sara, I gotta confess—I *wanted* something to happen, something to confirm in my mind that I had *some* of the ability Loren had to attract a woman. But I obviously didn't know how to handle one once I caught her, because then—then Marlene wrapped her arms around my neck and planted a big one on me.''

For some reason Sara could see the scene with perfect clarity, at least what Cade must have looked like then: young and earnest, without a clue as to his effect on women or the power in his presence.

''I just froze,'' he stated. ''It was like someone had gotten me with the business end of a cattle prod. Whatever I'd been aiming for, I knew for sure I didn't want *this* happening. But I knew I'd encouraged it, too, of my own free will. I had my hands on her waist, trying to get her off of me. When Loren walked in to find his fiancée and his brother in one pretty damning situation. I knew how in love Loren was with Marlene, so I took the blame. He left the next day, taking her with him—and believin' his brother had betrayed him.''

He reached out then, and took her mittened hand, tucking it in the crook of his elbow and holding it there with his own gloved one. At his touch, warmth spread through Sara like melting butter. Why had she been so worried?

"At least I understand now why you were so shocked, thinking I was Loren's wife." She slanted him an empathetic glance. "And cynical about things working out for the better."

His laugh was short and sardonic. "I thought I'd hit the mother lode of bad luck. But the reason I'm tellin' you all this is because, for a long time, I denied to myself that it wasn't bad luck at all. I'd set myself and Marlene up for that encounter happening. I sure enough felt guilty, even if I couldn't figure out why. It was only recently that I realized I'd seen the signs of Marlene's attraction and had literally put them out of my mind—along with the competitive urge in me to see if I could attract her."

He dropped his chin, expression serious as Sara had ever seen it. "I can see now, too, that had I faced the situation squarely and looked into my heart, I would've seen what was goin' on, and maybe avoided a whole lot of heartache, not just for me, but for a whole slew of people."

Sensing how hard it had been for him to tell her this, Sara squeezed Cade's arm in support. "Cade. You mustn't continue to blame yourself for what happened. It's past. And even if I hadn't seen it for myself in that first dream of him that I had, every instinct in me tells me Loren certainly doesn't blame you."

"And I thank you for that assurance, now and from before. I don't blame myself, not anymore. You're right, what's happened has happened. I can't change it."

He turned to her, and with infinite gentleness extracted his arm from her grasp. That sense of portent infused her again. "But I do have a choice in how I deal with what's happened between us...with what's happened to you."

"What do you mean?" she asked, searching his face for clues.

He didn't bat an eyelash but held her gaze. "The only way I know to play this out, Sara, is with complete truth between us. And much as I wish to God it weren't true, I really believe that if there's a reason you're not remembering your past, it's me."

He was right, of course. Whenever she got close to that edge that seemed to fall off into the nothing of her past, he'd been there to pull her back.

Something in his tone, though, in his eyes, made her heart stop with completeness. "What are you saying, Cade?"

"You don't need me anymore. You've got Sarah Ann and Loren. Baby Cade. I'm askin' you to release me from my promise to you."

"But...why, Cade?"

His face had gone pale as marble, was as immobile and cold. Except for those golden-brown eyes that burned bright with emotion.

"Because the only way you'll remember your husband, Sara, is if I leave you."

Chapter Ten

"You're…l-leaving?" Sara repeated numbly. Suddenly, she felt as if she'd topple over and reached out blindly for Cade's support.

To his credit, he hesitated not a second but responded by clasping her upper arms, shoring her up. It gave her the least bit of hope she could talk him out of this silly notion.

Because it was wrong! Wrong for both of them. She knew it in her heart.

"Yes," he answered calmly. "Tomorrow. If it helps at all, Sara, I'd be going even if it weren't for the situation between us. I have to—for myself and my future. I entered Destiny in a cutting show in Austin, and from there I figure I'll stay on the road and hit as many stock shows and horse shows as I can to try to scare up some interest in my horse-training skills. That aim hasn't changed at all, Sara."

"Why, though? Why must you leave?"

"Because—because I don't seem to be able to stop myself from doin' just this, Sara.'' His fingers clenched around her arms.

His face was ravaged by the guilt she'd seen in him so often, as well as the anger. "It's like I've got no choice in the matter. There's somethin' in me that won't be denied. But it has to be! I'm keepin' you from remembering. As long as I'm here, it's not going to happen.''

Sara seized upon those words. "What about what you said, though, that you can't make anything happen in training Destiny? How you can only *let* it happen by making that your goal—to simply let what happens happen.'' She clung to his jacket front, almost as if she were afraid he'd disappear before her eyes. "Why can't you do that with anything else in your life? Why can't you trust that'll happen with me?''

"It seems to me I'm not the one with the problem with trusting, Sara,'' Cade said, sounding ever so cold, all of the sudden. "Otherwise, why would you try to erase your past from your mind? Why've you blocked your husband from your mind?''

A jolt of fear charged through her. "I told you, I don't know—''

"You say you can't stop loving me any more than you can stop yourself from loving your baby, but you can't change or outrun your destiny, either, and that's what you've done with Greg Childress.''

He shook her slightly. "What was it about his dying that you couldn't bear, so much so you had to make it not've happened, if only in your own mind?''

"I don't know!'' Sara tore herself from Cade's grasp and whirled, running away from him, her direction aimless. But he was right. She couldn't escape him or the truth he bore....

She found herself at the corral, with no notion of how

she'd gotten there. The corral, where she and Cade had first confronted the forces at play in both of them.

There was nothing wrong in those emotions, nor in the connection they gave rise to between Cade and her! There was nothing wrong, either, with where such feelings sprang from within them, or with her and Cade's expression of them. Never in a million years would he convince her of that!

That wasn't what he was trying to do, though, and deep down she knew it. That's why she'd run.

Sara grabbed hold of the top railing on the wooden fence as if it would somehow keep her from being wrested from this time and place. Her breath was coming in huge gulps of air as she tried to stay oriented to the here and now, tried to stay calm.

Then she remembered: Cade's promise. Even if he did leave, she still had that precious gift. The thought was like finding a refuge with chaos raging all around.

Sara turned to find Cade standing a few feet away, breathing hard, his cheeks red with cold and exertion, his whiskey-brown eyes no longer cold but blazing with worry and fear. He'd apparently shadowed her every step here, ready to catch her if she stumbled.

Yes, she still had that precious gift he'd given her.

"I don't know why I've forgotten Greg Childress," Sara said simply. "And I don't know why I would have wanted to block him or our life together from my mind. But whatever the reason, I have to believe the forces that be will make that reason clear to me when the time is right, and not before."

She lifted her chin. "And if you think that means I'm running from my responsibilities—to my child, or his father, or even to myself—then go ahead. I—I simply can't play this out any other way at the moment."

He said nothing for a long moment. Then he nodded.

"I'm—I'm glad to hear it, Sara. Because then you can appreciate why *I* have to do what I believe is right, to be true and good. For you, and for Baby Cade."

"Which is to leave?" she asked. "Because don't for one second fool yourself, Cade, that you're not running from your fate, too, the love between us that was born the night Baby Cade was, whether either of us wanted it to or not!"

He took an angry step forward. "Damn it, Sara, I'm *not* runnin' from my responsibilities. Or my destiny. Training horses *is* what I've always been meant to do, and maybe for the first time in my life I'm following my heart. But as long as I stay, I feel like I'm keepin' you from *your* fate—from remembering your past."

He took another step closer, and she could see actually that he wasn't angry but desperate. "Think about it. What if I stayed, let us both get more involved, and you did regain your memory and discovered you couldn't let go of your love for your husband? I *know* you, Sara—it'd tear you apart to know that love in all of its force and realize how you'd forsaken it, whatever the reason."

A muscle leaped in his jaw as he clenched it before going on hoarsely. "And I gotta be completely honest here. I won't be happy so long as I feel you're not able to bear the pain that kind of love brings along with its joy. Sure, we knew some of that joy up close and personal, bringin' Baby Cade into the world. But it's stayin' steady through the rough times, the darkest times, that carves that love into two people's souls, so that they make a promise to fulfill their destiny together in this lifetime, and the next. And if that's what you had with Greg, that's not gonna be good for any of us in the long haul."

He swallowed audibly, and she knew then she'd never seen a man look so bleak.

"That's why I have to go," Cade continued raggedly.

"I have to. I'm not sayin' it's for forever. It's just...the only way I can think of to keep both of us from making more of a mistake."

Sara wrapped her arms about her body, trembling with the strength of her emotions. He was wrong to leave! She knew it with every fiber of her being.

Perhaps that wasn't the issue here, though. Cade stood before her, obviously as torn as ever, but trying with all of his might to do what he believed was right for her and her baby. To do what was right for him, even, which could only benefit them all. Yes, it would destroy something within him to stay, even if she felt something equally as important within her would die to have him leave.

She could scarce draw a breath, so at war with herself was she, as if she again fought a life-and-death struggle, only this time it was for this man.

"So just what would you have me do until that moment of truth arrives, and all is revealed, Cade?" Sara asked.

"Just keep keepin' the faith, Sara, like you've done all along. Knowin' that you are...well, it might just be the only thing that gets me through."

She saw then how scared he was, too, and what he stood to lose. And yet, as ever, Cade was facing the challenge squarely. She must show the same strength of spirit.

"All right, then." Sara set her shoulders, and somehow found a smile within her and pasted it on her face. "We'll miss you, Baby Cade and I. And we won't f-forget you, no matter how long you're gone."

He reached out a hand as if to touch her cheek, but let it fall between them. "I know, Sara," was all he said. "I know."

Sara held out until he'd left, and then sagged against the fence. Despair, as sharp and desperate as ever, attacked her from all sides, giving rise to that awful, terrible fear, now so familiar to her she wondered if she would ever know a time without it. But it was inescapable. Her fate was inescapable; she saw it stretching out before her in stark clarity: she would lose this fine man if she did not fight with everything in her to face down that monstrous fear and know it for what it was.

She had to, even if it went against every instinct in her.

It may be her only chance to bring Cade McGivern back into her life, this time for good.

Five o'clock came way too soon, even if Cade had lain awake all night waiting for the hour to chime.

He rose in the dark and dressed except for his boots, which he carried with him to the bathroom and from there down the stairs. He'd put his duffel next to the back door last night, set the coffeemaker on automatic perk, wanting his exit this morning to cause as little disturbance to the household as possible.

All he lacked was loading Destiny into the stock trailer. Then he'd be gone.

He poured three quarters of the pot of coffee into a Thermos, the rest of it into some sort of tipless travel cup Loren had urged upon him last night, telling Cade he'd need it with as much time as he'd be spending on the road.

Taking a few hot swallows to warm his insides before he ventured out into the frigid cold, Cade took a last glance around the kitchen. It had been a different house since Loren and his wife had come. The evenings were filled with the smells of good home cooking and lively conversation. Even Virgil had seemed to forgive him, of a fashion, and it had almost seemed like old times, the three of them together again.

It would be one of the toughest things he'd ever done, leaving here.

But while once he had hoped for nothing more than

exactly that, Cade now found it wasn't enough for him. He wanted more than the past back. He wanted…

"Cade?"

He whipped around, almost spilling his coffee. Sara stood at the kitchen doorway in her long flannel nightgown, her wavy black hair spilling over her shoulders.

"Sara. It's five o'clock. What're you doin' up?"

Her hands clenched the folds of her nightgown. "You— you weren't going to leave without saying goodbye, were you? You know, to Baby Cade?"

"I—I didn't want to wake y'all up," he said by way of explanation, which was really an excuse.

Her eyes were huge in her wan face. He set his coffee cup on the counter. "Of course I couldn't leave without seein' the little mite."

Brushing past her, he walked down the hall and into the darkened room, lit only by the diffused illumination of the hall light. The baby was awake in his cradle but not at all fussy, his dark eyes bright and alert, tiny mouth working as his pink tongue darted in and out in curiosity.

Feeling like he had to swallow around his entire heart, Cade lifted the young one, holding him before him so he could take in every bit of him, imprint him on his mind.

The baby had lost most of that newborn look, his features rounding out and not so squished and pruny-looking. There was no denying, though, that that shock of black hair was as wild as ever, and Cade wondered if it always would be so. It struck him that there was a possibility that he'd never know. Not that he would never see Sara or the baby again, not by choice. But things happened that parted loved ones, just as they had happened to her husband.

"Well, pardner," he said, having to clear his throat three times to get even that much out, "guess we won't be seein' each other for a while. Y'all be good for your mama, you hear? Time with her is precious. I know. I lost my own mama when I was ten."

Baby Cade snuffled, making a face like he'd swallowed a bitter pill. "Hey now. I didn't mean to upset you or anything. Like as not, you'll both have all the time in the world with each other. Just...don't forget what I said."

Cade brought him closer to bestow a tender kiss on his forehead. "Don't forget...me," he whispered against that silky-soft surface, as if to imprint himself on the little one's brain.

Settling the babe back into his cradle, he turned. Sara stood at the entrance to the room, her hand covering her mouth and tears sparkling in those sapphire blue eyes of hers.

"U-oh, *Cade*," she choked out.

He held his arms out to her, and she came swiftly into them. He crushed her to him, lips pressed to the top of her head—as if to imprint himself on her and her on him— and arms steeled around her in support as she cried as if she'd never stop.

His own tears crowded his throat. He wondered how he'd ever find the strength to let her go.

"I'm s-sorry for crying," Sara sobbed, trying to pull away and making a brave attempt to sniff back her tears. "You don't need this right now."

Cade wouldn't hear of it. Holding her closer still, he whispered, "Aw, don't be sorry, darlin'."

He lifted her chin, brushing her hair back and wiping away her tears with a soft, "Don't worry, it'll be all right." But she cried all the harder, until he was miserable with her sorrow.

"Sara. Sweet, sweet Sara." He dipped his head, kissing first one, then another of her tears from her cheek. "It'll be all right, I promise."

He kissed another drop that had trailed all the way to

her chin, kissed the ones still dampening her eyes and on her wet, tear-soaked lips...

Cade drew back, hands framing her face. She stared up at him, black lashes starred around those blue, blue eyes, that tender, crooked mouth of hers glistening and trembling no longer from her tears but from his kiss.

"We won't forget you, either of us. I could never forget you, Cade," she vowed passionately. "Not for anything, anything in the world."

"Promise?" he asked thickly.

"With all my heart..."

It did Cade no good to discover he couldn't have stopped himself, not for anything, as slowly, inevitably, he leaned closer, then closer still, until his mouth was upon hers.

She still tasted of salty tears, but only for an instant as he washed them away with the stroke of his tongue. Then he was tracing that lush curve of her lower lip, the sensitive swell at the center of her upper lip, before plunging inside to taste her completely.

Choking back a sob, she surged against him, her warm, soft flesh yielding under the pressure of his hands.

She was so sweet! If heaven had a taste, or touch, or even a scent, surely it was the honey in Sara's kiss, the silken softness of her lips, the head-spinning perfume of her womanliness.

Of which he knew so little. Cade lifted his head. Her eyes remained closed, features soft and rapt, as if she were immersed in that hundred-year sleep he'd first found her in, held bound in a dream of such wonderful scope that waking up didn't bear contemplating. She even made that same sound in the back of her throat, half moan, half sigh.

Except this dream was the result of the spell he'd cast upon her, and not another man.

He could stand it no longer, but lowered his mouth to

take hers again, to try with all his heart to make those dreams come true, if only for a few moments.

Her fingers clenched and unclenched on his shirtfront, then climbed upward to bury themselves in his hair. He gathered her closer still, pressing the soft length of her against him, her full breasts crushed against his chest and wringing a moan from him.

He couldn't resist. His hand slid over her ribs, up from her waist, to press his palm to her breast.

Sara gasped, making him jerk away.

"I—I'm sorry," Cade rasped, forehead against hers and eyes screwed shut in regret. "I just...you're so sweet, I had to touch you."

"Cade, no! Don't be sorry!" He felt her tugging his head up and he opened his eyes to find her gaze upon him, soft and loving. "I want you to touch me."

She moistened her lips, just as she'd done the first time he kissed her, and it aroused him now as it had then. "Please. I need you to."

"A-all right." With shaking fingers, he fumbled at unbuttoning her nightgown, and she waited patiently until he'd reached the last button at her waist. Then it was she who parted the sides, revealing herself to him.

Cade could only stare in reverence. In the faint light, her skin appeared whiter and finer than ever, the curve of her full breasts looking carved from marble, with only the dark rose of her nipples and the tracing of delicate blue veins to color their surface.

And between them the band of gold.

He couldn't go on.

"You're so...perfect," Cade whispered miserably. "So beautiful." He raised his hands before him. "Look at me. I'm rough and callused and clumsy...and—"

He shoved his fingers into his jeans pockets, disgusted.

"What are you trying to say, Cade?" Sara asked softly.

He couldn't bring himself to answer her for a moment. But he had to be scrupulously honest with her, if they were to have a chance in that ever so uncertain future.

"I've never been much of a hand when it came to women or relationships, you know that," he said. "So I just gave up long ago thinkin' that kind of happiness was to be mine this go-round on earth."

He didn't take a breath but plunged on while he still had the nerve to be completely honest with her. "The thing is, Sara, you have had happiness, so much that you totally wiped a man from your heart and mind to keep from contemplating a life without him."

He hesitated over the last part, but he couldn't stop now. He had to say it or he'd never feel himself a man of character. "I don't know that I have what it takes to fill the hole he left in your heart, that's all. And I know I won't be satisfied being the man you don't need to forget."

He turned his head momentarily, jaw working with the strength of his emotions. He had never felt so helpless, vulnerable or exposed in all his natural-born life.

With the last bit of his courage, he looked at Sara, and heaven help him, her eyes filled with tears again. Then she was shaking her head and fumbling for his wrist to press her lips to his palm, press his palm to her cheek.

"No! No, Cade. How can you say that? How can you even think it?" She grabbed his other hand and brought it to her lips to kiss it, over and over again. "Oh, these strong, capable, tender hands that first held my baby and gave him life!"

She gave a sob, then went on fiercely, "You *do* have what it takes within you, you always have, right here." She laid her hand over his heart. "And you're right, I never will forget you. I couldn't—because you are and always will be right here."

Never taking his eyes from hers, she took the hand against her cheek and placed it upon her own heart.

She had given him a gift, Cade realized. One different from the gift she claimed he had given her, but he didn't doubt the same life-changing impact it would have upon him.

Slowly, he slid his hand to curve around underneath her breast so that he took the weight of it in his palm. Then, with infinite gentleness, he stroked the edge of his thumb over the taut, swollen nipple.

Sara's eyes drifted closed. "Oh, *Cade,*" she gasped.

In one movement he'd swept her into his arms and laid her back on the bed. Hands on either side of her as he bent over her, he gazed at Sara in all her glory.

He wanted this to be good for her. Wanted, he realized in a rush, to brand another memory into her mind, that of the two of them, like this, so that if or when she rediscovered her past and remembered her husband, this experience would be there, too, for whatever it was worth.

It was selfish of him, to be sure. But he couldn't stop himself from wanting to share this one last moment with her. And then he'd go.

"Show me," he whispered, lowering himself beside her.

All the while holding his gaze, she lifted his hand in both of hers and set it upon her cheek. Spontaneously, he stroked his thumb back and forth across her soft, creamy skin. "Like this?" he whispered.

She didn't answer but tugged his wrist ever so slowly downward, so that his fingers caressed her throat, then her collarbone. Cade took it from there, trailing his fingertips lower still to the slope of her breast.

He lowered his head and tasted her.

Sweet. All other description failed him as he tongued that rigid peak of flesh. Sara arched beneath him, urging him on, and he wouldn't see her denied.

Even if it was only for this moment that she needed him, then that was what he would give her. He couldn't have denied her that even if his soul depended upon it. Couldn't deny this desire that was a force, in and of itself, to be reckoned with.

Heat pooled in his loins, and he tried mightily to ignore it. He wanted this to be for her. But Sara must have had other ideas, as she pulled his shirt from his jeans and slid her hand under it. Her slender fingers traced the muscles of his chest and stomach, feathering lower and lower to bump over his belt buckle, then the fly of his jeans.

Through the denim, she pressed her hand flush against him.

Cade gritted his teeth.

"Sara," he moaned, "I can't...*you* can't...it's too soon after the baby...."

"I know. I know..."

They lay twined together, breathing ragged and shallow. Damn it, he was anything but in control here, and he had to be. He had to be—for her.

"Believe me, Sara, I'd like nothin' better right now than to make love to you, but it's not to be." He raised himself up on one elbow. "So let me just...give you this, make this moment about *you*."

She looked at him with amazement and tenderness. "You are the dearest man."

Lowering his head, he took her into his mouth again with tender nips and shifting suction that made her writhe beneath him. Sliding her gown upward along her slender thigh, then her hip, Cade cradled the sweet mound of her belly, remembering how he'd touched her so when she'd been pregnant.

Someday, he thought fervently. *Someday our own child might grow here within her.*

Such a day, however, might never come. Yet it didn't

matter. That didn't stop him from wanting to give her this moment. Even if that someday never came, the pain then would be worth it, because of the joy in this moment.

Tenderly, gently, not knowing if this might be both the first and the last time he would touch Sara this way, Cade skimmed his hand lower, finding the hot, sensitive core of her, and stroked her.

Sara sucked in a jagged breath. "Oh...yes."

He stroked her again as, his mouth fierce as his touch couldn't be, he took her lips to his, setting up another rhythm with his tongue, taking the kiss deep, then pulling back, then more deeply still, until Sara squirmed beneath him. He was going on instinct here, knowing nothing of what she liked or how, but something told him all he need know was already within his ken, as he caressed her intimately.

And then, like a miracle, she was shuddering against him, fingers mindlessly clutching his shoulder, his hair, as every inch of her trembled violently.

He shook, too, shook with the power of holding such ecstasy within his very hands. He'd never known anything like it, and it was like a gift to him, perfect and whole.

She didn't open her eyes, even after her breathing had evened out, but lay with the pale morning light upon her face, at peace for now. And he knew it for sure then, in all its bittersweetness.

The joy now was worth the pain later.

He left them both sleeping, Sara and the baby. The morning wind coming off the plains was frigid as he'd ever felt it as he let down the back of the stock trailer and loaded Destiny onboard. Thank God he was headed south, into relatively warmer temperatures. Once he finished the cutting show in Austin, he planned to head across to a stock show in Houston. He'd been too late to register for it, but he could do some networking. The crowd there would be exactly the people who'd be apt to hire him to train their horses.

The cab of the pickup warmed up quickly once he got on the road. Even with the defrost on full blast, though, the windows fogged over. That'd have to change. With the trailer on the back, he had only the use of his side mirrors to see behind him. The window on his side he could clear with the swipe of his sleeve, but the passenger side was a bit of a stretch.

Cade was reaching for a bandanna in the side pocket of his duffel laying next to him on the seat when his fingers met with something unfamiliar. Puzzled, he pulled out a large brown envelope. Steering with his left hand, he flicked on the dome light and set the envelope on his thigh to open its clasp.

He decided he'd better pull over, once he saw what was inside.

Motor still running, the dually chugged in the thin cold air as with stiff fingers, Cade slid a pale gold brochure from a rubber-banded stack of them and held it up to the light. There on the front were the words in bold, no-nonsense letters, just as he'd seen them in his mind: *Cade McGivern, horse trainer.*

And underneath was what he hadn't seen in his mind but that struck the perfect note: a photo of him and Destiny in the corral that had been taken who-knew-when. It showed him and the gelding in action, Destiny's head held high and his conformation perfect. He didn't look too bad himself, Cade realized, relaxed and assured in the saddle.

Sara must have stayed up all night putting this together! He couldn't imagine it had been easy for her, given she had just started getting familiar with her computer and re-membering her skills.

Eagerly, he opened the brochure. All the information

needed was there in short, concise bullets. There was even a short bio on him that Loren had to have helped her with.

But it was the quote on the facing side that stopped Cade in his tracks.

"With horses," it read, "you don't *make* anything happen. Training a horse is more about letting him deal with the choices he's been given, making him feel he's the one in control. Fix it up for him and let him find it by making the wrong thing difficult to do, and the right thing easy. And you make sure you feel it yourself, all the way through your body on down to your toes, letting go yourself and just thinking and feeling the movement as it comes."

His name followed as the author of such reasoning.

Cade sat for a long time before rousing himself. When he did, it was to cast a glance, now misted of its own accord, into his side mirror and down the road he'd just come. If she had wanted to capture the very sum and substance of him and what he believed in, she couldn't have done it better. Or touched him as greatly.

In that moment, Cade never loved a person on earth more than he loved Sara. It took every bit of his willpower not to crank the wheel of the dually and head back to the ranch.

But they were doing the right thing here. Maybe that was what Sara was trying to tell him with this brochure— that, and how much faith she had in him and in them, and in destiny. What would be would be, and it would all turn out for the good of everyone.

He wasn't one to predict the future, but Cade knew then that holding on to that one thought *would* be the only thing to get him through the next several weeks.

He only hoped it wouldn't have to be for years.

Chapter Eleven

Cade lifted the saddle off of Destiny's back and set it on the rack provided in the stall he'd been assigned to on the back of the arena at the Fort Worth Stockyards. Steam rose from the saddle blanket, throwing off the pungent smell of horse sweat and oiled leather that Cade found not at all unpleasant. That could have been because he was steeped in both odors himself. Or that he was on a natural high, he and Destiny having just taken first in the calf roping competition. In any case, he'd wash Destiny down, water him and set him up with a ration of feed before seeing to his own washing up, followed by his usual celebratory steak and a beer.

Such was the life of a horseman.

He had been away from the ranch for six long weeks. Six weeks of living out of motels, or bunking at friends' homes. Six weeks of stock and cutting shows, even taking in the odd rodeo, where he and Destiny would compete in the calf roping, and as today like as not end up in the money. Six weeks of talking to folks about their training problems, about technique and method, and of course about that favorite subject of horses in general, on which Cade discovered he had a lot to say.

So apparently did other people. He'd signed up four clients, had lines on another six, and hadn't felt so encouraged and purposeful in years.

Yup, he was making things happen, was sure enough in charge of his life and his future. And was lonely as hell.

He phoned Loren about once a fortnight, and his brother was charitable enough to keep Cade up to date on what was going on with Sara and the baby. Baby Cade was growing like a weed, Loren told him, smart as a whip and with such a sunny disposition you were hard-pressed to leave the house for fear of missing him doing something cute and have to satisfy yourself with merely hearing about it that evening at the supper table.

Come to think of it, Cade reflected, there wasn't anything in the least charitable about Loren.

The conversation inevitably ended with a one-sided discussion about Sara's progress. She'd started seeing a therapist in Amarillo once a week, with hopes of getting to the root of her amnesia. So far, Loren said, she still didn't know what had made her lose her memory—or what was holding her up from remembering.

So was this self-imposed exile from each other just another exercise in futility? Cade wondered, leading Destiny to the washing area. He couldn't go back to the ranch, however, firstly because he really did believe his presence kept her from remembering. And secondly, he didn't know how he could go back—for his own good. What if, instead of Sara remembering without it affecting her feelings for him, he one day looked into her eyes and realized he was only someone she used to love?

The mere thought of that happening wasn't to be borne.
No, he was better off going on with his life. He was done
with waiting for happiness to find him.

"Cade! Cade McGivern!"

Cade turned to see a short, barrel-chested man in jeans
and a buff-colored suede sport coat hurrying to catch up
with him.

"Hey there, Dick. Been awhile, hasn't it?"

He stuck out his free hand, and Dick Olin took it, pump-
ing his arm enthusiastically.

"Talk about a phoenix rising from the ashes!" the older
man said. "I don't think I've seen hide nor hair of you
since you took over runnin' your granddad's cow-calf operation."

"And you know how that goes," Cade returned amiably. "Always somethin' to get done or to worry about not
getting done."

"I don't get out much these days myself. Hip replace-
ment last March, and afore that had a pacemaker put in."

"Don't tell me you're slowin' down," Cade said with
a lift of his eyebrows.

"Hell, no." Dick fell into step beside him. "You know
me. I've always had a finger in just about every pie in the
Panhandle. Diversifyin' is what they've taken to calling it
these days. Creatin' your own luck, is the label I've always
pinned on it."

"I see we're of a mind on that one, Dick," Cade said
on a laugh.

"That's for sure. I've been gettin' all kinds of good
news about you lately. In fact, your brother called me couple of weeks ago."

"Loren?" Cade asked, surprised.

"Yup." Dick beamed at him. "Braggin' you up and
down, he was, about how you'd been running the ranch

and what a bang-up horse trainer you were shaping up into.''

Cade couldn't speak, touched as he was by his brother's support. He hadn't known how much he missed it these past weeks.

"So Loren's back working the ranch, and married with a little one on the way, is he?" Dick blithely went on.

"Yes, and looking forward to both. He's always been the real rancher in the family, to tell the truth.'' He gave a private nod. "It'll be a good life for them all. His wife's trained as a nurse, and I believe she's looking to continue that kind of work after the baby is born.''

"Loren said his wife's cousin was staying there, too. Sara Childress, I believe her name was?''

Cade's heart broke its rhythm. "It is.'' Then out of the blue, something made him ask, "She's trying to start up business as a graphic designer. Do you need one?''

Dick scrubbed a hand over the back of his neck. "Frankly, I don't know if I'd have a use for a graphic designer or not, since I'm not sure what someone like that could do for me.''

"Actually, I've got somethin' here Sara worked up for me that might give you an idea, at least, of what *she* can do.''

Stopping, Cade pulled one of his gold horse training brochures from the inside pocket of his coat and handed it to Dick.

He in turn removed his reading glasses from his jacket pocket and peered at Sara's brochure for a long moment as Cade waited anxiously. What an opportunity for Sara if she could get on doing work for Dick! He was probably one of the most successful businessmen in the Panhandle, with, as he'd said, any number of interests that Sara would be able to help with.

Finally, Dick glanced up at him. "Well, I haveta say, she sure makes you sound like one helluva horse trainer."

"That'd mean she's pretty damn good, wouldn't it?" Cade said with a grin of relief.

Dick laughed. "Guess I better give the gal a call and find out what she can do for me."

Ruminatively, he scored the edge of the brochure with his fingernail. "Speakin' of horse training, though…I've always kept a bunch of horses on that operation of mine south of Amarillo, and I haven't had much luck finding a man with a good eye and a way with horses to help me decide which to train up and how. You think you could help me out there?"

Cade's spirits soared. If he proved himself to be competent with Dick's horses, the businessman wouldn't be shy about spreading the word. He'd send more business Cade's way than he could whip up in a year of networking.

"Why thanks, Dick," he said. "I wasn't expecting such an opportunity when I showed you that brochure, but I'll sure take it." He sidestepped himself and Destiny out of the way of another horse trying to get past. "I'll be up that way next week, in fact."

"Give me a call then, when you get to town," Dick said. He gave Cade a broad wink. "See what I mean 'bout creatin' your own luck? Cain't very well be in the right place at the right time sittin' at home."

After Dick left, Cade stood in the middle of the aisle as people streamed past him like the river's flow around a crag jutting out of its bed. The man had a point. Who knew whether Cade would have ever stumbled into this golden opportunity if he hadn't taken that first step of leaving the ranch to follow his destiny?

Of course, he wouldn't have left at all if destiny hadn't already found him in the form of Sara and her baby.

Life sure enough did seem to be a subtle mix of fate

and free will, although it was damned difficult sometimes
to tell which was which.

But what could be the harm in trying? Cade wondered.

Juggling her portfolio under her arm, Sara tugged fu-
tilely at the motel restaurant door. The blustery March
wind swirled debris and an assortment of candy wrappers
around her ankles and upward. Just what she needed, to
go into her best opportunity in two months with bits and
pieces of last fall's leaves sticking to her new outfit, and
her hair in a stir.

She gave a huff, ready to put her back into giving the
door a good yank, when above the handle in bold black
letters she read Push.

The signs definitely didn't bode well for her.

Not that she was too terribly worried about her meeting.
From what she gathered, the gentleman already liked what
he'd seen of her work from the samples she'd sent him,
and settling the terms was just a formality. But she'd
learned the hard way never to take anything for granted,
because there was always a chance, however slim, of the
unanticipated happening. Always.

In any case, she got a booth and ordered a cup of coffee,
prepared for a wait and glad she'd have some time to com-
pose herself. Her weekly appointment with her therapist
had ended early, making her a good hour before her meeting time.

Bending, Sara shook out the hem of her ankle-length
broomstick skirt before straightening and brushing at the
imaginary specks of dust on her bolero-style jacket. The
outfit had been an indulgence, to be sure. The jacket was
navy wool with gold buttons, the pattern in the skirt a
mixture of every shade of blue and then some. She thought
it made her look both professional and feminine, and she'd

simply needed the boost it gave her to look like a woman again and not so much a mother.

When her coffee came, Sara gulped down half the cup, hoping the caffeine would kick in soon. The therapy sessions always left her drained. Her counselor seemed to think they were making progress, but rather than feeling she was getting closer to discovering her lost memory, Sara had the distinct sensation of moving farther and farther away from that happening, no matter how hard she tried to move toward it. And she'd done everything her counselor suggested: at home, she'd surrounded herself with images of Greg, thinking that would spark at least a glimmer of her past. She and her cousin talked about him, as much as Sarah Ann knew of Greg. Loren had even driven her back to Oklahoma City for a few days, where she visited hers and Greg's old house, talked to friends and business acquaintances who knew him. It had helped to learn how devoted they'd been to each other.

Yet while there was nothing, as there hadn't been regarding Loren, to raise a red flag in her mind, neither was there much that struck a chord in her. Even with Baby Cade, who certainly presented her with the strongest image of Greg, she got not even the least flicker of a memory.

No, rather than arousing memories of his father in her, Baby Cade was a constant reminder of the man he was named after. When she looked at her son, she inevitably saw Cade...Cade cradling him for the first time in those strong hands of his...singing to him as he howled like a siren...holding the baby before him and begging the infant not to forget him....

Now, there was an avenue of thought she simply couldn't go down. Because what hindered her progress more than anything was that, while fighting to remember Greg, she fought another battle to forget, at least for the time being, Cade. Try as she might, though, she was finding it impossibly draining to repress thoughts of him, put him out of her mind and heart so she could let another in.

And she simply didn't believe that any amount of time or distance in the world would make that happen. Whoever she'd been and however she felt before her amnesia, she simply wasn't that person anymore. She couldn't continue to look backward. She had a baby to raise and a life to live. She needed to go on. But how to convince everyone else of that? How to convince Cade?

To her dismay, tears of frustration started in her eyes, and Sara barely managed to blink them back as she tried to turn her mind to other subjects and away from the one that inevitably led her to experience that certain hopelessness she'd been feeling more and more of late. She simply couldn't go into this meeting looking as if she'd been crying.

Reaching into her purse, she pulled out her compact and dropped it on the Formica tabletop with a prodigious clatter that had heads at two other tables beside her turning in curiosity. She must be even more nervous than she thought. Snatching it up, she clasped the blasted compact in both hands. She definitely needed to get a grip on herself.

Maybe she shouldn't have come today. It was obvious she wasn't ready for this kind of meeting. But if not now, then when? When might she get another chance?

She closed her eyes, taking deep breaths to calm herself. It didn't help. With effort, she tried to clear her mind, and suddenly she remembered Cade's way of dealing with these things: *Just forget about the past for now, set your worry about the future aside, and focus on the here and now,* his voice in her head told her.

And amazingly, she felt a small measure of peace descend over her, even as she realized it had happened when she didn't fight thoughts of him. But then, she didn't see how she could anymore.

Gripping the compact firmly, Sara opened it and checked her makeup. Nothing damaged. Hopefully, the French twist she'd managed to wrestle her hair into this morning was holding. She hadn't done anything with her hair since the baby's birth other than pull it back in a clip. The new hairstyle was, she realized, yet another attempt to demonstrate outward change and progress.

She tilted her head, trying to see in the mirror how her hair was holding. She almost didn't dare touch it. Lifting the mirror, she tried for a better angle.

Sara froze at the image in the mirror. A man sat two booths back from hers, one hand on the coffee cup before him, the index finger of his other hand pressed to the underside of his lower lip in purposeful contemplation...of her.

Sara lowered the mirror, and as if in a trance, turned around.

Cade didn't move. Didn't have to, for the bond between them was as strong and alive and intense as ever as it stretched across those fifteen feet, drawing them toward each other as surely as a magnetic field—or another, even more powerful, force of nature.

How could she have even begun to believe she could put out of her mind those eyes like molten gold, that springy, thick chestnut hair? That mouth that last time she'd seen him had branded her flesh.

And those hands...oh, what they'd done to her.

No, she hadn't regained her memory, but even with no clue as to what her past or future held, Sara knew, as she'd always known, this was the one man she would never, ever forget.

Gaze never leaving hers, he rose, tossing a few bills on

the table and picking up his hat before coming toward her with that ambling cowboy gait of his.

He stopped next to her booth, looking down at her. "Sara. What a coincidence."

"It is, isn't it?" Her swallow was audible, her head was tipped back at such an angle to drink in every long, lean inch of him. He wore that chocolate-brown suede jacket, the one he'd had on the day in the corral when he'd first kissed her, the same black brushed felt Stetson in his hands. "Wh-what are you doing here?"

"I'm passin' through Amarillo on my way to Reno for a horse show day after tomorrow." He gave a nod toward the bank of windows next to her. "The motel here is cheap but clean, and the owner lets me turn Destiny out in the field on the other side of the restaurant. In fact, I was just on my way out to give him a mornin' spin around the pasture."

So he'd stayed here in the past when he'd been in the area. "Were you...were you going to stop by the ranch to see everyone since you were so close?" she asked.

There was a measuring beat, then he shook his head. "No," he said gently.

"I see." Sara dropped her chin, trying to submerge the hurt and succeeding only passably.

"And you're here because...?" Cade asked.

She pressed her palms against her ribs under opposite arms. She was cold, all of a sudden. "I've got a meeting in an hour or so with an old friend of Loren's he arranged for me to meet. As a potential client, I mean. Maybe a big one. I'd like to be working more than I am."

"So you've been able to pick up your skills again all right?"

Sara lifted her shoulders. "Most of them. It's been difficult, going through the projects I completed before and trying to get a sense of how or why I did something a certain way. I've had to move ahead, in any case," she said, adding pointedly, "I can't let what I don't know keep me from using what I do."

His lashes flickered imperceptibly. "Well, good luck. I hope you don't go away disappointed."

Oh, but I will, she thought, searching her mind frantically for a way to detain him, because that was a goodbye if she ever heard one.

But no. "Speakin' of the rest of the family," Cade said abruptly, "how's the little mite?"

"You mean Baby Cade?" She wouldn't shy away from using her child's given name, even if he still couldn't bring himself to. "I'm not one to brag, but he's getting cuter every day."

He gestured toward her purse with his hat, held by its crown. "I'm guessing that means you wouldn't be caught dead with a picture of him anywhere on you."

"Of course I would!" Sara said, flashing an indignant glance up at him before she caught the gleam in his eye. "Oh…you."

It was the same way she'd reacted when he'd teased her that very first time. She felt as flushed and flustered as then, too.

Suddenly, Sara was almost anxious for Cade to leave, so she wouldn't make even more of a fool of herself—over him.

"So, can I have a look?" he asked.

"Oh…sure." She delved into her pocketbook as, uninvited, he took a seat across from her. She came up with the Mom's Brag Book album she kept with her and slid it over to him.

"That's Baby Cade getting a bath—Sarah Ann was the one who bought him all those bath toys, not me," she said, pointing. "At least we won't lack for them when her baby comes along. And that's him in the cowboy outfit Loren found I don't know where. Isn't it cute? It's got a little cowboy hat and everything. There's Loren holding him in it. He'll make a great daddy. And there's one of Virgil somewhere…. Wait—'' She flipped a few pages forward. ''There it is. The baby's asleep on Virg's chest. Isn't that just the sweetest thing you've ever seen?''

She glanced up to find Cade had lost his aloofness and was devouring the photos with his gaze, the expression on his face one of such acute longing and aloneness it took her breath away. How often had she felt so herself during the long winter days and nights?

It was abundantly clear to her how much he had missed them all.

''Cade.'' She flattened her palm on the surface between them. ''This is ridiculous, can't you see that? We miss you—terribly so. All of us, Baby Cade included. O-or maybe it's me who misses the way you had with him, never doubting you had the power to soothe his fears and dry his tears, even when he was most upset.''

He set the album aside purposefully, not looking at her. ''Are you sure?''

''Sure—about what?''

''That it's me you're missin'.''

Her mouth fell open. She snapped it shut. ''Yes! Life is so short. Why should you be away from home, from the people you care for and who care for you?''

''You think I want to be?'' He looked at her then, his eyes fierce and intense. ''I'm tryin' to do what's best for all of us—what's best for you, Sara.''

She sat back against the cushioned seat, her coffee cup clasped so tightly between her hands it seemed she'd break it. She stared at him, shaking her head slowly. ''I—I have to be honest with you, Cade. I'm not getting any closer to regaining my memory. Your leaving doesn't seem to have helped.''

The sun streaming in the window cast his face half in light, half in shadow, which matched the expression on his face, one that mixed gladness with gloom.

"So the solution is to just give up tryin'?" he asked, his voice low and intense. "'Cause that's pretty much what would happen if I came back, and we both know it."

His fingers clenched into fists on the tabletop as his eyes squeezed shut in almost the same way she had sought to block certain images from her mind's eye. "We—we just get too caught up in each other. You know that. I mean, even if the situation turned out differently in the end, I *was* willin' to betray my own brother over this—this connection we have with each other."

"And that's a bad thing?" Sara countered. "Cade, look at me."

He opened his eyes to gaze at her, looking as torn as she'd ever seen him.

"Whatever I do know, it's this—a connection such as we have between us, as strong as it is, it doesn't come along every day. If it won't be denied, maybe it's because it can't be."

"Even when it leads a man to brand his touch on a woman's memory and body while supposedly in the act of helpin' her remember another man's claim on her?" he asked in that brutally honest way he had.

She could only be as candid in return. "Even then, Cade. I refuse to see the love that's grown between us as wrong," she whispered. "I can't."

"I'm not sayin' it is," he answered, his own voice hoarse. "But how can it be completely right until you know why you've lost your memory?"

"So we both put our lives on hold while I keep up this futile trying that's like banging my head up against a wall? I'll lose my mind for sure, Cade!"

His gaze was laser-sharp. "And who's to say that's not what's needed to set things right at last?"

Sara stared at him. Was he right? Did she really need to experience that unmitigated fear again in order to regain her memory? Was that the only way her buried past could be revealed to her, through a shocking, savage exhuming that would leave her just as devastated as when she'd lost it?

Yet what she stood to lose if she didn't—the love and respect of this good man, whom she knew waged his own internal battle for courage every day—didn't bear contemplating.

She *must* have courage, too!

Sara lifted her chin. "If that's the only way, then yes. And I guess it's best to get it done with."

His features seemed chiseled from stone, except for his eyes, which burned as brightly as gems in the face of an idol. "So we're right back where we were a month and a half ago," he said, his tone steeped in finality, "and nothin's changed."

She shook her head slowly, gaze never leaving his. "No, nothing's changed."

He gave a nod. "Then I'll keep headin' on up the road for now."

Once he'd risen, though, setting his hat on his head, he hesitated. Then, as if he still thought better of making the gesture, Cade stuck out his hand to her.

Sara took it, unable to even think of doing anything different, and it was as forceful and magnetic as ever, that connection between them, as the warmth of his hand crept up her arm through her very bones and straight to her heart.

Too soon, he released her, and was gone.

The ensuing cold enveloped her, just as it had that first night when she'd thought he meant to leave her. He hadn't then, and in her mind she could tell herself that while he'd left now, it wouldn't be for forever.

Yet would they be doomed always to be separated by this one point of contention between them? In the scheme of things, it was such an absurd argument! Silly, really.

Really. It doesn't seem silly to me.

Sara stiffened as a jolt of pure fear shot up her spinal cord like electricity through a live wire. No, it wasn't silly! The matter was dead serious—almost one of life and death. And one, she knew in a flash of precognition—or was it exactly the opposite?—she couldn't let happen again.

Sara was out of her seat in a trice and headed for the front of the restaurant, her portfolio banging painfully against her hip. She tore out the door, gaze scouring the parking lot for his dual-wheeled pickup, but there was no sign of it, or Cade.

Where had he gone? He couldn't leave! She wouldn't let him, not this time, not without saying what she needed to say.

Perhaps he'd gone back to his room. Dashing inside again, Sara very nearly attacked the desk clerk. "Cade McGivern," she panted. "Can you tell me what room he's in?"

"Well, he *was* in room 293," she said, riffling through a stack of receipts. "Just paid his bill, said he'd leave the key in the room since he had a few things to take care of before—"

"Thank you!" She was already on her way out the door.

What a sight she must be! Sara thought, her long skirt catching between her legs as she ran in the unfamiliar boots, the portfolio literally an albatross on her shoulder.

At least she was able to find Room 293 with little difficulty. She pounded on the door.

"Cade? Cade!" She had to catch her breath or she'd pass out. "Are you in there? It's me, Sara."

She tried the knob and the door opened. Stumbling inside, Sara searched the room frantically, but the situation was clear: he was gone.

She bent her head as her portfolio slid to the carpet and she pressed both hands to her mouth to stifle a sob of despair. Oh, had she blown her one and only chance at—

Destiny. Sara's head shot up. He'd said he was going for a ride on Destiny before loading him into the trailer.

Sara whirled, prepared to run for her life. She came up short, however, at the sight of a man standing in the doorway, his silhouette outlined by the morning sun streaming in behind him.

"Cade!"

In two strides he had caught her in his arms, holding her in a crushing embrace.

"When I went back to the restaurant you'd already left," he whispered raggedly into her hair. "I thought you were gone for good—"

"No, I came looking for you—"

"—and I thought, just my luck, runnin' into you and then missin' by only a minute telling you how I feel—"

"So." Sara lifted her head, taking his face between her hands. "Is that what you believe? *Was* this just a coincidence today, us running into each other here?"

"What would you call it?" he asked, low.

"You know how I feel, Cade, and I can't do it any longer." She stepped away from him, and never had she seen such bleakness in a man's eyes. But she had to be strong.

"Meanin'?" he asked.

"I'm sorry, Cade. I can't keep focusing on recovering this forgotten past of mine. I can't chase after my fate any more than you can run from yours. I *won't* do it, not anymore. I won't let what I don't know keep me from believing in what I do. And what I believe in is this," she gestured between them ''—this bond, this force, this love that connects us. And you said it yourself, Cade. Such love requires you to forge through the doubts and fears, not knowing the future but trusting you'll be able to face it— together.''

A tear fell to her cheek and she swiped it away as she would a pesky fly. She *would* not cry!

"Don't you see? It's not about me and Greg any longer. Whatever life we had together, that's what *was*. Now is *our* time, Cade, and nothing can change the way I feel about you—that I won't forget you, couldn't forget you, and would never forsake our love. And if you can't believe that, if you can't believe in the rightness of our love and that it's meant to be…well, then, maybe you're right, and i-it isn't.''

Another tear, another mad swipe at her eyes. "But not because of me. *You're* the one who's giving up on us, not me. Because I know I can't change the fate I've been handed, and that fate is, I love you, Cade McGivern! With all my heart. If that doesn't fit into your grand scheme of things, then that's just too damn bad!''

She'd wanted to be logical, convincing. Her words, though, were tumbling out in a hodgepodge, helped not a bit by the tears she still tried to stifle. But it was just too important to her! He was too important to her.

"I'm not leaving—*you're* not leaving,'' she continued, ''until we work this out, even if it takes the rest of our lives!''

No, she wouldn't let him go without putting up the fight of her life. But his stubbornness was legend. She could see the hard, cold determination in his eyes, and she wondered suddenly if, truly, their love wasn't meant to be, or that it was all a delusion of hers born out of desperation not to face her past.

Then Cade spoke.

"So you think it's too damn bad you can't stop loving me, do you? Well, let me tell you somethin'. I can't walk away from you either, woman, even if it's for both our good. The short of it is, I don't have a choice. Whatever brought us together—call it destiny or fate or some kinda hoodoo straight out of the twilight zone—it's sure enough given us this chance together."

Pushing back the tail of his jacket, he set his hands on his hips with a short nod. "I've had some time to think, and you're right. Love like that requires you to forge through the doubts and fears, not knowing the future but trusting you'll be able to face it, together."

"So what are *you* saying, Cade?" Sara asked, her heart in her throat, and most likely in her eyes, too.

He widened his stance, as if facing a shoot-out at high noon. "I'm sayin' that, if or when you get back your memory, if that means having to work through your love and loyalty to your dead husband, then—then I'll be here for you, however you need me to be. I won't give up on you— and I won't leave you."

He cracked a one-sided smile that broke her heart. "I'd say I've already got the waitin' part down pat, and that you can depend on."

"Oh, *Cade,*" Sara sobbed.

And, tears blinding her, she ran into his arms.

Cade caught her to him. His mouth was wild against hers, parting her lips with his own, stroking inside with his tongue until her knees buckled.

Oh, how she'd thought she'd die for want of just this connection, so strong and sure!

Still, she needed more.

"Make love to me, Cade," Sara whispered.

Without a word, he kicked the door closed behind him before lifting her and carrying her to the bed, where he laid her down with infinite tenderness. She kept her arms wrapped around his neck, remembering how she'd done the same that very first night. Yes, those memories were a part of her now. Cade was a part of her. He'd always be in her heart, never to leave.

And just like that night, his gaze fell to the ring at her throat. Without a word, Sara reached behind her neck and unclasped the chain. For a moment, she grasped the gold band in her hand as it rested against her heart. Then, with infinite care, she laid it aside, and opened her arms to him again.

There was no need to rush this time as Cade ever so slowly tugged her skirt down her hips, slid her jacket and blouse from her shoulders. She herself took deliberately agonizing long minutes unbuttoning his shirt, sliding his belt from its buckle, savoring the sensual sound of his fly rasping open.

Yet even when at last they lay naked, the exploration became more leisurely, as Sara grazed her fingertips over the muscles of Cade's hard chest, up and across those wide, sturdy shoulders, down his strong arms to those large, capable, gentle hands of his that she would always think of as life-giving, in so many ways.

Then, as he watched, lids heavy and eyes glowing, she lifted one of those hands to her lips and kissed its rough, callused palm before pressing it to her breast, needing to know that exquisite reawakening again.

His fingers clenched. "Ah, Sara, Sara. What you do to me."

The simple stroke his thumb across her nipple made her suck in her breath as desire stirred hot within her core. And grew hotter as Cade kept up the caress, taking her moans of pleasure into his own mouth.

She arched against him, a silent plea for more, and he wouldn't see her denied.

Yet when he moved over her, parting her thighs gently,

she stayed him with her hand upon his shoulder. Cade looked up, questioning.

"Tell me again," she said simply, and his eyes glinted in perfect understanding.

"Wherever you came from," he said huskily, "whatever happened before, you're here now in my arms, exactly where you need to be, with me."

He took her hand, weaving her fingers in his, and brought them between their chests, so that their clasped hands were pressed against both their hearts. "And I won't ever let you go."

Hands still threaded together, he slid into her, eliciting a groan from him, a sigh from her. They made love, hearts, bodies and souls completely attuned, the bond between them as powerful as ever. Fated, as if it had been carved into time itself. Every thought, emotion and action in the universe seemed to converge deep inside her, and needing to look into Cade's eyes, needing something else, something more, that was still missing, Sara tugged at his hair, desperately urging his chin up. When their eyes met, she found what she sought, once more and forever. The force of that ultimate connection resounded to her core like the stroke of a clock, bright and clear and vibrant, that pealed over and over again.

As if in echo to that soundless throbbing, Cade shuddered against her in completion, and Sara shed tears of joy to know this one perfect moment, for within it nothing else mattered.

Yes, this was right where she belonged, where they both belonged.

And that's when she knew…knew it all, past, present—and future.

She blinked. "Cade."

Forehead against her shoulder, he brushed her hair back

with infinite tenderness, his breathing still ragged. "What, darlin'?"

"I remember," she said simply.

He moved not a muscle, but Sara felt every inch of him turn to stone.

He lifted his head and asked, "You do?"

"Yes."

Apprehension entered those whiskey-brown eyes of his, but only for an instant before it was replaced with caring concern. "Are you all right?"

"I'm…fine," Sara said wonderingly. It was so strange, like an out-of-body experience in reverse as her mind seemed to settle back in to her head, and all that had been missing was suddenly just *there*. Including Greg—and what had transpired that fateful day two months ago.

"Really," she told Cade quietly, "everything is…fine."

He shifted to the side and helped her sit up against the headboard, the covers tucked up under her arms for warmth.

"So what do you remember?" he asked, propped on one elbow and hand in her lap as she clutched it between hers. "Tell me."

She tried to sort it out chronologically. "I was…driving to Albuquerque when the storm started to blow into the Panhandle. The movers had taken two hours longer than I'd thought they would to pack up my stuff, so when they finally finished and left I was in a hurry to get on the road and forgot to check the weather, like Loren said."

She gave an involuntary shiver. "Stupid of me, I guess. That alone could have been disastrous for me."

"Aw, I wouldn't be too hard on yourself, Sara," Cade consoled, his thumb rubbing the back of her hand. "Even if you had checked the weather report, I don't know that you wouldn't still have decided to make your trip as scheduled. Nobody knew that cold front was gonna turn into an all-out blizzard.''

She gave him a grateful smile for his support. "At least when I realized I was heading straight at that big gray cloud I stopped at that café to call you to see if you'd mind me waiting out the storm.''

"So I was who you called?''

"Yes, and when there was no answer, I decided to come anyway, thinking if you still weren't home, surely having to break into your house for shelter would be preferable to trying to beat the blizzard. But once I got off the main road, I discovered my purse had been stolen from my car while it was in the café parking lot.''

Sara bit her lip. "I was...pretty distraught, what with the stress of the movers and leaving O.K.C. late and the storm coming on. By that time, my emotional reserves were pretty low. Plus I'd been feeling twingey all day. That's when the labor pains started.''

The fear she'd experienced at that moment came pouring back. She found it disturbing, but not debilitating.

"But you didn't go into labor till you got to my place,'' Cade pointed out.

Sara shook her head slowly, trying to keep straight the feelings and impressions flying at her. "Not in earnest, no. But I was terrified to think I might be starting to have this baby. I knew if I had him out in the middle of the Texas Panhandle as early as I believed he was going to be, I'd lose him.''

She gave another of those involuntary shudders, and Cade squeezed her hand tighter. "The thought wasn't to be borne. I'd already lost Greg—I simply wasn't going to accept fate dealing me another such loss.''

She looked at him. "I was so set on denying it in my mind, in defying fate, I repressed...everything. When I came to, it was with the piece of paper with your name on it in my hand, and the certainty that if I could just make it to you, everything would be all right. And everything was, thank goodness—except for the loss of my memory.''

They sat silently for some time, both of them absorbing all that had happened to bring them to this moment.

Chin down, Cade asked, ''So—so how do you feel now about what you've remembered. Y'know, about—Greg?''

Greg. She could picture him in her mind so clearly now, it was almost surreal. Everything was so sharp and distinct, she could see only now how much of a state of suspended animation she *had* been living in, even before she'd lost her memory. A state of grief.

''Sarah Ann was right,'' she said, ''I *was* completely devastated by his death in that car accident, especially coming as it had on the heels of that…silly little argument we had.''

She pulled her knees to her chest, hugging them. ''To tell the truth, I *still* can't remember what it was about, it was so trivial. When he walked out, I'm sure it was simply because he felt he could do with some perspective and nothing more. And for the same reason, I let him leave.''

Resting one cheek on her knees, Sara admitted, ''Knowing what I know now, I wouldn't have let him go. That must have been the reason why, even without memory of it, I was terrified to let you leave.''

His chin shot up. ''God, I'm sorry, Sara! I didn't know.''

''Of course you didn't. *I* didn't.'' Tenderly, she feathered her fingers through his thick chestnut hair, her hand lingering at his nape. ''But this I do know. Greg will always be in my heart for what we shared and the son he gave me. I can see now that my amnesia wasn't so much about not being able to think about living without him, because my heart did know that that's part of life and loving. It was my mind that couldn't put it together. So I guess I had to forget him in order for my heart to lead me where my mind didn't dare go. And that was to let myself believe in life again. To have faith that I did have some say in finding happiness again.''

Her voice dropped to a whisper. "To have faith that I could fall in love again."

"You never gave up faith," Cade vowed. "You've always had it right there inside you. It's you who gave it to me again."

Tears stung behind her eyes as she realized the gift she'd been given in having two such men in her life. She would never forget either of them, ever again.

She smiled tremulously at the one who'd seen her through that valley of darkness. "Do you know how much I love you, Cade McGivern? I have from the first. I couldn't have stopped myself from falling in love with you, can't stop myself from loving you now, any more than I could stop myself from loving Baby Cade."

A teardrop fell, trailing down her cheek, but she couldn't be bothered to brush it away this time. Not when it was one of joy. "And that will never change, no matter what happens."

She could tell Cade was as moved, his features ravaged with the strength of the emotion he felt, too, as he said roughly, "I love you, too, Sara with the blue eyes."

He slid his hand behind her nape to draw her close, and she let him, offering herself to the touch of his kiss, which she knew with all her heart she'd never grow tired of, would never stop wanting. Would never, ever forget.

After a few moments, Cade pulled away, his brow furrowed. "Why do you expect you recovered your memory now, of all times? And without that awful fear sendin' you into a tailspin?"

"I don't know. Although...remember what you said

when you were explaining to me about how you trained Destiny, how you can't make anything happen?''

For some reason, he lowered his gaze, giving an embarrassed cough. ''Sure, I remember.''

''Maybe that's what happened with both of us. We were both fighting loving each other so I could remember my past. But we couldn't *not* love each other. So when we stopped trying to do the wrong thing, the difficult thing, and let ourselves do what was easy and right—loving each other—then that's how we got to the place where we needed to be.''

''That's quite a theory,'' Cade drawled, a wry smile playing at his lips as he concentrated unduly on his finger tracing the life line, heart line, and love line of her palm.

''But it makes sense, doesn't it?''

He shrugged one muscled shoulder. ''Only if you don't forget the most important part.''

''What's that?''

His lashes lifted and he hit her with those rich, whiskey-brown eyes again. ''It only works as long as we give ourselves up to feeling the right thing for each other.''

He reached out and stroked her jaw with the back of his index finger, then trailed it down her throat to bump tantalizingly over her nipple, making Sara go weak with want for him in an instant as he whispered, ''Feel it all the way through our bodies on down to our toes.''

Their mouths found each other again in a kiss that flowered within her, blooming and spreading even more completely as Cade caressed her breast.

''Damn,'' he said breathlessly minutes later, his teeth doing wonderful things to her earlobe. ''Please tell me we've got time for me to make love to you again.''

''Time?'' Over his shoulder, she glimpsed the bedside clock. ''Oh my heavens! I was supposed to meet that client fifteen minutes ago!''

There was a mad scurry for underwear and crumpled clothes, which they hurried into as best they could for all the laughing and kissing going on. Sara managed to smooth out her skirt and jacket but could only gaze hopelessly into the mirror at her bedraggled hairdo. One side of the French twist had come completely loose and hung down over her ear. Hairpins stuck out all over. She had no choice but to take them out and wear her hair in a tumble around her shoulders. Speaking of a tumble…

"Do I look thoroughly ravished?" she asked Cade worriedly, pressing her hands to her flushed cheeks to cool them.

He only grinned and slid his arms around her waist from behind. "Not by half."

She blushed even more furiously. "Oh…*you.*"

Once dressed, they hurried down the stairs and across the parking lot to the restaurant. Inside, Sara searched the patrons at the tables for a self-described Texas good old boy, short on hair and wide of waistline, in glasses and a brown Stetson. But no one in the restaurant fit that description.

Dismay washed over her. "Darn! I can't have missed him. I needed to thank him—I mean, t-to talk to him about this opportunity."

"Wait a sec." Cade pointed out the window. "Is that who you're looking for?"

They ventured outside again, picking their way across a parking lot littered with cars to a man fitting the description Sara had been given. He stood at a white pipe fence, one boot propped on the lower rail and hand outstretched to scratch the broad nose of Destiny, who looked to be loving the attention he was getting.

The man turned at their approach. A smile broke out on his face. "Well, there she is," he boomed. "You're Sara, of course. We've talked on the phone so much, I feel like we're old friends already.''

"So do I, Dick," she said quickly, closing the last distance between them to offer the older man her hand, which he took between both of his. "Sorry to be late."

He brushed away her apology. "No problem a'tall."

He released her hand to turn and take Cade's with as much enthusiasm. "Hey there, Cade. Didn't expect to see you for another half hour or so," he said rather pointedly.

Sara lifted her eyebrows in question. She'd grasped the fact that of course, Cade would know Dick Olin. Loren had mentioned he was an old friend of their grandfather's.

"Dick's who I've got the lunch meetin' with at noon," Cade explained, "to talk about my doing some work for him, too."

Dick looked from one to the other. "And you two know each other?" He struck his forehead with the heel of his hand. "That's right, y'all are kissin' cousins, of a fashion. I guess I plumb forgot to mention it to y'all that I was meetin' with each of you one right after the other."

Beneath his gray eyebrows, his eyes were bright with inquisitiveness. "But I guess you both figured out for yourselves what was goin' on, am I right?"

"Of a fashion," Cade said cryptically as Sara became even more intrigued. What was going on here?

She indicated her portfolio. "Did you want to get a table in the restaurant so we could discuss some possibilities as to what I might be able to do for you?" she asked.

"Well, don't know as that I even needed to meet with the either of you." He clapped Cade on the back. "I've known you since you were just a li'l shaver, Cade, and you always were a wonder on horseback, no doubt about it. That's why I'd like you to take over buyin' and trainin' the entire string of horses on my operation. I'm of a mind to expand that side of the business, make a name for the ranch—and give you the chance to make one for yourself, if you'd like it."

Under the brim of his hat, Cade's ears turned red with embarrassment. Such a modest man! But still, sure of his talents and purpose.

"I'd be honored, Dick," he answered, adding, "I'll look forward to not havin' to move from town to town like a wanderin' cowboy." He slid her a glance. "Look forward, too, to bein' close to family again."

"Then it's settled."

He and Dick shook on it before the older man turned expansively to her, making her feel like Dorothy just before the Wizard bestowed his last gift upon her. "And you, young lady, I like what I've seen of your stuff, especially that brochure you did up for Cade. I'm gonna be needing some work done to get the word out 'bout him and buildin' the horse-training business on the ranch, plus a bunch of other businesses I got goin'."

He gave her a shrewd look. "Now, it's not full-time, but you'd be able to work from home most of the time so's you could be there for that little one of your'n."

Sara actually got tears in her eyes. "I'd love to!" she enthused sincerely.

She couldn't help herself; when Dick offered his hand to her as well, she threw her arms around him and gave him a kiss on the cheek, to which the older man responded with the flaming of his ears, too.

"Enough of that, now, young lady," he said gruffly.

Letting go, Sara turned to Cade and found herself caught up in a bear hug that left her even more giddy, especially when he released her and smiled down at her, love sparking those glowing gold eyes of his to an even greater incandescence.

She realized they were staring at each other like a couple of fools only when Dick coughed discreetly.

"So it's settled," he said. "Let's talk next week to firm up the details."

He peered at them, and Sara thought she saw what looked suspiciously like a smile of satisfaction lurking around his lips. "Now if it's all right with y'all, I'm of a mind to read the newspaper while I enjoy my lunch. 'Sides, I'm sure you two young'uns've got better things to do."

It was everything she could do not to look at Cade at that moment as she commanded herself not to blush. Then, as Dick turned to go, she ventured a quick glance up at Cade just in time to see him give a wink to the older man—in thanks.

He shrugged innocently when he saw her staring at him, openmouthed, for it just occurred to her: Cade's brochure hadn't been in the samples of her work she'd sent Dick.

"Cade...?"

He didn't even have the decency to look ashamed as he leaned back against the fence, drawing her into his arms again.

"Just a little lesson in what I like to call creatin' your own luck," he drawled triumphantly.

"Oh really? Well, I wouldn't gloat if I were you," she said, arching an eyebrow, "because from where *I'm* standing, it definitely looks to me as if destiny is firmly back in the saddle again, making things happen."

He groaned. "Don't tell me this's *still* gonna be a point of contention between us?"

Before she could respond, he dropped his chin to take her mouth again in a soulful kiss that had her snaking her arms up his chest and around his neck to pull him closer still.

Minutes later, Cade lifted his head. "So, is it?"

"I hate to tell you this, cowboy," Sara purred, "but I'm

going to take a lot more convincing than that to change my mind.''

"How much convincin'?"

"Oh, say, for the rest of our lives," she whispered, offering her lips to him again.

But it was probably a good thing, Sara decided, that Cade hadn't seen *her* wink—also of thanks—that she'd given Dick Olin in parting.

* * * * *

▼™ SILHOUETTE
SPECIAL EDITION®

AVAILABLE FROM 20TH APRIL 2001

THE BABY QUILT Christine Flynn

That's My Baby!

When a sophisticated Chicago lawyer rescued Emily Miller and her baby no one would've expected anything to come of it. But the young mum and her newborn touched something in Justin Sloan…

MATT CALDWELL: TEXAS TYCOON Diana Palmer

He was rich, powerful and every woman's fantasy, but no woman had caught this sought-after bachelor's eye until his new employee roused his temper and his dormant desires.

THE MD SHE *HAD* TO MARRY Christine Rimmer

Conveniently Yours

All her adult life Lacey Bravo had loved Logan Severance, but the good doctor had never—well, just *once*—made an improper advance towards her. And the soon-to-be mum knew Logan would come after her demanding marriage…

THE SHEIKH'S KIDNAPPED BRIDE Susan Mallery

Desert Rogues

Swept away by the passionate Prince Khalil Khan, Dora Nelson revelled in her new fairy-tale life as Princess of El Bahar—until she discovered Khalil had lied to her…

SULLIVAN'S CHILD Gail Link

Years ago, blind ambition tore Rory Sullivan from Caitlyn Kildaire's tempestuous embrace, before she could tell him that he was about to become a father. But now he was back to take up where he had left off!

THE BRIDE SAID, 'I DID?' Cathy Gillen Thacker

The Lockhart Brides

Dani Lockhart had married her handsome enemy Beau Chamberlain…and couldn't remember doing it! She also didn't know how it was that she was expecting his child!

AVAILABLE FROM 20TH APRIL 2001

Intrigue
Danger, deception and suspense

INTIMATE SECRETS BJ Daniels
RENEGADE HEART Gayle Wilson
INADMISSIBLE PASSION Ann Voss Peterson
THE SECOND SON Joanna Wayne

Desire
Intense, sensual love stories

YOUR BABY OR MINE? Marie Ferrarella
TALLCHIEF: THE HOMECOMING Cait London
SEDUCTION, COWBOY STYLE Anne Marie Winston
RIDE A WILD HEART Peggy Moreland
A ROYAL MARRIAGE Cara Colter
HER BABY'S FATHER Katherine Garbera

Sensation
Passionate, dramatic, thrilling romances

I'LL BE SEEING YOU Beverly Bird
ROGUE'S REFORM Marilyn Pappano
IN A HEARTBEAT Carla Cassidy
HER SECRET GUARDIAN Sally Tyler Hayes
HEART OF MIDNIGHT Fiona Brand
A CERTAIN SLANT OF LIGHT Terese Ramin

0401/23bb

Silhouette Stars

Born this month.

Lord Snowdon, Prince Edward, Harold Wilson,
Michael Caine, Dudley Moore, Jessica Lange,
Bruce Willis, William Hurt, Malcolm Muggeridge.

Star of the month

Aries

A year of change and although some will be due
to circumstances out of your control, you will
feel able to embrace all life has to offer. Career
moves are highlighted and you will feel proud of
what you achieve. Your love life is looking good
with spring bringing a sparkle into relationships.

SILH/HR/0401a

Taurus

A decision needs to be made and although you may feel the choices are limited you will soon be moving forward again. A romantic meeting late in the month puts you in a positive mood.

Gemini

Take a break and restore your energy levels as you have been overdoing life lately. Finances are improving and you should feel positive about planning some home improvements.

Cancer

Romance and travel are both highlighted in a positive way so relax and enjoy this stress free period. Communications are subject to delay so double check anything important.

Leo

Onwards and upwards Leo, you may have been beset by problems lately but this phase is passing and a more positive one starting. Romance is well starred with someone new coming into your life.

Virgo

An important trip made this month will change your outlook on your life and what you need from others. Mid month a lucky win could lead to a celebration or a great shopping trip.

Libra

Long term plans should start to come to fruition and you feel confident about the way your life is heading. Beware the jealousy of a so called friend as they may cause trouble.

 Scorpio

Positive events that happened last month continue to affect your life and you will achieve the results you desire. A journey made late in the month brings an old face back into your life.

Sagittarius

An excellent time to take up a new sport or fitness regime especially where it involves mixing with a new group of people. A family gathering occupies most of your time late in the month.

 Capricorn

You need to take some time out to consider future plans and changes. Listen to those close as they may have some solutions. Finances improve and there may be a reason to celebrate.

Aquarius

Socially a brilliant month with lots to do and people to see. New people entering your life will bring a breath of fresh air making this a very positive and fulfilling time.

 Pisces

You need to face up to any difficulties as and when they present themselves. You also need to know exactly what you need to do to change the situation to your advantage. Late in the month a new opportunity lifts your spirits

Look out for more
Silhouette Stars next month

2 FREE

books and a surprise gift!

We would like to take this opportunity to thank you for reading this Silhouette® book by offering you the chance to take TWO more specially selected titles from the Special Edition™ series absolutely FREE! We're also making this offer to introduce you to the benefits of the Reader Service™—

- ★ FREE home delivery
- ★ FREE gifts and competitions
- ★ FREE monthly Newsletter
- ★ Exclusive Reader Service discounts
- ★ Books available before they're in the shops

Accepting these FREE books and gift places you under no obligation to buy, you may cancel at any time, even after receiving your free shipment. Simply complete your details below and return the entire page to the address below. *You don't even need a stamp!*

YES! Please send me 2 free Special Edition books and a surprise gift. I understand that unless you hear from me, I will receive 4 superb new titles every month for just £2.80 each, postage and packing free. I am under no obligation to purchase any books and may cancel my subscription at any time. The free books and gift will be mine to keep in any case.

E1ZEA

Ms/Mrs/Miss/Mr ....Initials....................................
BLOCK CAPITALS PLEASE

Surname ....

Address ....

....

....Postcode.................................

Send this whole page to:
UK: FREEPOST CN81, Croydon, CR9 3WZ
EIRE: PO Box 4546, Kilcock, County Kildare (stamp required)